TVS

INTRODUCTION

Twice Loved by Wanda E. Brunstetter
The end of World War II finds Bev Winters, a war widow with a young daughter, out of a job and struggling with her faith. Dan Fisher, still grieving for the wife he lost two years ago, wants to help those in need and offers Bev a job at his used toy store. Can anything strengthen the couple's faith and bring purpose to their lives again?

Everlasting Song by DiAnn Mills
Olivia Howard is devastated when her cherished possessions are destroyed by a fire, but when fireman, Nate Forester, finds her family Bible in the ashes and rubble, she searches for strength to rebuild her life and continue her calling as a teacher. Love captures Olivia and Nate, but sometimes changes aren't easy to accept. Will God work things out in the midst of confusion?

Remnants of Faith by Renee DeMarco
Unemployment cruelly thrusts Natalie Thorsett and her children onto the cold and dangerous streets of Seattle. Miles away, her frantic and estranged husband, Mark, desperately searches to find "his girls." Will the bonds of love Mark and Natalie once shared be flexible enough stretch the miles between them? And will Mark find God and the Thorsett women in time to protect his family from the evil that tracks them?

Silver Lining by Colleen L. Reece
Major Gavin Scott, U.S. Air Force "Raven" reconnaissance pilot, soars higher than the white hawk for which he is named. He thanks God for the job he loves and the most wonderful fiancée in the world. Suddenly, catastrophic engine failure darkens his dreams and raises the burning question: Will Alaskan nurse Christa Jensen Bishop, who fell in love with a dashing pilot, feel the same if he is permanently grounded?

PATCHWORK
HOLIDAY

Published by Barbour Publishing, Inc., P.O. Box 719, Uhrichsville, Ohio 44683, www.barbourbooks.com

Our mission is to publish and distribute inspirational products offering exceptional value and biblical encouragement to the masses.

 Member of the
Evangelical Christian
Publishers Association

Printed in the United States of America.
5 4 3 2 1

PATCHWORK HOLIDAY

*One Heirloom Quilt Comforts
Four Couples in Search of True Love*

WANDA E. BRUNSTETTER
DIANN MILLS
RENEE DEMARCO
COLLEEN L. REECE

BARBOUR
PUBLISHING

TWICE LOVED

by Wanda E. Brunstetter

Dedication

To Dean Thompson, a special uncle
who survived the bombing at Pearl Harbor.
To Dr. Bob and Delva Lantrip,
who make all their patients feel "Twice Loved."
And to my sister, Joy Stenson,
who, like Amy in this story, loved to play with dolls
and stuffed animals when she was a little girl.

Who comforteth us in all our tribulation,
that we may be able to comfort them which are in any trouble,
by the comfort wheewith we ourselves are comforted by God.
2 CORINTHIANS 1:4

Introduction

Japan's unconditional surrender to the Allies on September 2, 1945, ended World War II. America and her allies rejoiced. The idea of peace had never seemed more precious than to those who had given faithful service on the home front, as well as those who had served on the battlefield.

Yet much needed to be done before peace could be achieved. Those who had lost loved ones grieved. Families of those who were classified as prisoners of war or missing in action hoped and prayed for the day when their loved ones might return home. Factories that had been engaged in the production of war materials returned to their former pursuits. Thousands of "Rosie the Riveters," women who had replaced men who had been called to defend their country, were no longer needed. Returning military personnel further flooded the job market.

There were rejoicing and mourning, newly created problems, and the adjustment from war to peace; but the spark of hope that had kept people through the dark days of war, rationing, and personal sacrifice burned high. A weary world looked forward to a season of peace on earth, good will to men.

Prologue

Dan Fisher went down on his knees in front of the sofa where his wife lay. Darcy had been diagnosed with leukemia several months earlier, and short of a miracle, he knew she wouldn't have long to live.

"I'm almost finished with this quilt," Darcy murmured, lifting one corner of the colorful patchwork covering she had been working on since she'd first gotten sick. It was made from various shapes of cotton and velveteen material, in shades of blue, scarlet, gold, and green, and had been hand tied. She'd been able to do much of the stitching while lying in bed or on the sofa, where she spent most of her waking hours.

Dan nodded. "It's beautiful, honey—just like you."

"I want you to have it as a remembrance of me." Tears gathered in the corners of Darcy's dark brown eyes, and she blinked them away. "It will bring you solace after I'm gone and help you remember to comfort others in need."

Unable to voice his thoughts, Dan reached for Darcy's hand. When she squeezed his fingers, he was amazed at the strength of her grip.

"There are things we must discuss," she whispered.

Dan nodded, wishing they could talk about anything other than his wife's imminent death.

"Please promise you'll keep Twice Loved open."

Dan knew how important Darcy's used-toy store was to her, and to all the children she had ministered to by providing inexpensive or free toys. Little ones whose fathers were away at war and those who'd been left with only one parent had received a measure of happiness, thanks to Darcy and her special store.

"I'll keep the place going," he promised. "Whenever I look at this quilt, I'll remember the labor of love that went into making it, and I'll do my best to help others in need."

Chapter 1

September 1945

B ev Winters shut her desk drawer with such force, the cherished picture of her late husband toppled to the floor. Her hands shook as she bent to retrieve it, but she breathed a sigh of relief to see that the glass was intact and Fred's handsome face smiled back at her.

Joy Lundy poked her head around the partition that separated hers and Bev's workspaces in the accounting department at Bethlehem Steel. "What happened, Bev? I heard a crash."

Bev clutched the picture to her chest and sank into the office chair. She reached for the crumpled slip of paper on her desk and handed it to her coworker. "What a nice thing to give someone at the end of the day. I've got two weeks to tie up loose ends and clear out my desk."

Joy scanned the memo, her forehead creasing as she frowned. "I heard there would be some cutbacks, now that the war is over and many of our returning men will need their old jobs back. I just didn't realize it would be so soon, or that you'd be one of those they let go."

Bev pulled the bottom drawer open and scooped up her pocketbook. "It's probably for the best," she mumbled. "I was thinking I might have to look for another job anyway."

"You were? How come?"

Bev hung her head, feeling the humiliation of what had transpired yesterday afternoon.

Joy touched Bev's trembling shoulder. "Tell me what's wrong."

"I—I—it's nothing, really." Bev was afraid to admit that their boss had tried to take advantage of her. What if Joy told someone and the news spread around the building? Bev's reputation could be tarnished, and so would her Christian testimony. Here at Bethlehem Steel, she'd tried to tell others about Christ through her actions and by inviting them to attend church. No, it would be best if she kept quiet about what had happened with Frank Martin. She'd be leaving in two weeks anyway.

Joy tapped Bev gently on the shoulder, driving her disconcerting thoughts to the back of her mind. "I'm here if you want to talk."

Bev nodded, as tears clouded her vision. "I–I'd better get going. I don't want to be late picking Amy up at the sitter's."

Joy returned to her own desk, and Bev left the office. Bev had only taken a few steps when she bumped into a tall man with sandy blond hair. She didn't recognize him and figured he must not work here or could be a returning veteran—perhaps the one who would be taking her bookkeeping position.

When the man looked down, Bev noticed that the latch on his briefcase had popped open, and several black-and-white photographs were strewn on the floor.

"I'm so sorry," she apologized.

"It's my fault. I wasn't watching where I was going." He squatted down and began to collect the pictures. "I'm here to do a photo shoot for management and can't find the conference room. Do you know where it is?"

"Two doors down. Here, let me help you with those." Bev knelt on the floor, unmindful of her hose that already had a small tear in them. As she helped gather the remaining photos, she almost collided with the man's head.

For a few seconds, he stared at Bev with a look of sympathy. Could he tell she'd been crying? Did he think she was clumsy for bumping into him, causing his briefcase to open?

She handed the man his photos and stood, smoothing her dark green, knee-length skirt. "Sorry about the pictures. I hope none of them are ruined."

He put the photos back into his briefcase, snapped it closed, and rose. "No harm done. Thanks for your help."

"You're welcome."

The man hesitated a moment, like he wanted to say something more, but then he strode down the hallway toward the conference room.

Bev headed in the opposite direction, anxious to get her daughter and head for home.

❦

As Dan strolled down the hallway, he thought about the young woman he'd bumped into a few minutes ago. She wore her dark hair in a neat pageboy and had the bluest eyes he'd ever seen. If he wasn't mistaken, there'd been tears in her eyes, and he figured she must have been crying before they collided.

It's none of my business, he admonished himself. *My desire to help others sometimes clouds my judgment.*

Dan spotted the conference room and was about to open the door, when a middle-aged man with a balding head stopped him. "Hey, aren't you Dan Fisher?"

Puzzled, Dan only nodded in reply.

"I'm Pete Mackey. We met back in '39 when we were photographing the pedestrian suspension bridge that links Warren and Valley streets. That was shortly after it was damaged by a severe storm."

"I remember. That was quite a mess," Dan said. "The new bridge is holding together nicely, though."

"Yeah, until the next hurricane hits the coast."

"I hope not."

Pete's pale eyebrows drew together. "Say, didn't you lose your wife a few years ago? I remember reading her obituary in the newspaper."

"Darcy died of leukemia in the fall of '43." Dan's skin prickled. He hated to think about how he'd lost his precious wife, much less discuss his feelings with a near stranger.

"That must have been rough."

"It was."

"Do you have any children?"

"No, but we wanted some."

"Me and the wife have five." Pete gave his left earlobe a couple of pulls. "Kids can be a handful at times, but I wouldn't trade mine for anything."

Dan smiled and glanced at his watch. In about two minutes, he would be late for his appointment.

"You here on business?" Pete asked.

"Yes. I've been asked to photograph some of the managers. How about you?"

"Came to interview a couple of women who lost their husbands in the war."

"I see. Well, it was nice seeing you again." Dan turned toward the door, hoping Pete would take the hint and be on his way.

"Say, I was wondering if you could do me a favor," Pete said.

Dan glanced over his shoulder. "What's that?"

"I'm working for *Family Life Magazine* now, and I've been asked to write an article on how people deal with grief. Since you lost your wife, I figured you might be able to give me some helpful insights."

Dan pivoted on his heel. "Are you suggesting an interview?"

"Yep. I'm sure the article will reach people all over the country who lost a loved one during the war. Some might be helped by your comments or advice, same as with the folks I'll be interviewing here today."

Dan's face warmed, and his palms grew sweaty. Even though it had been two years since Darcy's death, it was still difficult to talk about. Hardly a day had gone by that he hadn't yearned for her touch. He wasn't ready to share his feelings—not even to help someone going through grief.

"Sorry," Dan mumbled. "I'm not interested in being interviewed for your magazine, and I'm late for an appointment." He hurried off before Pete could say anything more.

Chapter 2

Dan leaned against his polished oak office chair and raked his fingers through the back of his hair, preparing to look over some proofs from a recent wedding that he'd done. Things had been busy lately and would soon get even busier, with Christmas only three months away. Many people wanted portraits taken to give as gifts, and he hoped those who did wouldn't wait until the last minute to schedule an appointment. That had happened in the past, and there were days when he wondered why he'd ever become a photographer.

Dan thought about his first career choice, and how he had wanted to join the navy shortly after he got out of high school. However, due to a knee injury he'd received playing football, he had been turned down for active duty.

Guess it's just as well, he thought. *If I'd gone into the navy, I might never have met Darcy. Might not be alive today, either.*

He thought about the radio broadcasts he'd listened to

during the war and the newspaper articles that had given account of the battles, often mentioning those in the area who'd lost their lives in the line of duty. War was an ugly thing, but he knew it was a price that sometimes had to be paid in order to have freedom.

Dan's thoughts were halted when the telephone rang. Knowing it could be a client, he reached for the receiver. "Fisher's Photography Studio. Dan speaking."

"Hi, Danny. How are you this evening?" The lilting voice on the other end of the line purred like a kitten, and he recognized it immediately.

"I'm fine, Leona. How are you?"

"Okay." There was a brief pause. "You said you enjoyed my spaghetti and meatballs last week when you came over for supper, so I was hoping you'd join me tonight for my meat loaf special."

"I appreciate the offer, but I'm busy right now, Leona."

Dan's next-door neighbor's placating voice suddenly turned to ice. "I hope you're not giving me the brush-off."

"Of course not. I've got work to do in the studio, and I'll be here until quite late."

"I'm really disappointed, Danny."

Dan clenched the phone cord between his fingers. Leona Howard was a nice enough woman, but why did she have to be so pushy? "Can I take a rain check?" he asked.

"Okay, but I plan to collect on that rain check soon."

"I'd better get back to work, so I'll talk to you later. Good-bye, Leona." Dan hung up the phone with a sense of relief. He didn't want to hurt the woman's feelings, but they weren't right for each other. At least, she wasn't right for him. Leona was nothing like Darcy. In fact, she was the exact opposite of her. Leona usually wore her platinum blond hair in one of those wavy updos, with her bangs swept to one side. Darcy's chestnut brown hair had been shoulder length and worn in a soft pageboy. Leona plastered on enough makeup to sink a battleship, and Darcy had worn hardly any at all.

Dan massaged his forehead, making little circles with the tips of his fingers. *Who am I kidding? I'm not ready to commit to another woman, and I may never be. Besides, Leona is not a Christian, and that fact alone would keep me from becoming seriously involved with her.*

A couple of times, when Leona first started inviting him to her house for a meal, Dan had asked her to attend church with him. She'd flatly refused, saying church was for weak people who needed a crutch. Leona wasn't weak, and she'd proved that when her husband was killed on the USS *Arizona* during the bombing of Pearl Harbor. Leona had become a nurse and picked up the pieces of her life so well, it made Dan wonder if she'd ever loved her husband at all.

A rumble in the pit of Dan's stomach reminded him that it was nearly suppertime. He momentarily fought the urge to call his wife on the phone and ask what she was fixing tonight. He glanced through the open door of his office, leading to the used-toy store on the other side of the building. There was Darcy's quilt hanging over the wooden rack he'd made. The coverlet was a reminder of her undying love and brought him some measure of comfort.

Bev sank into a chair at the kitchen table and opened the newspaper. Yesterday had been her last day at Bethlehem Steel, and she hoped to find something else right away. She *needed* to, as the meager savings she'd put away wouldn't last long.

She scanned the HELP WANTED section but soon realized there were no bookkeeping jobs available. "They've probably all been taken by returning war veterans," she grumbled.

Her conscience pricked, and she bowed her head. "Forgive me, Lord. I'm thankful that so many of our soldiers have come home. I only wish Fred could have been one of them."

Tears stung Bev's eyes as she thought about the way her husband had been killed, along with thousands of other men and women who'd been at Pearl Harbor on December 7, 1941. For nearly four years now, Bev had been without Fred, but at least she'd had a job.

She returned her attention to the newspaper. Surely there had to be something she could do. She was about to give up and start supper when she noticed an ad she had not seen before. "Wanted: Reliable person to manage used-toy store. Must have good people skills and be able to balance the books. If interested, apply at Twice Loved, on the corner of North Main and Tenth Street, Easton, Pennsylvania."

She pursed her lips. "Maybe I should drop by there tomorrow after I take Amy to school. Even if I don't get the job, I might be able to find an inexpensive doll or stuffed animal I could put away for her Christmas present."

As if on cue, Bev's six-year-old daughter burst into the room. Her blue eyes brimmed with tears, and her chin trembled like a leaf caught in a breeze.

Bev reached out and pulled Amy into her arms. "What's wrong, honey?"

"I was playin' with Baby Sue, and her head fell off."

"Why don't you go get the doll, and I'll see if I can put her back together."

Amy shook her head as more tears came. "Her neck's tore. The head won't stay on."

Bev knew enough about rubber dolls to realize that once the body gave way, there was little that could be done except to buy a new doll.

Her gaze came to rest on the newspaper ad again. *I really do need to pay a visit to Twice Loved.*

Chapter 3

Bev stood in front of Twice Loved, studying the window display. There were several stuffed animals leaning against a stack of books, a toy fire truck, two cloth dolls, and a huge teddy bear with a red ribbon tied around its neck. Propped against the bear's feet was a sign that read: HELP WANTED. INQUIRE WITHIN.

Bev drew in a deep breath and pushed open the door. Inside, there was no one in sight, so she made her way to the wooden counter in the center of the room. A small bell sat on one end, and she gave it a jingle. A few minutes later, a door at the back of the store opened, and a man stepped out.

Her heart did a little flip-flop. He was tall with sandy blond hair and wore a pair of tan slacks and a long-sleeved, white shirt rolled up to the elbows.

Bev recognized him, but from where? She'd never been in this store before. She was tempted to ask if they'd met somewhere, but that might seem too forward.

The man stepped up beside her. "May I help you?"

Bev moistened her lips, feeling as though her tongue were tied in knots. "I—um—do you have any dolls?"

He smiled and made a sweeping gesture with his hand. "All over the store, plus toys of all sorts."

"I'm looking for something inexpensive that's in good condition."

"Shouldn't be a problem. Most of the toys are in pretty fair shape."

"Would you mind if I have a look around?"

"Help yourself." He stepped aside, and Bev walked slowly around the room until she came to a basket full of dolls. Surely there had to be something here Amy would like. If they weren't too expensive, maybe she could buy two—one to replace Amy's Baby Sue and the other for Amy's Christmas present.

Bev knelt in front of the basket and rummaged through the dolls. A few minutes later, the man pulled up a short wooden stool and plunked down beside her. "Have we met before? You look familiar."

She felt the heat of a blush creep up the back of her neck. "I'm—uh—not sure. You look familiar to me, too."

They stared at one another a few seconds, and his scrutiny made Bev's cheeks grow even warmer. Suddenly, she remembered where she'd seen the man. It was at Bethlehem Steel, the day she'd rushed into the hallway in tears after receiving her layoff notice. She had been mortified when she bumped the man's briefcase and it opened, spilling his photographs. But no, this couldn't be the same man. The man she'd met was obviously a photographer, not a used-toy salesman.

"I'm Dan Fisher, and I have a photography studio in

the back of this building," he said, reaching out his hand.

"I'm Bev Winters." She was surprised by the firm yet gentle handshake he gave. "You're a photographer, not the owner of Twice Loved?"

"I do both. The used-toy store was my wife's business, and I took it over after she died two years ago from leukemia."

"I'm sorry for your loss." Bev's heart went out to Dan. It was plain to see from the way his hazel-colored eyes clouded over that he still missed his wife. She could understand that, for she missed Fred, too.

"Were you at Bethlehem Steel a few weeks ago?" she questioned.

He nodded. "I was asked to take some pictures for management, and—" Suddenly, his face broke into a smile. "Say, you're that woman I bumped into, aren't you?"

"Actually, I think I bumped your briefcase."

"Ever since you came into the store, I've been trying to place you."

"Same here."

He motioned to the basket of dolls. "What kind of doll are you looking for?"

"I might buy two. One needs to be a baby doll, because my daughter's favorite doll is broken beyond repair. I'd also like to find something to give her for Christmas."

"How about this?" he said, pointing to a pretty doll with a bisque head.

Beth looked at the price tag and released a sigh. "I'm sure Amy would like it, but I can't afford that much right now." She plucked a baby doll from the basket. Its head was made from compressed wood, and the body was cloth.

"I think this could replace Amy's rubber doll. How much is it? I don't see a price sticker."

"Some of the dolls in that basket came in last week, and I haven't had a chance to price them yet. How does twenty-five cents sound?"

Her mouth fell open. "You can't be serious. The doll probably cost at least three dollars when it was new."

He shrugged. "Maybe so, but it's used now, and twenty-five cents seems fair to me."

Bev sat a few seconds, thinking about his offer and trying to decide how best to reply. *I shouldn't have told him I couldn't afford the other doll. He probably feels sorry for me or thinks I'm a charity case.* She pinched the bridge of her nose, hoping to release some of the tension she felt. "Maybe I'll take this doll now. If I find a job soon, I might be able to purchase the bisque doll later."

His eyebrows lifted in obvious surprise. "You're not working at Bethlehem Steel any longer?"

She shook her head. "I was laid off. A returning soldier used to have my bookkeeping position."

"I'm sorry." The compassion Bev saw in Dan's eyes made her want to cry, but she couldn't. It would be humiliating to break down in front of someone she barely knew.

"I understand that a lot of women who were filling job slots during the war are now out of work," he commented.

"Which would be fine if my husband were coming home."

"He was in the war?"

She nodded, willing her tears not to spill over. "Fred was killed during the Pearl Harbor attack. He was aboard the USS *Maryland*."

"I'm sorry," Dan said again. He reached out his hand as though he might touch her, but quickly withdrew it and offered Bev a crooked grin instead.

She felt relief. One little sympathetic gesture and she might give in to her threatening tears.

"An elderly lady from church worked here part-time for a while," Dan said, as though needing to change the subject. "Alma fell and broke her hip a few weeks ago, so she had to quit. I've been trying to run both Darcy's toy store and my photo business ever since. It's become an almost impossible task, so I'm looking for someone to manage Twice Loved." He released a puff of air. "You think you might be interested in the job?"

Interested? Of course she was interested. That's one of the reasons she'd come here today. "I did notice your HELP WANTED sign in the window," Bev admitted.

"I put it there yesterday. Also placed an ad in the newspaper."

"I read that ad in last night's paper," Bev said, feeling the need to be completely honest with him.

"You did?"

"Yes, but that's not the only reason I came here this morning. I really do need a doll for my daughter."

"I appreciate your truthfulness," he said with a smile. "I'm a Christian; I believe honesty and integrity are important—especially where business matters are concerned."

"I'm a Christian, too." Bev fingered the lace edge on the baby doll's white nightgown. "I would have told you right away that I was interested in the job, but I was taken by surprise when you stepped into the room and I couldn't figure out where we had met."

He chuckled.

"So, about the position here—what hours would I be expected to work, and what would the job entail?"

"The store's closed on Sundays and Mondays, so I'd need you to work Tuesday through Saturday from nine to five. Could you manage that?"

Bev nibbled on the inside of her cheek as a sense of apprehension crept up her spine. Would he refuse to hire her if he knew she couldn't work Saturdays?

"Is there a problem?" he asked. "I sense some hesitation."

"The woman who watches my little girl after school is not available on weekends, so it would be difficult for me to work on Saturdays."

Dan shrugged. "That's not a problem. Bring your daughter to the store."

"You wouldn't mind?"

"Not at all. I have no children of my own, but I like kids." He shrugged. "Besides, a lot of kids come here with their folks. Maybe your daughter could keep them occupied while their parents shop. In between customers she can play with the toys."

Bev could hardly believe the man was so accommodating. Her boss at Bethlehem Steel would never have considered such a thing. Of course, there weren't a bunch of toys available there.

"What type of work would be expected of me?" she asked.

"Keeping the books, waiting on customers, going

through boxes of toys that have been donated; that sort of thing."

"I think I could handle it." She felt her face heat up again. "That is, if you're willing to give me a try."

Dan stood and motioned her back to the counter.

Bev followed, wondering what he had in mind.

He reached underneath, pulled out a dark green ledger, and flipped it open. "If you're a bookkeeper, you should be able to tell me if there's any hope for this store."

Bev peered at the page and frowned. The figures showed a decided lack of income, compared to the expenditures. "Why are so many of the toys given away for little or nothing?" she questioned.

"I donate a certain percentage of the proceeds from Twice Loved to children in need. It was something Darcy started before she died, and I plan to continue doing it." His forehead wrinkled. "So many kids had to do without during wartime."

"There have been so many people affected by the war, children who have lost a parent, most of all." Bev drew in a deep breath and decided to ask the question uppermost on her mind. "How can you afford to pay me if the toy store operates in the red?"

"I make enough as a photographer to cover your wages." He motioned to the ledger. "And maybe you'll figure out a way to sell more toys and put Twice Loved in the black. My only concern is whether you'll be able to handle some of the repairs."

She lifted one eyebrow in question.

"The dirty toys that come in aren't such a problem. I usually take them home and soak them in the tub.

However, I'm not good with a needle and thread, the way my wife was." Dan nodded toward a colorful patchwork quilt draped over a wooden rack on the opposite wall. "Darcy finished that shortly before she died."

Bev studied the item in question, taking in the vivid colors mixed with warm hues. "It's beautiful."

"Can you sew?" he asked.

She nodded. "I don't quilt, but I can mend. I've made most of Amy's and my clothes."

"Great. I think you'll do just fine."

"Is there anything else?"

He ran his fingers through the back of his hair, sending a spicy aroma into the air that tickled Bev's nose. "You know anything about electric trains?"

Chapter 4

On her trip home, Bev sat at the back of the bus, thinking about the job. Had she made a mistake in accepting Dan Fisher's invitation to work at Twice Loved? She was sure she could handle the books because bookkeeping was something she had been doing for the last four years. But what did she know about fixing broken dolls and stuffed animals? And a toy train, of all things!

Bev winced. Had Dan been kidding about her repairing the broken train, or did he really expect her to tackle such a job? She would have asked about it right away, but he'd received a phone call that interrupted them. When he hung up, Bev paid for the baby doll; and not wanting to miss the next bus, she had left in a hurry and forgot to ask about the broken train.

She glanced at the small box lying in her lap. Amy's new doll. The one she'd paid a quarter for. She figured it was an act of charity, but since money was tight, she'd set her independent spirit aside.

I still can't believe he suggested that I bring Amy to the store. But tomorrow's Saturday, and I can't leave her alone. I hope things will go okay during my first day on the job.

"Excuse me, but is this seat taken?"

Bev was glad for the interruption, as her worrisome thoughts were taking her nowhere. "No, you're welcome to sit here," she said to the elderly woman who stood in the aisle.

The woman slid in next to her, pushing a strand of gray hair away from her eyes. "Whew! I almost missed the bus."

"I'm glad you made it." Bev could relate to what the woman had gone through. Since Bev didn't own a car, she usually rode the bus and had dashed for it many times when she'd been late. When she worked at Bethlehem Steel, which was several miles outside of town, Bev rode to work with a coworker who owned a Hudson and lived near her apartment. With her new job being downtown, though, she would ride the bus every day.

As the bus continued on its route, Bev watched the passing scenery—The Karldon Hotel, Easton City Hall, Maxwell's Book Store. How long had it been since she'd bought a book to read? Money was tight; America had begun rationing things during the war. She had a feeling that despite the end of the war, some things might continue to be rationed for a while.

Even though Bev had Fred's monthly veteran's pension, it was small and not enough to provide all the essentials she and Amy needed. Bev wished her wages at Twice Loved wouldn't be coming from Dan's photography business. She hoped to find a way for the toy store to make more money and get out of the red, while keeping prices low.

Bev closed her eyes and leaned against the seat, willing herself to relax and give her troubles to the Lord. After all, He had provided her with a new job, and so quickly, too. She needed to trust Him and believe He would care for her and Amy in the days ahead.

Sometime later, Bev arrived at her apartment and was surprised to find a note taped to the door. She waited until she was inside to read it, dropping her coat and the box with the doll in it onto the couch. Then she took a seat and opened the folded paper.

Dear Mrs. Winters:
  This is to inform you that due to the expected rise in heating costs this winter, I need to raise your rent by five dollars a month. The increase will take effect on the fifteenth of October.
  Thank you.

  Sincerely,
  Clyde Smithers,
  Manager

Bev moaned. This kind of news was not what she needed. The rent on her small two-bedroom apartment was already sixty dollars a month, and she didn't think she could afford another five. With the addition of bus fare to and from work every day, and the fact that her wages at Twice Loved wouldn't be as much as what she had made at Bethlehem Steel, she couldn't afford the rent increase.

Maybe I should look for an apartment closer to town so I can walk to work. That would save money, and perhaps I can find something cheaper to rent.

Bev dismissed that thought as quickly as it came. She had heard that apartments in the heart of the city were in demand, and with so many men and women returning from the war, it would be difficult to find one that wasn't already rented, let alone cheaper.

Bev massaged her pulsating forehead. Just when she thought the Lord was watching out for them, another problem had come along. Ever since Fred died, it seemed as if her whole world were out of control. Bev attended church on Sunday mornings, read her Bible regularly, and prayed every day. Yet her faith was beginning to waver.

Blinking back tears, she closed her eyes and prayed, "Lord, show me what to do about the increase in my rent. If there's something closer to town, please point the way."

For the last couple of hours, Dan had been sitting at his desk going over some paperwork. Trying to run two businesses by himself had put him behind in the photography studio. But that was about to change. Now that he'd hired Bev Winters to run Twice Loved, things would get back to normal. At least he hoped they would. What if Bev didn't work out? He didn't know much about the woman other than that she had worked as a bookkeeper, had a young daughter, and was widowed. He hadn't thought to ask for a résumé or any references. He'd based his decision to hire Bev on her need for a job. That and the fact that she said she was a Christian.

A beautiful one at that, Dan thought, tapping his pencil on the edge of the desk. It wasn't just Bev's dark hair and luminous blue eyes that attracted him. There was something about her demeanor that reminded him of Darcy.

He rapped the side of his head with the pencil. "Get a grip on yourself. You hired the lady to run Twice Loved, not so you could become romantically involved."

The phone rang, and he grabbed for it, glad for the interruption. "Fisher's Photography. May I help you?"

"Hello, Dan. This is Pete Mackey, with *Family Life Magazine*. We talked at Bethlehem Steel a few weeks ago, remember?"

Dan's gaze went to the ceiling. "I hope you're not calling about that article you're doing on grief, because, as I told you before, I'm not interested in being interviewed."

"I'd hoped if you had a few weeks to think it over, you might change your mind."

"Nope. Sorry, Pete."

"Here's the phone number where I can be reached, just in case."

Dan studied a set of negatives on his desk as Pete rattled off his number. There was no point in writing it down because he had no intention of doing that interview.

"I appreciate your time," Pete said. "Please call if you ever want to talk."

"Okay, thanks. Good-bye, Pete."

Dan had no more than hung up the phone when he heard a knock on the door of his studio. *Wonder who it could be? I don't have any appointments scheduled for the rest of the day.*

When Dan opened the door, he discovered Leona Howard holding a casserole dish wrapped in a towel with a paper sack balanced on top.

"Hi, Danny," she said, offering him a pleasant smile. "Since you've been too busy lately to have dinner at my place, I decided to bring a meal over to you this evening. It's chicken noodle supreme."

Leona wore a maroon-colored, knee-length skirt with a single-breasted jacket that had wide lapels and padded shoulders. It looked like something a woman might wear when she went out to dinner, but not to drop off a casserole for a neighbor.

"I'm working right now," Dan said as she swept into the room, her fragrant perfume leaving a trail of roses behind.

"Surely you're ready for a break. I'll be disappointed if you don't try some of my yummy casserole." Leona nodded at the paper sack. "I even brought some dishes, silverware, and napkins, so all you need to provide is a place for me to set the table."

Dan was sure the woman wasn't going to take no for an answer, so he removed the negatives and paperwork from his desk and slipped them into a folder. "You can put the food here." He pulled out his desk chair, grabbed another one for Leona, and sat down.

She quickly set out the dishes, opened the lid of the casserole dish, and served them both a hefty amount. "Oh, dear, I forgot to bring something to drink," she said with a frown. "Do you have anything cold on hand?"

He reached into the bottom drawer of his desk and grabbed a Thermos. "It's coffee, so it's not cold."

She smiled. "That will be fine."

"Mind if I pray before we eat?"

She shrugged. "If it makes you feel better. I wasn't planning to poison you, Danny."

He bit back a chuckle. That thought had crossed his mind.

After the prayer, Dan poked his fork into the gooey mess she'd put on his plate and took a bite. Ugh! The stuff tasted worse than it looked. He grabbed his Thermos, twisted the lid, and gulped down some coffee.

Leona's lower lip protruded. "You don't like it?"

Searching for words that wouldn't be a lie, Dan mumbled, "It's—uh—different." He set the Thermos lid down and wiped his mouth on the cloth napkin she had provided.

"I'm really not hungry."

Leona pushed her chair aside, and it nearly toppled over. "I can tell you'd rather not eat it."

Dan opened his mouth to reassure her, but Leona gathered her things so quickly, he barely had the presence of mind to say he was sorry.

"I'll try something different next time," she said as he followed her to the door. "Something I know you'll like."

Chapter 5

Dan took a swig of coffee and glanced at the clock on the far wall. Bev Winters should be here any minute and would be bringing her daughter along. He moved across the room and put the OPEN sign in the window. It was almost nine o'clock. Better to have the store ready for business on time, even if his new employee wasn't here yet.

I wonder if her bus was late, or maybe she had trouble getting her daughter out of bed. Sure hope I did the right thing in hiring her.

Dan thought about his favorite verses of scripture— 2 Corinthians 1:3–4. It reminded him that God is our comforter, and because He comforts us in all our troubles, we should comfort those who have trouble, as well. Through God's Word and the godly counsel of his pastor, Dan had been comforted many times since Darcy's death. It was only right that he should offer comfort to Bev, who was probably hurting from the loss of her husband, and also her job. He'd known yesterday that he needed to give her a chance. If hiring her to work at Twice Loved could help them both during their time of need, then so much the better.

Dan's gaze came to rest on the clock again. It was now ten minutes after nine. Bev was late. Maybe she'd changed her mind about the job and wasn't coming.

The bell above the front door jingled, and his thoughts were halted. Bev entered the store holding a metal lunch pail in one hand and a brown pocketbook in the other. A young girl stood at her side, clutching the same doll he'd sold Bev yesterday afternoon.

"I'm sorry we're late." Bev patted the sides of her wind-blown hair and smoothed the wrinkles in her knee-length, navy blue dress covered by a short, black jacket. "The bus was late, and there was more traffic this morning than I've seen in a long time."

"It's okay," Dan said with a nod. "There haven't been any customers yet." He smiled at the little girl who stood beside Bev. She was a beautiful child—curly black hair like her mother's and the same brilliant blue eyes. She wore a beige-colored tweed coat with a pair of dark green overalls with patched knees peeking out from underneath. "So, this must be Amy."

"Yes." Bev's generous smile seemed to light up the room.

Darcy used to smile like that, Dan noted.

"Amy, this is Mr. Fisher, and he owns this store where I'll be working."

The child smiled shyly and glanced around the shop. "I like it here."

"Me, too." Dan swallowed around the lump in his throat. He and Darcy had wanted children, but that wasn't to be. Did Bev Winters know how fortunate she was?

"Why don't you find a book to read?" Bev said to her daughter.

"Mommy needs to begin working now."

Dan pointed across the room. "There's a table in the corner where you can sit if you want to read or work on a puzzle. Feel free to play with any of the toys that are in baskets sitting on the floor."

Amy didn't have to be asked twice. She slipped out of her coat and handed it to her mother. Then she sprinted across the room, grabbed a fat teddy bear from a wicker basket, and helped herself to a book from the bookcase. A few seconds later, she sat at the table, wearing a contented grin.

Dan turned his attention back to Bev. "Should we take a look at some of the toys that need to be fixed?"

Her eyes widened. "Uh—about the toys—"

"What about them?"

"Yesterday you mentioned a broken train, and I thought I should let you know that I'm not the least bit mechanical."

He chuckled and led her over to the desk. "I was only kidding. The train will have to be sold as is."

A look of relief flooded her face. "There's an elderly man at my church who collects old trains. I could speak to him and see if he might be able to look at the broken train."

"That would be great."

Bev set her pocketbook and lunch pail on the desk, removed her jacket, and draped it and Amy's coat over the back of the wooden chair. "Which toys did you want me to see about fixing?"

"First, I'd like to tell you something."

"What's that?"

You're beautiful. Dan shook his head, hoping to clear his ridiculous thoughts. "Uh—the dress you're wearing might not be practical here at the store."

She crossed her arms. "Too dressy?"

"It's not that." Dan paused. How could he put this tactfully? "Sometimes you'll have to get down on the floor, in order to sort through the boxes of toys that come in. You'll also be working with glue and other repair items. It might be better if you wear slacks to work from now on."

She blinked. "You wouldn't mind?"

He shook his head.

"I was expected to wear a dress at Bethlehem Steel, so I figured—"

"Wear whatever you're comfortable in here, Bev. I trust you to use good judgment."

"Thank you, Mr. Fisher."

"Dan. Please call me Dan."

Bev's cheeks turned pink as something indefinable passed between them, and she looked quickly away. "Guess you'd better show me what to do, so I can get to work."

He glanced toward the room where his studio was located. "That makes two of us."

～◦～

Bev's stomach growled as her gaze went to the clock on the wall across from her. It was almost noon, and she couldn't believe how quickly the morning had passed. She'd mended two doll dresses, stitched a stuffed kitten's eyes in place, and waited on several customers. In all that time, Amy had hardly made a peep. She'd kept herself occupied with various toys, books, and puzzles. Dan excused himself soon after showing Bev what needed to be done, and he'd been in his photography studio ever since.

Should I ask him to cover for me so I can see that Amy is fed, or should I serve Amy her lunch and try to eat my sandwich while I keep an eye out for customers? Guess the latter would be better, she decided. *No point in bothering Dan. He's probably busy and might not appreciate the interruption. After all, he hired me so he could be free to operate his own business and not have to run back and forth between Twice Loved and his photography studio.*

"Amy, please have a seat at the table again, and I'll bring your lunch," Bev instructed her daughter, who was now on her knees in front of a stack of wooden blocks.

"Okay, Mommy." Amy lifted her baby doll by one arm. "Can Baby Sue eat lunch with me?"

Bev smiled, pleased that the child had accepted the new doll so readily and had even given it the same name as her old doll. "Sure, sweetie. Just don't give her anything to drink, all right?"

"Okay."

A few minutes later, Amy and Baby Sue were seated in the small wooden chairs opposite each other, a peanut butter and jelly sandwich and a cup of cold milk in front of Amy.

Bev said a quick prayer, thanking God for the food, then took her bologna sandwich and the remaining milk over to the desk so she could look at the ledger while she ate. From time to time she glanced up, wondering if or when Dan might emerge from his studio. But he didn't. The only evidence that he was in the back room was the occasional ringing of his telephone.

After lunch, Bev encouraged Amy to lie on a piece of carpet next to the bookcase and take a nap. Amy slept with Baby Sue tucked under one arm and a stuffed elephant under the other.

Bev decided to use this quiet time to sort through some boxes she'd found in one corner of the room. She soon discovered they were full of Christmas decorations, and it put her in the mood to decorate the store for the holidays. Perhaps it was too soon for that, though. It was early October, and most of the stores didn't set out their Christmas things until sometime in November. She set the box aside, planning to ask Dan if he would mind if she decorated Twice Loved a little early. If she put some Christmas items in the store window, it might attract more customers. Besides, it would help Bev get into the spirit of the holiday season. For the past several Christmases, she'd forced herself to put up a tree. Christmas wasn't the same without Fred, but for Amy's sake, Bev had gone through the motions.

Pushing the decorations aside, she turned her attention to another box. This one was full of old train cars, reminding her that she should speak to Ellis Hampton when she saw him at church tomorrow morning. She hoped he would be willing to look at the broken train. It would be cute, set up in the store window under a small, decorated tree with several dolls and stuffed animals sitting off to one side.

Bev blinked back tears as a feeling of nostalgia washed over her. Christmas used to be such a happy time, first when she was a child growing up near the Pocono Mountains, and then after she'd married Fred and they moved to Easton.

She closed her eyes and thought about their last Christmas together. She could almost smell the fragrant scent of the evergreen tree they'd cut down in the woods that year. Amy was only two, and Bev remembered the touching scene as Fred carried their daughter on his shoulders while they trudged through the snow. They'd laughed and thrown snowballs, eaten the chewy brownies Bev had made, and drank hot chocolate from the Thermos she'd brought along.

Unwanted tears seeped under Bev's eyelashes and trickled down her cheeks. *Those happy days are gone for good.* Her mother and father had been killed in a car accident five years ago, and the ugly war had taken Fred away. It was hard not to feel bitter and become cynical when there were so many injustices in the world. But for Amy's sake, Bev was determined to make the best of her situation.

"Ah! I caught you sleeping on the job, didn't I?"

Bev jumped at the sound of Dan's deep voice.

"I—I wasn't sleeping." She sat up straight and swiped a hand across her damp cheeks.

"I was kidding about you taking a nap, but your daughter certainly is." Dan motioned across the room, where Amy lay curled on her side.

Bev nodded. "I suggested she rest awhile. I hope you don't mind."

"Why would I mind?"

She merely shrugged in reply. Dan didn't seem like the type to get upset over something like a child falling asleep inside his toy store. In fact, from the look on his face, Bev guessed he might be rather taken with her daughter.

Dan left the desk and headed across the room. When he reached the wooden rack where the colorful patchwork quilt was draped, he pulled it down. Turning to give Bev a quick smile, he moved over to where Amy lay sleeping. Then he bent at the waist, covered her with the quilt, and reached out to push a wayward curl off her forehead.

The sight was so touching, Bev's heart nearly melted. She barely knew Dan, yet she could tell he had a lot of love to give. How sad that he hadn't been blessed with any children of his own.

She swallowed around the lump in her throat. Why was life so unfair? Shouldn't only good things happen to good people?

Chapter 6

On Tuesday morning, Bev showed up at Twice Loved wearing an olive green, two-piece trouser suit; a pale yellow blouse; brown lace-up shoes; and the same jacket she'd worn on Saturday.

When Dan greeted her, she offered him a radiant smile. Then, as her fingers curled around the strap of her pocketbook, a little frown pinched her forehead. "I was wondering if it would be all right if I left the shop during my lunch hour today. There's an apartment for rent in the building two doors down, and I'd like the opportunity to look at it before it's taken."

"You're planning to move?"

She nodded. "My rent's going up to sixty-five dollars in a few weeks, and since I live on the south side of town and have to catch the bus to get here, I thought if I could find something closer, it would be the wise thing to do."

Dan's heart went out to Bev. He could see by her troubled look that she was probably struggling financially. Many people had been faced with financial hardships during the war. "Mend and make do." That was the motto for the women in America.

From the looks of the patches he'd seen on the knees of Amy's overalls the other day, Dan figured Bev had done her share of mending.

He rubbed his chin and contemplated a moment. "Maybe I can increase your wages."

Bev stared at the floor, twisting the purse strap back and forth. "Today's only my second day on the job, and I've done nothing to deserve a wage increase."

"I know, but—"

She held up her hand. "I don't need your charity, but I do need to look at that apartment today. Is it okay if I leave the store for an hour during lunch?"

"Sure, that'll be fine." Bev was obviously a proud woman, and he really couldn't fault her for that. Maybe he could find some other way to help.

"Thank you, Dan." She pursed her lips. "Well, I'd better get busy."

"Same here. I've got some phone calls to make."

She started across the room but turned back around. "I almost forgot to ask. . . . Would you mind if I decorate the store window for Christmas a little early?"

Dan's eyebrows drew together. Other than attending the candlelight Communion service at church on Christmas Eve, he hadn't done much to celebrate Christmas since Darcy died. His parents, who lived in Connecticut, had invited him to come to their place for the holidays, but Dan always turned them down, preferring to be alone.

He glanced around the store as bittersweet memories flooded over him like waves lapping against the Jersey shore. When Darcy was alive, she had decorated every nook and cranny of Twice Loved for the holidays.

"If you'd rather I wait until after Thanksgiving, I understand," Bev added. "I just thought it might bring in more customers if we had the window decorated a little sooner."

Dan tapped his foot against the hardwood floor. Would it hurt if the store were decorated? It didn't mean he would have to celebrate Christmas, and it wasn't as if he would be giving up memories of Darcy by allowing Bev to do something festive here. In fact, if Darcy were alive, he knew what she would do.

"Sure, go ahead. Do whatever you'd like with the store window," he conceded.

"I'll start on the decorations when I return from my lunch break," Bev said sweetly.

"Take as long as you need to look at that apartment. I'll be praying it's the right one."

"Thanks. I appreciate that."

❧

Bev wanted to pinch herself. Not only was the apartment she had looked at within walking distance of Twice Loved, but the rent was five dollars cheaper than what she was paying now. Without hesitation, she had signed the lease, and she hoped that by the next weekend she and Amy would be in their new home.

The move would mean Amy had to change schools, but she was young and adjusted easily. It would solve the problem of her needing a babysitter after school, too, which meant one less expense. Since the closest elementary school was only a few blocks away, Amy could walk to Twice Loved after school on the days Bev was working. Of course, she knew she would have to check with Dan first and see if he approved of the idea.

Bev smiled as she pulled out the box of Christmas decorations. Everything was working out fine. She'd been worried for nothing.

For the next hour, Bev worked on the window decorations. She had spoken to Ellis Hampton after church on Sunday, and he'd agreed to look at the broken train.

She knew it was too early to get a cut tree. She certainly didn't want it drying out and dropping needles everywhere.

For the time being, Bev hung several Christmas ornaments in the store window, along with some red and green bows. She also placed three dolls and a couple of stuffed animals in the center and included several small empty boxes, which were wrapped like Christmas presents.

It looks rather festive, she told herself as she stood off to one side and studied her work. She allowed herself a satisfied sigh. She began humming the words to "White Christmas," swaying to the music.

"The window display looks great. Your humming's not so bad, either."

Bev whirled around. She hadn't realized Dan had come into the room and stood directly behind her. Her face flushed. "Thanks. I think it will look even better once the train is fixed and set up under a small tree." She chose not to mention her off-key music.

"Did you speak to that man from your church?" he asked, leaning against the inside casing of the window display and looking at her intently.

Bev nodded and moistened her lips. *Why do I feel so jittery whenever Dan's around?* "Ellis said he would come by sometime this afternoon," she said.

Dan smiled, but there was sadness in his hazel-colored eyes. Was he nostalgic about trains, or could something else be bothering him?

"I'll be anxious to hear what the train expert has to say." He took a few steps toward Bev but then backed away, jamming his hands into the pockets of his brown slacks. "How'd things go with the apartment hunt?"

"It went well. If I can get some of the men from church to help transport my furniture, I'll be moving to my new place next Saturday. After I get off work here, of course."

"If you need the whole day to move, that won't be a problem. In fact, why don't we close the store that day and I can help you?"

Bev noticed the look of compassion on Dan's face. Help her move? Was there no end to this man's charitable offers?

She opened her mouth to decline, but he interrupted her. "I can't get much into my Studebaker, but I know someone who has a pickup truck. I'm pretty sure I can borrow it."

"That's nice of you, but I really couldn't accept your help." Bev appreciated his generosity, but he'd already done enough by hiring her and allowing her to bring Amy to the shop on Saturdays.

He lifted his hand and leaned forward, almost touching her lips with his fingertips, but then he quickly lowered it. "I wish you'd reconsider."

Bev swallowed around the lump in her throat. Why was it that whenever anyone was nice to her, she felt all weepy and unable to express herself? She'd been that way since Fred was killed. And why was she so determined to do things on her own? Maybe she should accept Dan's help—just this once.

"Thank you," she murmured. "I appreciate your thoughtfulness."

His ears turned pink. "Just helping a friend."

Chapter 7

Bev closed the door behind a customer and glanced around the toy store. She couldn't believe she'd been working here three weeks already. So much had happened in that time—moving, getting Amy situated in her new school, and learning more about her job. She felt she was doing fairly well, for she'd sold twice as many toys in the last few days as she had the previous week. Working at Twice Loved was proving to be fun, with not nearly as much stress as her last job. No overbearing boss making unwanted advances, either.

Bev had felt such relief when Dan agreed to let Amy come to the store after school. He even said having the child there might make some customers stay longer, since those who'd brought children along could shop at their leisure while Amy kept their little ones occupied.

There were times, like the Saturday Bev and Amy had moved, when Dan seemed so friendly and approachable. Other times he shut himself off, hiding behind the doors of his studio and barely saying more than a few words whenever he was around. Bev figured he was busy with pre-Christmas portraits, but it almost seemed as if he'd been avoiding her.

Have I done something wrong? she wondered. *Is he displeased with the way I do the books or how I run the store?*

She studied the room more closely. Everything looked neat and orderly. Cleaning and organizing was one of the first things she had done. She'd also placed some of the more interesting toys in strategic spots in order to catch the customers' attention when they entered the store. The Christmas decorations she'd put in the store window looked enticing, even though the train wasn't part of the display yet. Ellis had phoned yesterday, saying the train should be ready later this week and that he would bring it by.

Bev picked up the ledger from her desk and thumbed through the last few pages. Twice Loved was making more money than it had in several months; the profit column was proof of that.

So why did Dan seem so aloof? Was he dreading the holidays? If so, Bev couldn't blame him. This was the first year since Fred's death that she hadn't experienced anxiety about Christmas coming.

"It's probably because I'm working here among all these toys," she said with a smile. "I feel like a kid again."

Bev closed the ledger and moved across the room to the sewing area. *Maybe I should invite Dan to join Amy and me for Thanksgiving dinner. It would be nice to have someone else to cook for. I could bake a small turkey, fix mashed potatoes, gravy, and stuffing. Maybe make a pumpkin and an apple pie.*

Bev took a seat at the sewing table and threaded her needle, prepared to mend the dress of the bisque doll she had chosen to give Amy for Christmas. Once the dress was repaired and the doll's wig combed and set in ringlets, she planned to put the doll in the storage closet at the back of the store until closer to Christmas. Then she would wrap it, take it home, and when Amy wasn't looking, slip it under the tree she hoped to get for their new apartment.

Thinking of a tree caused Bev to reflect on the day they had moved. Her daughter's enthusiasm over the large living room with a tall ceiling was catching.

"We can have a giant Christmas tree, Mommy!" Amy had exclaimed. "Uncle Dan can help us decorate and climb the ladder to put the angel on top."

Bev didn't know what had prompted Amy to call Dan "Uncle," but he didn't seem to mind. In fact, the man had been patient and kind to Amy all during the move, even rocking her to sleep when she'd become tired and fussy that evening.

The bell above the door jingled, forcing Bev's thoughts aside. When Amy skipped into the room, Bev hurriedly slipped the doll's dress into a drawer.

"Mommy, Mommy, guess what?" Amy's cheeks were rosy, and she was clearly out of breath.

"What is it, sweetie?" Bev asked, bending down to help her daughter out of her wool coat.

"No, I can't take my coat off yet," Amy said, thrusting out her lower lip.

"Why not?"

" 'Cause it's snowing, and I want to play in it!"

Bev glanced out the front window. Sure enough, silvery flakes fell from the sky like twinkling diamonds. And here it was only the second week of November.

"It's beautiful," she murmured.

"Can we build a snowman?" Amy's blue eyes glistened with excitement, as she wiggled from side to side.

"Simmer down," Bev said, giving her daughter a hug. "There's not nearly enough snow to make a snowball, let alone a snowman. If we had a place to build one, that is."

"We can put it out on the sidewalk in front of the store. I'll give it my hat and mittens to wear." Amy reached up to remove her stocking cap, but Bev stopped her.

"Whoa! You need your hat and mittens—you would get cold without them."

"What about the snowman? Won't he get cold without anything on his head or hands?"

Bev chuckled. "Oh, Amy, I don't think—"

"What's all this about a snowman?"

Bev and Amy turned at the sound of Dan's deep voice. Then Amy darted across the room and grabbed hold of his hand. "It's snowing, Uncle Dan! Can we build a snowman?"

"Amy, I just told you there's not enough snow," Bev reminded. "Besides, Uncle Dan—I mean, Mr. Fisher—is busy and doesn't have time to play in the snow."

Dan shook his head and gave Amy's hand a squeeze. "Who says I'm too busy to have a little fun?"

"Yippee!" Amy shouted.

Bev took a few steps toward him. "Do you really have the time for this?"

"For Amy and fun in the snow—absolutely!" His face sobered, and he bent down so he was eye level with the child. "There's not enough snow to build a snowman, but we can run up and down the sidewalk and catch snowflakes on our tongue." He glanced over at Bev and smiled. "How about it, Mommy? Why don't you slip into your coat and join us?"

She laughed self-consciously. "Oh, I couldn't do that."

"Why not?"

She made a sweeping gesture with her hand. "Who would mind the store?"

Dan tweaked Amy's nose and gave Bev a quick wink. "Let the store mind itself, because I think we all deserve some fun!"

⌇

Dan couldn't remember when he'd felt so exuberant or enjoyed himself so much. Certainly not since Darcy had taken ill.

For the last half hour, the three of them had been running up and down the sidewalk, slipping and sliding in the icy snow, catching snowflakes on their tongues, and singing Christmas carols at the top of their lungs. Some folks who passed by joined in their song. Some merely smiled and kept on walking. A few unfriendly people shook their heads and mumbled something about it not being Christmas yet. One elderly woman glared at Dan and said, "Some people never grow up."

Dan didn't care what anyone thought. He'd been cooped up in his studio for several days and needed the fresh air. He drew in a deep breath, taking in a few snowflakes in the process. *If I had known this was going to feel so good, I would have done it sooner.*

The sidewalk was covered with a good inch of snow now, and feeling like a mischievous boy, Dan bent down and scooped up a handful of the powdery stuff. He then trotted up the sidewalk, grabbed hold of Bev's collar, and dropped the snow down the back of her coat.

She shrieked and whirled around. "Hey! That was cold!"

"Of course it's cold. Snow's always cold." Dan winked at Amy, and she snickered.

"Stop that, or I won't invite you to join Amy and me for Thanksgiving." Bev wrinkled her nose. "That is, if you have no other plans."

He grinned. "I have no plans, and I'd be happy to have dinner at your place."

Bev smiled, and Amy clapped her hands.

"Can I bring anything?"

She shook her head. "Just a hearty appetite."

Before Dan could respond, two teenage girls strode up to them. Each held several wreaths in their hands. Dan recognized them and realized they attended his church.

"Hi, Mr. Fisher," Dorothy said. "Looks like you're havin' some fun today."

"Sure am," he replied with a smile.

"We came by to see if you'd like to buy a wreath for your front door," Amber put in.

He glanced at Bev. "Might be nice to have one hanging on the door of Twice Loved. What do you think?"

She nodded. "Sounds good to me."

Dorothy moved toward Bev. "Would you like to buy one to take home?"

"Thanks anyway, but it will be all I can do to afford a tree."

Dan was tempted to give Bev the money for a wreath, but he figured she would see it as charity. She'd made it clear that she didn't want his help and was making it difficult for him to do anything nice for her and Amy. So he kept quiet and paid the girls for one wreath, then went to hang it on the door of Twice Loved.

Just as the teens were leaving, an elderly couple showed up, wanting to buy something in the store.

"I had better get back inside," Bev said, hurrying past Dan.

He nodded. "Amy and I will be there in a minute."

Bev and the couple entered the store, and Dan reached for Amy's hand. "How would you like to give your mother a special Christmas present this year?"

She grinned up at him with snowflakes melting on her dark, curly lashes. "What is it?"

"Can you keep a secret?"

She bobbed her head up and down.

"Let's go inside my photography studio, and I'll tell you about it."

Chapter 8

I'm sorry, Leona," Dan said into the phone, "but I can't come to your place for Thanksgiving."

"Why not?"

"Because I've made other plans."

There was a long pause, and he could almost see Leona's furrowed brows.

"Are you spending the holiday with your folks this year?"

"No. I'll be staying in town."

"But you're having dinner with someone?"

Dan tapped his fingers along the edge of his desk, anxious to end this conversation. He still had some book work to do, and another photo shoot was scheduled in half an hour. "I've been invited to eat with Bev Winters and her daughter, Amy."

"Bev Winters? Who's she?" Leona's voice sounded strained, and Dan had a hunch she might be jealous. Of course, she had no right to be. He'd never given her any hope that he was interested in starting a relationship. Besides, Bev was an employee, not his girlfriend.

"Danny, are you still there?"

"Yes, Leona, although I do need to hang up. I've got a client coming soon."

"First, tell me who this *Bev* person is."

"She's the woman I hired to run Twice Loved."

Leona made no reply.

"I really do need to go. Thanks for the invite."

Leona sighed. "Have a nice holiday, and I'll see you soon." She hung up the phone before he could say good-bye.

Dan massaged his forehead, feeling a headache coming on. He reached for his cup of lukewarm coffee and gulped some down as the picture of Darcy hanging on the far wall caught his attention. Even though it had been two years since her death, he still loved her and always would.

~∞~

Bev had been scurrying around her apartment all morning, checking the turkey in the oven, dusting furniture, sweeping floors, setting the table, and preparing the rest of the meal. Amy was in the living room with her new coloring book and crayons. Last week, shortly after their romp in the snow, Bev had seen her daughter go into Dan's studio. When Amy emerged a short time later, she had a box of crayons and a coloring book, which she said were a gift from Dan.

Bev glanced at the clock on the far wall. It was one-thirty. Dan should be here soon, and she still needed to change clothes and put on some makeup.

"I'll be in the bedroom getting ready," Bev called to Amy. "If anyone knocks on the door, don't answer it. Come and get me, okay?"

"All right, Mommy."

A short time later, Bev stood in front of the small mirror hanging above her dresser. She'd chosen a dusty pink rayon and crepe dress with inset sleeves to wear. It was homemade and last-year's style, but she felt it looked presentable.

When Bev reached into her top dresser drawer for a pair of hose, she discovered that her one and only pair had a run in one leg that went all the way from the heel up to the top.

"I can't wear this," she muttered. "Maybe I should draw a line down the back of my leg, like I've seen some women do when they have no hosiery."

Bev rummaged around in her drawer until she found a dark brown eyebrow pencil. Craning her neck, she stretched her left leg behind her and bent backwards. Beginning at the heel of her foot, she drew a line up past her knee and then did the same to the other leg. "That will have to do," she grumbled, wishing she had a full-length mirror so she could see how it looked.

A knock at the door let Bev know Dan had arrived. She clicked off the light and left the bedroom. When Bev opened the front door, she was surprised to see a wreath hanging there.

Dan smiled at her. "Happy Thanksgiving."

"Same to you." She pointed to the wreath. "This is pretty, but I told you not to bring anything except your appetite."

He shrugged and turned his hands palm up. "It was there when I got here."

Bev squinted at the item in question. It hadn't been there this morning when she'd gone next door to borrow a cup of flour to make gravy.

"Looks like a mystery Santa Claus paid you a visit," Dan said with a chuckle.

Bev had no idea who it could be, but the pretty wreath with a red bow did look festive, so she decided not to worry about who the donor was. She opened the door wider. "Please, come inside."

～◎～

Dan sniffed the air as he entered Bev's apartment. "Umm—something sure smells good."

Bev nodded toward the kitchen. "That would be the turkey. Would you mind carving it for me?"

"I'd be happy to."

"Follow me."

Dan stopped at the living room to say hello to Amy, then he caught up to Bev. When she'd opened the door to let him in, he had noticed how pretty she looked in her frilly pink dress. He hadn't yet seen the backs of her legs, but now, as she led the way to the kitchen, Dan couldn't help but notice the strange, squiggly dark lines running up both legs.

"What happened, Bev?" he queried. "Did Amy use her new crayons to draw on your legs?"

Bev whirled around, her face turning as pink as her dress. "I—I didn't have a decent pair of hose to wear, so I improvised."

Dan tried to keep a straight face, but he couldn't hold back the laughter bubbling in his throat.

Bev's eyes pooled with tears, and he realized he had embarrassed her. "I'm sorry. If you'd told me you needed new hosiery, I would have given you the money."

She lifted her chin. "I don't need your money or your pity, and I'm sorry you think my predicament is so funny."

"I don't, really." He glanced at the crooked lines again and fought the temptation to gather her into his arms.

Bev craned her neck and stuck one leg out behind her. When she looked back at him, she wore a half smile. Soon the smile turned into a snicker. The snicker became a giggle, and the giggle turned into a chortle. She covered her mouth with the palm of her hand and stared up at him. "You had every right to laugh. What I did was pretty silly. But I was worried that if I didn't wear any hose, you'd think I wasn't properly dressed."

Dan shook his head. "I'd never think that, and as far as your being worried. . .I have a little quote about worry hanging in my studio."

"What does it say?"

"'Worry is the darkroom in which negatives can develop.'"

She pursed her lips. "Your point is well taken. I do have a tendency to worry."

He wiggled his eyebrows. "Still want me to carve that bird?"

"Absolutely." She turned toward the door leading to the hallway. "While you do, I think I'll change into a comfortable pair of slacks."

"Good idea." Dan winked at Bev, and she scurried out of the room.

~◎~

The rest of the afternoon went well, and Bev felt more relaxed wearing a pair of tan slacks and a cream-colored blouse than she had in the dress. After they'd stuffed themselves on turkey and all the trimmings, Bev, Dan, and Amy played a game of dominoes in the living room.

Soon Amy fell asleep, and Dan carried the child to her room. When he returned a few minutes later, he took a seat on the sofa beside Bev. She handed him a cup of coffee and placed two pieces of apple pie on the coffee table in front of them. It was pleasant sitting here with him. Bev hadn't felt this comfortable with a man since Fred was alive. Dan seemed so kind, so compassionate, and he was a lot of fun. If she were looking for love and romance, it would be easy to fall for a man like him.

She glanced at Dan out of the corner of her eye. Was he experiencing the same feelings toward her? Had he enjoyed the day as much as she had?

As if he could read her thoughts, Dan reached over and took Bev's hand. "Thanks for inviting me today. I had a nice time, and the meal was delicious."

"You're welcome. I'm glad you came."

"I'd like to reciprocate," he said. "Would you and Amy go out to dinner with me some night next week?"

Bev moistened her lips, not sure how to respond. If she agreed to go to dinner, would that mean they were dating?

Of course not, silly. He just wants to say thank you for today.

Bev leaned over and handed Dan his plate of apple pie. "A meal out sounds nice, but you're not obligated to—"

"I know that, Bev." He forked a piece of pie into his mouth. "Yum. Apple's my favorite."

"Thanks. My grandmother gave me the recipe."

They sat in companionable silence as they drank their coffee and ate the pie. When Dan finished, he set his empty plate and cup on the coffee table and stood. "Guess I should be going."

"Amy will be disappointed when she wakes up and finds you are gone."

He reached for his coat, which he'd placed on the back of a chair when he first arrived. "Tell your daughter I'll see her bright and early tomorrow. Since she has no school until Monday, you'll be bringing her to work with you, right?"

Bev nodded. "The day after Thanksgiving should be a

busy time at the store."

"Which is why I plan to give you a hand, at least for part of the day."

"I appreciate that." Bev walked Dan to the door, and when she opened it, he hesitated. She thought he might want to say something more, but he merely smiled and strolled into the hallway.

"See you tomorrow, Bev."

Chapter 9

B ev plugged in the lights on the small Christmas tree she and Amy had picked out that morning for Twice Loved, after Dan had given her some money to purchase it. Amy could decorate the tree with silver tinsel and shiny red glass balls, while Bev waited on customers.

The decorations would look even better if the toy train were here, Bev thought as she scrutinized the window display. *I wonder why Ellis hasn't come by yet. He was supposed to have it ready last week. If he doesn't show up soon, I may give him a call.*

"Isn't the tree pretty?" Amy asked, pulling Bev's thoughts aside.

"Yes, it's very nice. Now be sure to drape the strands of tinsel neatly over the branches," Bev said as Amy dove into the box of decorations.

"I will."

The bell on the front door jingled, and Bev turned her head to see who had entered the store.

A young woman with platinum blond hair piled high on her head swept through the door holding a cardboard box in her hands. She wore a black wool coat with a fur collar, and a blue, knee-length skirt peeked out from underneath. The woman stood there a few seconds, fluttering her long lashes, as she glanced around the room.

"May I help you?" Bev asked.

"I came to see Danny. Is he here?"

Bev motioned toward the back room. "He's in his studio, but I believe he plans to work in the toy store later today. May I give him a message?"

The woman stared at Bev with a critical eye, and it made Bev feel uncomfortable. "Are you the person he hired to run Twice Loved?"

Bev nodded. "I'm Bev Winters. Are you a friend of Dan's, or are you here looking for a used toy?"

"My name's Leona Howard. I'm Danny's neighbor and a good friend." She tapped her long, red fingernails along the edge of the box. "I have no need for used toys, but I would like you to tell Danny I'm here and wish to speak with him."

Bev glanced at the back room again. "I believe he's on the phone, and I would hate to interrupt him. So if you'd like to wait—"

"Fine. I'll get him myself." Leona pushed past Bev, bumping her arm with the box.

"I—I really don't think—"

"Just go back to whatever you were doing," Leona called over her shoulder.

Bev stood there dumbfounded as the brazen woman entered Dan's studio without even knocking. Then with a shrug, she took a seat at the desk, knowing she needed to make price stickers for some newly donated stuffed animals and get them set out.

Some time later, the door to Dan's studio opened. Leona and

Dan stepped into the hall.

"Thanks for the pumpkin pie, Leona."

"Now don't forget that rain check you promised me, Danny," Leona said sweetly. "How about one night next week?"

Bev put her head down and forced herself to focus on the project before her. It wasn't her nature to eavesdrop, but it was hard to think about anything other than Dan and his lady friend. She glanced up once, and it was just in time to see Leona kiss Dan on the cheek. He grinned kind of self-consciously, and his ears turned red.

That's what you get for thinking you might have a chance with Dan, Bev fumed. Was that what she believed? Could she and Dan have a relationship that went beyond boss to employee, or friend to friend? Probably not, if he was dating his flamboyant neighbor. Besides, after Fred died, Bev had decided that she didn't need another man in her life. It would be easier on her emotions if she could learn to manage on her own. Of course, the absence of romantic love had left a huge void in her life.

Dan walked Leona to the front door, glancing at Bev as he passed. She averted his gaze and tried to concentrate on the price stickers in front of her.

"See you soon, Danny," Leona said, reaching for the doorknob. The door swung open before she could turn the knob, and in walked Ellis Hampton with a large box.

"I've brought the train," he announced.

Glad for the interruption, Bev pushed her chair away from the desk. "Oh, good. I'm happy you came by today, Ellis."

"I'm sorry it took me so long to get the engine repaired, but I ran into a few problems," he apologized.

"That's all right. Let's get it set up under the tree in the display window." Bev was almost at Ellis's side when Leona took a step backward. The two women collided, and Leona collapsed on the floor.

Chapter 10

"Are you all right?" Dan knelt next to Leona, who appeared to be more embarrassed than any-thing else. "I–I'm fine," she stammered, "but I think the heel of my shoe is broken." She pulled off her shoe and held it up for his inspection.

"Yep. The heel's almost off." He helped Leona to her feet. "Maybe I can put some glue on it to help hold it together until you can get the shoe properly repaired."

She glared at Bev. "This is all your fault. If you hadn't gotten in my way, I never would have fallen."

Bev's cheeks were pink, and she looked visibly shaken. "I–I'm sorry, but I wasn't expecting you to step backward."

Leona's face contorted. "So now it's my fault?"

"I didn't say that. I just meant—"

Dan stepped between the two women. "It was only an accident, but if it will make you feel better, Leona, I'll pay for the repair of your shoe."

"Thank you, Danny. I appreciate that." She batted her eyelashes at him.

"I'm glad you weren't hurt, and I'm sorry we bumped into each other." Bev reached her hand out to Leona, but the woman moved quickly away. Bev turned with a shrug and followed Ellis to the window display, where Amy was decorating the tree.

Leona removed her other shoe and handed it to Dan. "It might be a good idea if you check this one over, too."

He led the way to his studio, and once they were inside, he motioned to the chair beside his desk. "Have a seat, and I'll see if I can find some glue."

Leona dropped into the chair with a groan. "That woman you hired is sure a pain."

Dan looked up from the desk drawer he was rum-maging through. "What's that supposed to mean?"

"When I first came into the store, she wouldn't let me talk to you. Said something about you being on the phone. Then after I told her I was going to your studio anyway, she tried to stop me." Leona frowned. "I think she's jealous because I'm prettier than she is. That's probably why she tripped me."

Dan blew out a ragged breath. "I'm sure she wasn't trying to trip you, Leona. Bev's a nice lady."

"How would you know that? She's only been working for you a short time."

He squeezed a layer of glue onto the broken heel and gave no reply.

"Are you dating the woman? Is that why you've been giving me the brush-off lately?"

He squinted. "What? No!"

She smiled. "That's good news, because I wouldn't like it if you were interested in some other woman. I think we—"

Dan handed her the shoe. "Here. I believe this will hold until you get home."

"Thanks."

He leaned forward with both elbows on his desk. "Leona, I think I need to clarify a few things."

She blinked and gave him another charming smile. "What things?"

He cleared his throat, searching for words that wouldn't sound hurtful. "I'm not completely over my wife's death yet, so there's no chance of me becoming romantically interested in anyone right now."

Leona opened her mouth, but he held up his hand. "Please, hear me out."

She clamped her lips tightly together and sat there with her arms folded.

Dan reached inside another drawer and retrieved his Bible. When he placed it on the desk, she frowned. "What's that for?"

"I'm a Christian, Leona. I believe God sent His Son to die for my sins."

She shook her head. "Oh no, Danny. You're too nice to have ever sinned."

"That's not true. Romans 3:23 says, 'For all have sinned, and come short of the glory of God.' "

"Are you saying that includes me? Do you think I'm a sinner, Danny?"

"We all are," he answered. "Everyone needs to find forgiveness for his or her sins, and the only way is through Jesus Christ."

"I'll have you know I did a lot of volunteer work during the war, in addition to my nursing duties," she said with a huff. "I've always tried to be a good person, so I don't need anyone telling me I'm a sinner."

"I'm sorry you feel that way."

Leona wrinkled her nose. "And I don't see what any of this has to do with you and me developing a relationship." She relaxed her face and reached over to touch his arm. "I can make you forget about the pain of losing your wife if you'll give me half a chance."

"The Bible teaches that those who believe in Jesus should not be unequally yoked with unbelievers, Leona. So even if I were ready to begin a relationship, it would have to be with a woman who believes in Christ as I do."

Her face flamed. "You mean because I don't go to church and rub elbows with a bunch of hypocrites, I'm not good enough for you?"

"That's not what I'm saying."

"What then?"

Lord, help me, Dan prayed. His fingers traced the cover of the Bible. "As a Christian, I know it wouldn't be right to date someone who doesn't share my beliefs."

"What about that woman you spent Thanksgiving with?"

"What about her?"

"Does she go to church and believe in the same religious things as you?"

Dan closed his eyes as a mental picture of Bev flashed into his mind. She was a Christian, and as near as he could tell, she lived like one. Ever since he'd first met Bev, he'd been attracted to her sweet, caring disposition. She reminded him of Darcy in so many ways. He rubbed the bridge of his nose. *If that's so, then why can't I—*

Leona shook his arm, and Dan's eyes popped open. "Are you ignoring me?"

"No, but I—"

She pursed her lips. "I want to know one thing before I leave."

"What's that?"

"If you have no interest in me, then why have you been leading me on?"

Dan cringed. Had he led Leona on? He'd thought he was being kind and neighborly when he'd agreed to have dinner with her a few times. He was only trying to set a Christian example.

"If I led you on, I'm sorry," he said.

Leona stood and pushed her chair aside with such force, it nearly toppled to the floor. She grabbed her shoes and tromped across the room, but before she reached the door, she whirled around. "Just so you know—you're not the only fish in the Atlantic Ocean. When you turned me down for Thanksgiving dinner, I invited an old army buddy of my husband's over, and he was more than willing to share the meal with me."

Dan was about to comment, when she added, "I'll send you the bill for the shoe repairs!" The door clicked shut, and Leona was gone.

Dan leaned forward and continued to rub the pulsating spot on his forehead. *I never should have had dinner with her.* When he glanced at the picture of Darcy, he thought of Bev again, and feelings of confusion swirled around in his brain like a frightening hurricane.

∽◌∾

"Come and look at what I found, Mommy," Amy called to Bev.

Several minutes ago, the child had become bored with decorating the tree and had wandered over to a box of stuffed toys that had recently been donated to Twice Loved.

"I'm busy, honey. Can it wait awhile?" Bev asked over her shoulder. She and Ellis were still trying to get the train set up.

"That's okay. I can manage on my own if you need to see what your daughter wants," Ellis said with a grin. "I've got six grandkids, and I know how it is when one of 'em gets excited about something."

Bev smiled gratefully. "Thanks. I'll be back soon." She stepped across the room and knelt on the floor beside Amy. "Let's see what you've found."

Amy lifted a bedraggled-looking teddy bear from the box and gave it a hug. "He reminds me of Uncle Dan."

Bev tipped her head and studied the bear. One eye was missing, both paws were torn, the blue ribbon around its neck was faded, and some of the fur on the bear's stomach was gone. He didn't look anything like Dan, who was always nicely dressed, with his hair combed just right.

"What is there about the bear that makes you think of Dan?" Bev asked her daughter.

"He needs someone to fix him, Mommy," Amy said in a serious tone. "I think he's lonely and has no one to love." She pointed to the bear. "Can we take him home so he won't be sad?"

Bev's eyes stung with unshed tears. She didn't know why she felt like crying. Was it the touching scene with Amy and the bear; or did she feel sorry for herself because, like the tattered bear, she, too, was lonely and needed love? Was it possible that Dan felt that way, too?

"I'll tell you what," Bev said, giving Amy's arm a gentle squeeze. "If you promise to help me finish decorating the tree in the window, I'll see about buying that bear for you."

"Can he go home with us today?"

"Yes. After I patch him up."

"Okay, but I would love the bear just the way he is."

Bev smiled. "That's how Jesus sees us, and the best part is that He loves us the way we are." She held out her hand. "Should we go back and finish the tree now?"

Amy nodded and grabbed the bear by one torn paw. "Until we're ready to go home, I'm gonna put him in the window with the dolls and stuffed toys. That way he can see all the people who walk by the store."

As Bev started across the room, the door to Dan's photography studio opened. Leona marched through the toy store with a pained expression on her face.

Bev was tempted to say something, but the woman's angry glare made her decide to keep quiet.

A few seconds after Leona stormed out of the store, Dan emerged from his studio, wearing his coat, hat, and a pair of gloves. He looked upset, too. Was he mad at Bev for bumping into his girlfriend? Did he think she had done it on purpose?

"I'm sorry, but something's come up, and I won't be able to help you today after all." He nodded at Bev.

"I'm sure I can manage."

He was almost to the door, when he halted. "Uh—can we take a rain check on that dinner I promised you and Amy?"

She swallowed around the lump in her throat. "Sure. It's probably best if we don't go out anyway."

Dan merely shrugged and opened the door.

He's probably going after Leona. Bev reached into the cardboard box and removed the train's caboose. She was on the verge of tears. What had happened between yesterday's pleasant Thanksgiving dinner and today? *It must be Leona Howard.*

At that moment, Bev made a decision. From this point on there would be no more romps in the snow or friendly dinners. Her relationship with her boss must be kept strictly business.

Chapter 11

Holding tightly to Amy's hand, Bev trudged up the stairs to her apartment. Today was Thursday, and her work-week was nearly finished.

The last two weeks had been the hardest she had experienced since Dan hired her to run Twice Loved. Not only had there been more customers than usual, but despite her best intentions, she continued to struggle with her feelings for Dan. He seemed sweet and attentive where Amy was concerned, even allowing her to visit his photography studio a couple of times. He'd also taken the child Christmas shopping one afternoon, which gave Bev the freedom to wait on customers without any distractions. Around Bev, however, Dan was distant and appeared to be preoccupied. He'd been friendly and attentive until the day after Thanksgiving, and Bev didn't know what had happened to change things.

She'd thought at first that Dan's lack of interest in her was due to Leona Howard, but shortly after the woman's last visit to the store, Dan told Bev he had informed Leona he wasn't free to pursue a relationship with her because she wasn't a

Christian. He'd also made it clear that he hadn't fully recovered from his wife's death and didn't know if he would ever be ready for a relationship with another woman.

Bev opened the door to her apartment, allowing her thoughts to return to the present. She and Amy had purchased a Christmas tree at a reduced price, and the man at the tree lot would be delivering it soon. For the rest of the evening she planned for the two of them to decorate the tree, snack on popcorn and apple cider, and sing whatever Christmas songs were played on the radio.

That should take my mind off Dan Fisher, Bev told herself as she entered the living room and clicked on the light.

Amy went straight to her room and returned a few minutes later with Baby Sue. She placed the doll on the sofa and plunked down beside her. "We're gonna wait right here 'til the tree arrives," she announced.

"I think it's here already, because I hear the rumbling of a truck."

Amy jumped up and raced for the door. Bev caught her hand, and the two of them hurried down the steps and onto the sidewalk.

The delivery man was already unloading the tree from the back of his pickup. "Want me to haul this upstairs for you?"

Bev shook her head. "I'm sure I can manage."

"It's a pretty big tree, ma'am."

"Thanks anyway."

He merely shrugged and climbed back into his truck.

Grabbing hold of the cumbersome tree trunk and directing Amy to go ahead of her, Bev huffed and puffed her way up the flight of stairs until she stood in front of her door. She leaned the tree against the wall and studied it, wondering if the oversized tree could be squeezed through the doorway.

She turned to Amy. "Sweetie, I want you to go into the living room and wait for me. After I bring the tree inside, we can begin decorating it."

"Okay."

Amy disappeared inside, and Bev grabbed hold of the tree, lining the trunk up with the door. She gave it a hefty thrust, but it only went halfway and wedged against the door jam. *"Oomph!"* She pushed hard again, almost losing her balance and catching herself before she fell into the scraggly branches.

Bev dropped to her knees and crawled under the limbs. *Maybe I can grab hold of the trunk and push it through that way.* Grasping both sides, she gritted her teeth and gave it a shove. The tree didn't budge.

With a sense of determination, Bev reassessed her situation. This time, facing the hallway, she would back in under the branches, grab hold, and try to pull the tree as she scooted through the doorway.

Bev had backed part way through the evergreen tunnel when a pair of men's shoes appeared. She froze.

The branches above her head parted, and Dan grinned down at her. "Oops. Looks like I'm too late."

"Too late for what?"

"I—uh—brought you a tree."

"You did what?"

He shuffled his feet a few times, and Bev pushed against the branches of the tree again, hoping to dislodge it. In the process, her hair stuck to a prickly bough. "I'm trapped and so is the tree," she admitted sheepishly.

Dan reached through and untangled her hair. "See if you can back your way into the living room, and I'll try to follow with the tree."

Bev was skeptical but did as he suggested. Once she had clambered out from under the branches, she stood off to one side and waited to see what would happen.

To her amazement, Dan and the tree made their entrance a few minutes later. He obviously had more strength than she did.

After Amy greeted "Uncle Dan," Bev asked the child to go to her room and play. Then she turned to face Dan. "Now, what's this about you bringing another tree?"

He swiped his hand across his damp forehead. "I—I figured you probably couldn't afford to buy a nice tree, so I bought you one and was going to leave it outside your door."

"An anonymous gift?"

He nodded and offered her a sheepish grin. "To be perfectly honest, I've done a couple other secret things, too."

She frowned. "Such as?"

He pointed to the front door. "While I wasn't the one who actually hung the wreath there, I did pay for it and asked the girls from church to put it on your door Thanks-giving morning."

Bev sank onto the couch. "Anything else I should know?"

He shifted uneasily. "Well—"

She blew out an exasperated breath.

"I know the man who owns this building, and when you said you were interested in renting an apartment here but might not be able to afford it, I agreed to pay your landlord the extra twenty dollars he normally would have charged per month."

Bev's mouth fell open. "Why would you do such a thing without asking me?"

"When I offered to increase your wages, you flatly refused, and several times you've mentioned that you don't want any charity. I thought the only way I could help was to do it anonymously."

Bev's body trembled as she fought for control. How dare this man go behind her back! "Please take the tree and the wreath to your own home. I'll speak to Mr. Dawson in the morning about the rent."

"Does that mean you won't accept any of my gifts?"

She shook her head as tears pooled in her eyes.

"I'm sorry if I've offended you, Bev."

She made no reply.

"I–I'd better get going." Dan turned for the door. "I hope I'll see you at the store tomorrow."

As much as she was tempted to quit working at Twice Loved, Bev knew it would be difficult to find another job. Besides, she enjoyed the work she did there. "I'll make sure I'm on time," she mumbled.

❦

The following morning, Bev found it difficult to concentrate on her work. Last night, she and Amy had decorated their tree, and she'd lain awake for hours thinking about Dan and the gifts he'd given her in secret. She had lost her temper and hadn't shown any appreciation for his thoughtfulness. *I need to apologize, but he also has to understand that I won't accept his charity.*

She glanced around the store. Christmas was only a few days away, and most of the toys had been picked over. Most that were left needed repair. She'd been too busy with customers to get more mending done. She was also behind on the book work and wanted to finish that before the week was out. It was time to get busy and quit thinking about Dan.

Since there were no customers at the moment, Bev decided

to start with the book work. She seated herself at the desk, opened the drawer, and reached for the ledger, prepared to record the previous day's receipts.

Near the back of the drawer she discovered a folded slip of paper. Funny, she'd never noticed it before. Curious, she unfolded the paper and silently read the words.

> *One thing I have learned since I was diagnosed with leukemia is not to worry about things I can't change. Every day God gives me is like a special gift, and I am putting my trust in Him. I've also learned to accept help whenever it's offered. I used to be too proud to ask for assistance, thinking I could do everything in my own strength. But since I became sick, I have no choice except to rely on others. Dan has been especially helpful, often setting his own needs aside for mine. I know he would rather be in his photography studio than at the toy store, yet he works here without complaint.*

Bev blinked away tears. Dan's late wife had obviously written the note before she'd become too ill to be at the store, but for whom was it intended? Perhaps it was a letter to a friend or family member and Darcy had forgotten to mail it.

The poor woman had been through more than Bev could imagine, yet Bev realized Darcy had kept a positive, thankful attitude, despite her ill health. She'd learned not to worry and had been willing to accept help, two areas in which Bev often struggled.

She realized, too, that Dan had only been trying to help when he'd given money toward her rent and purchased the tree and wreath. Even so, she didn't want to feel beholden to a man who only saw her as his employee—a man who was still in love with his wife and might never be ready for a relationship with another woman. Too bad she hadn't been able to keep from falling in love with him.

∽◌∾

Dan stared at Darcy's Bible lying on his desk. He'd discovered it in the bottom drawer of their dresser this morning and felt compelled to bring it to work with him. Maybe it was because Christmas was fast approaching and he needed the comfort of having something near that belonged to his wife. This was Darcy's favorite time of the year, and every Christmas carol he heard on the radio, every decorated tree he saw in a window, and every Christmas shopper who came into the toy store reminded him of her.

Dan leaned forward and closed his eyes. *Help me, Lord. Help me not to forget my sweet Darcy.*

He had been fighting his attraction to Bev ever since she came into the store looking for a doll for her daughter, yet he hadn't succumbed to the temptation of telling her how he felt. He couldn't. It wouldn't be fair to his wife's memory.

Dan opened his eyes and randomly turned the pages of Darcy's Bible. To his surprise, an envelope fell out, and he saw that it was addressed to him. With trembling fingers, he tore open the flap and removed the piece of paper.

My Dearest Dan,
 If you're reading this letter, then I have passed from this world into the next. One thing you can be sure of is that I'm no longer in pain. Take comfort in knowing I am healed and in my Savior's arms.

Dan's throat constricted as he tried to imagine his precious wife running through the streets of heaven, whole and at peace. With a need to know what else she had written, he read on.

> *My greatest concern is that you will continue to grieve after I'm gone, when you should be moving on with your life. You're a wonderful Christian man who has so much love and compassion to give. Please don't spend excessive time mourning for me. Praise God that I'm happy, and ask Him to bring joy into your life again.*
>
> *Just as you and I have shared the love of Jesus with others, I pray you will continue to do the same—not only through what we've done at Twice Loved, but in your personal relationships.*
>
> *It's my prayer that God will bring you a special Christian lady, because I know you will be the same wonderful husband to her as you have been to me.*
>
> *As you know, I always wanted to give you children, and I pray the Lord will bless you and your new wife with a family. Please know that by loving and being loved in return, you will be honoring my wishes.*
>
> *May God richly bless you in the days to come.*
>
> All my love,
Darcy

Tears welled up in Dan's eyes and spilled onto his cheeks. Darcy's letter was like a healing balm, given at just the right time. He realized now that Darcy wanted him to be happy and to find love again. But could he find it with Bev? Was she the one God meant for him? If so, then he had some fences to mend.

Dan reached for the telephone. "First things first."

"*Family Life Magazine*," a woman answered on the second ring.

"May I speak to Pete Mackey?"

"One moment, please, and I'll see if he's in."

There was a brief pause, then, "Mackey here."

"Pete, this is Dan Fisher, with Fisher's Photography."

"Ah, yes, I remember. How are you, Dan?"

"I'm doing okay. Listen, Pete, I was wondering if you're still interested in interviewing me for that article you're writing on grief."

"Sure am. When can we talk?"

"I'll give you a call right after the New Year. How does that sound?"

"Great! Thanks, Dan. I'm glad you've changed your mind."

Dan smiled. "Actually, it was my late wife who changed my mind, but I'll tell you about that during the interview."

"Okay. I'll look forward to hearing from you."

Dan hung up the phone feeling as if a heavy weight had been lifted from his shoulders. Now he had one more hurdle to jump, and that *couldn't* wait until after the New Year. He pushed his chair away from the desk and headed down the hall for Twice Loved.

When he entered the store, he realized Bev was with a customer. He paused inside the door, waiting for her to finish wrapping a doll for an elderly gentleman. As soon as the man left, Dan stepped up to her. "If you have a minute, I'd like to speak with you."

She tipped her head. "Is something wrong?"

"Not unless you—"

The telephone rang, interrupting him.

"I'd better get that." Bev moved to her desk and picked up the receiver. "Twice Loved. May I help you?" Her face paled, and Dan felt immediate concern. "Thank you for letting me know. I'll be right there."

"What's wrong?" he asked as she hung up the phone.

Bev turned to face him, her eyes pooling with tears. "That was Amy's teacher. Amy fell from a swing during recess and has been taken to the hospital."

Chapter 12

Bev paced the floor of the hospital waiting room, anxious for some word on her daughter's condition. "You're going to wear a hole in the linoleum. Please, come sit beside me and try to relax," Dan said, patting the chair next to him.

She clenched her fingers and continued to walk back and forth in front of the window. "What if her leg's broken or she has a concussion? What if—"

Dan left his seat and went to stand beside her. "Whatever is wrong, we'll get through it together."

We? After the way I spoke to him last night, why is Dan being so nice? And what does he mean when he says, "we"? Bev glanced at him out of the corner of her eye.

"It's going to be okay," he said with the voice of assurance. "Amy's a tough little girl, and she's got youth on her side."

Bev nodded slowly. "I know, but—"

"But you're her mother and you have a tendency to worry."

"Yes."

"I understand, but worry won't change a thing." He took

Bev's hand and led her over to the chairs. "Let's pray, shall we?"

Bev glanced around the room. There was an elderly couple sitting across from them, but they seemed to be engrossed in their magazines. "You want to pray now?"

Dan offered her a reassuring smile. "Absolutely." In a quiet voice, he prayed, "Heavenly Father, we ask You to be with Amy and calm her if she's frightened. Give the doctors wisdom in their diagnosis, and help Bev remember to cast her burdens on You, the Great Physician."

Bev thought of a verse of scripture from Matthew 6:34 she had read the other evening. "Take therefore no thought for the morrow; for the morrow shall take thought for the things of itself."

Lately, she'd been trying not to worry so much, but staying calm was hard to do when something went wrong. Especially when that "something" concerned her daughter.

A few minutes later, a nurse entered the room and called to Bev. "The tests are done, and you may see your daughter now."

"Are her injuries serious?" Bev tried to keep her voice calm, but her insides churned like an eggbeater.

"The doctor will give you the details," the nurse replied, "but Amy's going to be fine."

Bev drew in a deep breath. *Thank You, Jesus.* She turned to Dan. "Would you like to come with me?"

He nodded and took her hand.

∾⌾∾

Dan stood at the foot of Amy's bed, relief flooding his soul. Her leg wasn't broken, but her ankle had been badly sprained. She did have a concussion, though it was thought to be mild. The doctor wanted to keep her overnight for observation.

Bev sat in the chair beside Amy, holding her hand and murmuring words of comfort. It was a touching scene, and Dan felt like an intruder.

Maybe I should leave the two of them alone.

He turned toward the door, but Amy called out to him. "Where ya goin', Uncle Dan?"

"To the waiting room, so you and your mom can talk."

Amy looked over at Bev. "We want Uncle Dan here, don't we, Mommy?"

Bev nodded. "If he wants to be."

Dan rushed to the side of the bed and stood behind Bev's chair. "Of course I want to be. I want—" What exactly did he want? Was it to marry Bev and help her raise Amy? He rubbed the bridge of his nose. No, it was too soon for that. They'd only known each other a few months.

"Can you come to our place for Christmas dinner, like you did on Thanksgiving?" the child asked.

Dan's gaze went to Bev, seeking her approval, or at least hoping for a clue as to whether she wanted him there or not.

She smiled. "I'm sorry for the unkind things I said when you stopped by our place with the tree."

"It's okay. I understand."

"No. I was wrong to refuse your help and the offer of gifts, and I hope you'll accept my apology."

"Only if you will accept mine for overstepping my boundaries."

She nodded. "If you have no other plans for Christmas, we'd love to have you join us."

He shook his head. "I don't think coming to your place is a good idea."

Tears welled up in Amy's eyes, and her lower lip trembled.

"Why not? We had fun on Thanksgiving, didn't we, Uncle Dan?"

Dan felt immediate regret for his poor choice of words. Leaning over the bed, he took the child's other hand. "I had a wonderful time on Thanksgiving. It was the best day I've had in a long time."

"Then why won't you come for Christmas?" This question came from Bev, whose vivid blue eyes were full of questions.

He smiled. "Because I'd like to have you and Amy over to my house for Christmas dinner."

Bev's mouth dropped open. "You're planning to cook the meal?"

He shrugged. "Sure, why not?"

Amy giggled. "Can ya make pumpkin pies?"

Dan grinned, then winked at Bev. "Actually, I was hoping you might furnish the pies, but I can roast the turkey and fix the rest of the dinner."

Bev's expression was dubious at first, but she gave him a nod. "It's a deal."

❦

Dan had been rushing around for hours, checking on the bird he'd put in the oven early that morning, peeling and cutting the potatoes and carrots he planned to boil later on, and placing presents under the tree. He wanted everything to be perfect for Bev and Amy. They might not realize it, but they had brought joy into his life, and they deserved to have a special Christmas.

Satisfied that everything was finally ready, Dan put the potatoes in a kettle of cold water, grabbed his coat and gloves, and headed out the door. It was time to pick up his dinner guests.

A short time later, he stood in front of Bev's door, glad she hadn't refused his offer of a ride. It would have been difficult for her and Amy to catch the bus, what with the child's ankle still slightly swollen, not to mention the weather, which had recently deepened the snow on the ground.

When Bev opened the door and smiled at Dan, it nearly took his breath away. She wore a lilac-colored gown with a wide neckline and a skirt that dropped just below her knees. And this time, she had on a pair of hose. "You're beautiful," he murmured.

"Thanks. You look pretty handsome yourself."

He glanced at his navy blue slacks and matching blazer. Nothing out of the ordinary, but if she thought he looked handsome, that was all right by him.

Bev opened the door wider. "Come in, and I'll get our coats."

Dan stepped into the living room and spotted Amy sitting on the sofa, dressed in a frilly pink dress that matched her flushed cheeks.

"Hey, cutie. Ready to go?"

She nodded and grinned up at him. "I can't wait to give you my present, Uncle Dan."

He leaned over and scooped the child into his arms. "And I can't wait to receive it."

❧

"That was a delicious meal," Bev said, amazed at how well Dan could cook. She was also surprised at the change that had come over him since Amy's accident. He'd driven Bev to the hospital and stayed with her until they knew Amy was okay. He had taken her home, back to the hospital the next day, and given them a ride to their apartment when Amy was released. Now, as they sat in Dan's living room inside his cozy brick home on the north end of town, Bev could honestly say she felt joy celebrating this Christmas.

"I'm glad you enjoyed dinner and equally glad I didn't burn anything." Dan nodded at Amy, who sat on the floor in front of the crackling fire he'd built earlier. "How about it, little one? Are you ready to open your presents?"

Amy scooted closer to the Christmas tree. "Yes!"

"Okay then. Who wants the first gift?"

"Me! Me!"

Dan chuckled and handed Amy a box. "I believe this one's from your mother."

Amy looked at Bev, and she nodded. "Go ahead and open it."

The child quickly tore off the wrapping, and when she lifted the lid and removed a delicate bisque doll, she squealed with delight. "She's beautiful, Mommy! Thank you!"

"You're welcome, sweetheart."

Amy smiled at Dan. "Can I give Mommy her present from me now?"

"Sure." Dan pointed to a small package wrapped in red paper. "It's that one."

Amy handed the gift to her mother and leaned against Dan's knee as Bev opened it.

"This is wonderful!" Bev exclaimed, as she held up a framed picture of Amy sitting on the patchwork quilt Dan's late wife had made. "How did you do this without me knowing?"

"When you were busy with customers, I took Amy into my photography studio and snapped her picture," Dan answered. "We bought the frame the day I took her Christmas shopping."

Bev kissed Amy's cheek and was tempted to do the same to Dan, but she caught herself in time. "Thank you both. I appreciate the picture and will find the right place to hang it when we go home."

"Here's my gift to you, Amy." Dan placed a large box in front of the child and helped her undo the flaps. Inside was a quilt—the same quilt that used to hang in Twice Loved and he'd used as a background for Amy's portrait.

Amy lifted the colorful covering and buried her face in it. "I love it, Uncle Dan. Thank you."

"It's a precious gift, Dan," Bev said, "but don't you think you should give the quilt to a family member?"

Dan took Bev's hand. "That's what I have in mind, all right."

Bev's heartbeat picked up speed. What exactly was he saying?

Dan reached into his jacket pocket and pulled out a flat, green velvet box. He handed it to Bev with a smile.

She lifted the lid and gasped at the lovely gold locket inside. "It's beautiful. Thank you, Dan."

"Open the locket," he prompted.

She did, and soon discovered there was a picture of Amy on one side and a picture of Dan on the other.

"I'm in love with you, Bev," Dan said, as he leaned over and kissed her.

Bev's eyes filled with tears, and at first she could only nod in reply. When she finally found her voice, she whispered, "I love you, too."

Amy grinned from ear to ear, then handed Dan a large gift, wrapped in green paper. "Here, Uncle Dan. This is for you, from me and Mommy."

Dan tore open the wrapping and lifted a brown teddy bear from the box. It had new eyes, patched paws, a pretty blue ribbon around its neck, and a sign on the front of its stomach that read:

"I am Twice Loved."

He tipped his head in question, and Bev smiled in response. "It was Amy's idea."

Dan gave Amy a hug, then lifted Bev's chin with his thumb. He kissed her once more and murmured, "I believe God brought the three of us together, and just like this bear and the quilt I gave Amy, we have been twice loved."

WANDA E. BRUNSTETTER

Wanda E. Brunstetter lives in Central Washington with her husband, Richard, who is a pastor. They have been married for forty-two years and have two grown children and six grandchildren. Wanda is a professional ventriloquist and puppeteer, and she and her husband enjoy doing programs for children of all ages. Wanda's greatest joy as a Christian author is to hear from a reader that something she wrote has touched that person's heart or helped them in some special way.

Wanda has written ten novels with Barbour Publishing's Hearstong Presents line, five novellas, and her Amish novel, *The Storekeeper's Daughter*, a best-seller. Wanda believes the Amish people's simple lifestyle and commitment to God can be a reminder of something we all need.

Visit her Web page at: www.wandabrunstetter.com.

EVERLASTING SONG

by DiAnn Mills

Those who sow in tears will reap with songs of joy.
PSALM 126:5 NIV

Chapter 1

October 1946
Tomball, Texas

Olivia Howard believed that in times of fear and peril, a woman looked for a hero. As the flames licked at her bedroom door and the heat fanned its hot breath of terror into her darkened room, Olivia realized that unless a hero were to arrive soon, she would be reduced to ashes along with everything she owned.

She tried to raise the window, but paint had sealed it shut. Her broken right arm, held against her body by a sling, hindered her even more. Olivia attempted to lift a rocker so that she could toss it through the bedroom window, but the chair's weight caused it to slip from her one-handed grasp. Smoke billowed beneath the door, signaling her impending death.

Think of something. Oh, dear God, help me.

The lamp resting on her dresser offered an escape from

the flames engulfing her home if she could manage to send it through the window with her left hand. Olivia yanked the lamp's electrical cord from the wall. She snatched the lamp up with her left hand and moved toward the window. Gasping for air while attempting to pray, she pitched the lamp through the window. Her sling offered scant protection to her face and eyes from the shattering glass, but she instinctively brought up her right arm to shield herself from the spray of shattered glass anyway.

Olivia pulled up her robe and kicked her bare foot through the jagged hole to clear enough glass for her to crawl through. Pieces of glass pierced her foot and leg, but she had no time to consider the pain.

"Help!" she called through the second-story window. "Fire!"

Below her, she saw Mr. Tanner, an elderly neighbor dressed in pajamas, peer up at her bedroom window. His wrinkled face shone in the fire's light. "The fire crew is on its way, Olivia, but you can't wait for them. Jump now, before it's too late!"

Just then, a truck, its siren blaring, rounded the corner and raced her way.

"I'm not afraid," Olivia said, more to reassure her own trembling heart than to convince Mr. Tanner.

The fire truck pulled up next to the inferno. Three men jumped from atop it. Two more trucks whipped in behind.

"You'll have to jump," one of the firemen called. "We'll catch you."

She drew her broken arm closer to her body and scooted feet first through the broken window. Sounds of the devouring flames roared in her ears.

"Now," the same fireman said, "just leap."

With her heart pounding hard against her chest, Olivia squeezed her eyes shut and jumped. She felt a momentary rush of air, and then, somehow, strong arms caught her, preventing her from striking the ground.

"Watch her arm," Mr. Tanner said.

"We got her," another man said. "Anyone else in the house?"

"No." She'd wanted to say she'd left her heart inside, but the words died in her throat.

The firemen attempted to let her stand, but the pain from the embedded glass in her foot, along with the limitations of the broken arm, caused her to ease back into the safety of their arms again.

"I don't think I can stand." Olivia winced. "Please, just place me on the ground." She swiveled her head to look behind her. "My house. Can you save my house?"

Once seated on the soft grass, Mrs. Tanner's arms around her, Olivia watched as the second floor crashed to the first, while yellow white flames lapped at what was left of her home. The streams of water that were intended to stop the destruction had accomplished little—like a sprinkle of rain on a parched earth. Never had she seen such a raging force; it had devoured everything she treasured.

This had been her parents' home, the security left to her when they passed on. Nothing remained.

Memories swept by of the little girl who had played with her dolls on the winding stairs. She recalled the enticing smells of days gone by, when she would arrive home from school to whatever Mama had baked that day. Past holidays and celebrations played before her eyes while the fire sought to snatch them all away. Smiles. Tears. The struggle to convince Daddy that she could go to college and be a teacher. The many notes from students and teachers who valued what she did for them.

Olivia struggled to hold back the tears, but visions of her cherished home and the people she loved continued to assail her. The worn, deep red sofa where she and Mama had shared so many happy hours must have been one of the first things the fire had taken. Grandma's fine china from Germany was no doubt gone. The embroidered pillows and handmade quilts were now ashes.

A fireman knelt beside her while the others battled the blaze. "Miss, you need to have a doctor look at your cuts."

Olivia peered up from the ground into the face of the man. The fire lit up his features, and she immediately saw the compassion radiating from his eyes, which were a striking blue.

"But—that's my home." Once again, she choked back the tears. "I'm sorry. This is just so horrible."

"Yes, it is." He stole a glimpse at the fire, then brought his gaze back to her face. "But you survived. Imagine how awful this could have been for those who care about you."

She understood that his comforting words were meant to yank her from self-pity. She turned toward the fire again, but he moved to block her view.

"Don't look, miss. There's nothing you can do."

She studied the man. "God must have brought you here tonight to help me. Without you and these other men, I'd have died."

He shook his head. "You would have jumped anyway, and you might have made it okay. I'm a volunteer, and I'm just glad we were here to catch you. Wish we'd been able to save your home, though.

"Your neighbor"—he pointed to Mr. Tanner—"woke your other neighbor, and they sent a boy on a bicycle to fetch us."

"I'll thank them all."

"Right now, let's get you to a doctor."

She nodded. "I taught the doctor's daughter last year."

"A teacher, huh?" He smiled. "I'll bet you're the best teacher in the school."

"I try to do my best, but there are many who have taught longer and are very good."

"What grade do you teach?"

Olivia knew he was trying to divert her attention. Talking did take her mind off the fire. "I teach second grade."

He nodded. "I hope it doesn't seem forward of me, but what's your name?"

"Olivia. I'm Olivia Howard."

He offered a warm smile. "Nate Forester here. It's a pleasure to meet you."

"Thank you, Mr. Forester."

"Miss Howard, I'd like to pick you up and help you into my truck so that I can drive you to see Doc Matthews."

"Oh, I can't leave. I might be able to salvage some things from the house once the fire is out."

"Attempting to sort through it all in the dark is impossible," Nate said. "And you can't do it with a foot and leg full of glass."

"Maybe one of my neighbors could pick out the glass."

Nate waved an arm at the crowd. "Is any one of them a doctor or a nurse?"

She knew the answer to his question. Suddenly she was self-conscious of wearing nothing but a robe and a nightgown underneath. She'd have to find clothes before she could be seen by the doctor.

Tears filled her eyes. "I don't want to leave my home." She silently begged him to understand.

Nate stared at her for a moment. "Please, Miss. There's nothing you can do here until morning."

Olivia picked at a loose thread in her robe pocket. She swallowed the hysteria threatening to burst out of her. "Everything is gone," she said.

"I'm afraid so."

"I have insurance, but it won't replace—" The floodgates opened, and she buried her face in her hands. Grief wrapped its dark blanket around her.

"Oh, the poor dear." Mrs. Tanner's soothing voice offered comfort while her arms pulled Olivia close.

"Would you try to convince Miss Howard to let me take her to the doctor?" Nate said. "Those cuts need to be looked at and cleaned, and she may need a stitch or two."

"Of course she'll go," Mrs. Tanner said. "And I'll ride along."

Olivia allowed them to have their way. She'd get her cuts tended to and not worry about her tattered robe. Her foot and leg stung like a thousand needles had danced across her skin, and she knew that by herself, she'd never be able to pull out all the glass slivers. When she glanced down at her leg, she saw that blood flowed from just below the knee to her toes. She could only imagine the blood and cuts in the light of day.

A few hours later, Nate brought Olivia and Mrs. Tanner back to where the house once stood. Olivia now had a bandaged leg and foot to go with the broken arm.

A sense of helplessness engulfed her. And she was afraid, like a child lost in a fog. Something dark inside tugged at her to watch as the final sparks snatched away the little that was left of what had once been so precious to her.

One fire truck lingered, apparently staying until the last ember had died. Clouds of smoke and steam rose as a monument to what was once her home. The smell of burning wood, which once had reminded her of home and security, now sickened her.

"Do you know what caused the fire?" Mr. Forester asked.

Olivia shook her head. "No, I don't. I cooked dinner, but nothing seemed amiss."

"We may never find out," he said. "I'm sorry, Miss."

So am I. How will I ever replace all my things? "Thank you," she said. "I really appreciate all your help."

"That's what I'm here for. Take care now." He walked away, his shoulders erect.

Did people ever fully comprehend what firemen went through to save lives and property? "God bless you, Mr. Forester."

He swung back around. "Just part of my job as a volunteer. I enjoy helping others. Guess it comes from being a soldier."

Olivia had assumed he'd been through the war by the way he carried himself. What should she say? Some men talked freely of their experiences in the war, while others chose not to discuss the tragic things they'd seen. But this man had already displayed his inner strength.

"Did you see action?" she finally asked.

He nodded. "At Normandy."

His reply spoke volumes about what he'd been through. "If I'd known, I wouldn't have asked."

He stood quiet in the darkness. "I reckon the good Lord thought I could handle the job. I'm alive to tell others about the sacrifice that so many fine men made to defend our country."

The sacrifice of blood. "And here I'm grieving for what *I've* lost." She shook her head. "I'm so selfish." Shame washed over her for leaning on the raven-haired fireman. "I must disgust you."

"Not at all. Grief comes in many forms." He jammed his hands inside his trouser pockets. "If you don't need me anymore, I'll head on home."

"Do you live far from here, Mr. Forester?"

"The name's Nate, remember? And I live west of Tomball with my parents. We have a dairy farm."

She nodded and lifted her free hand to wave. "Thank you again. I'll never forget you." Somehow that didn't sound right, and Olivia felt herself grow warm. At least the darkness hid her embarrassment.

"Don't imagine I'll forget you, either." Nate turned and walked toward his truck.

Olivia watched him drive away before she focused on what was left of her home. The stench of charred wood and the destruction caused her to shiver.

Mrs. Tanner wrapped her arm around Olivia's waist. "Come away from all this, dear. Tomorrow we'll sort through what needs to be done next."

Hot, stinging tears flowed over Olivia's cheeks. "Where do I begin?"

"With prayer."

The simple answer caused the tears to flow even more. "Why did God allow this?"

"I'm not sure, honey, but I'm praising Him for sparing you. Why, we'd all have been lost without our little Olivia and her sweet ways. And what about the children you teach? They love you, and so do their parents."

"You always seem to say exactly what's needed to encourage others." Olivia laid her head on the older woman's shoulder. "Thank you. Remember when I broke my arm?"

"Goodness. I should have known you were heading for a fall when you climbed that apple tree."

"And you rescued me. Doc Matthews said tonight that he was going to lock me in a closet if I didn't stop having accidents."

Mrs. Tanner laughed lightly. "He's a good man. I'm thanking God for him tonight, along with a long list of other things."

"Like Mr. Tanner, for seeing the fire."

"And Billy for riding his bicycle for help, and all of those wonderful firemen and folks who came to help. Especially for Mr. Forester. He's a real gentleman."

Olivia nodded. "He was a godsend tonight—a real hero."

"A very handsome hero. He liked you, Olivia. I could

see it in his eyes."

"That was just sympathy." The ordeal washed over Olivia again, giving her chills. She *would* never forget what Nate Forester had done for her this night.

Chapter 2

Olivia woke the next morning after only three hours of sleep. Before she opened her eyes, she wondered why the bed felt unfamiliar and the smells greeting her nostrils were of rose and smoke. Then she remembered the night before.

Fire had destroyed her home. Everything was gone. She didn't even have clothes to wear to school or shampoo to wash the smell of smoke from her hair. Despair settled over her as she looked ahead. She had to work. She needed go through the rubble that was once her home and search for something, *anything* that might still remain. The insurance company must be notified. *Thank You, God, for moving me to buy fire insurance.* Starting over would be difficult, considering all of the irreplaceable heirlooms, but the money would help her establish life again.

And I do have my life. I could have been killed.

Nate Forester came to mind. He'd been a godsend: strength, courage, and comfort in her time of need. Olivia recalled his prayer while driving to Doc Matthews. He'd prayed for healing of her spirit and praised God that she had been spared.

Olivia blinked and opened her eyes to the faint hint of sunrise peeking through the window. She had to get up and see if she could borrow something to wear from her dear friend Lydia. Olivia groaned. How could she approach Lydia wearing a smoky, dirty robe?

Normally Olivia was the strong one, the woman in charge of life and ready to help those in need. Now she felt so helpless, so much in need of a map to help her set out in the right direction. But she had that map; she had God and her Bible. She shivered at the realization that she no longer had her Bible, the one passed down from her great-grandfather to her father and then to her. It, too, was in ashes.

Tears trickled over her cheeks. She'd always had sympathy for all the people who had lost their homes and precious family and friends during the war, but now she felt empathy. What of those who didn't know Jesus? What hope lay ahead for them? The war had ended last winter, and she had joined others in giving thanks that Germany and Japan had been defeated, but never had she so fully understood the consequences of war as she did at this moment. The atrocities sickened her more this morning than ever before.

I guess I am selfish. Perhaps this had happened so she could be a better person—more giving and humble. *I can make another home for myself. I refuse to blame God and grow bitter.* Another tear slipped from her eye. She grieved for all the things she'd lost. No denying it. Olivia could not fathom the loss of old photographs and cherished items handed down from loved ones.

Tired of thinking about it all, she threw back the thin coverlet and swung her legs around. "Ouch," she said. Her bandaged leg hurt from the knee to her toes. How could she manage a classroom today? Teaching second-graders demanded all of her. The broken arm had been bad enough, but how could she walk? Classes had been in session for just a month, and she was working hard to build a relationship with each student. This was a severe complication.

Swallowing hard, Olivia sank back down onto the feather mattress. If paper and pencil were within reach, she'd begin a list of those things that demanded her attention. The stench of her hair assaulted her senses; a bath took the number one position on the list, followed by clothes to wear.

I'll hobble downstairs and ring up Lydia. Maybe she can drop by before she heads to school and bring something for me to wear. And I have to call Principal Hayden.

No matter how she looked at it, Olivia needed the day off to take care of matters. Determination reasserted itself. She'd make the telephone calls and deal with things one at a time.

❧

Nate Forester helped his dad finish scrubbing and disinfecting the milkers. He took one last look at the milk house to make sure it sparkled. You never knew when an inspector might stop by, and he surely didn't need to be cut off the route due to neglect.

"Today's going to be hard for you with only three hours' sleep," his dad said, drying his hands. He frowned.

"You don't have to help me. I can manage on my own."

Nate shook his head. "I'll be fine."

"I'm proud of all you do, son. Farmwork and volunteering for the fire department take a lot out of a man." The older man took a bristled brush and hung it upside down on a peg to dry.

"Sure glad the fire department doesn't need me every day." Nate chuckled. "Or I'd be mean and ornery from lack of sleep." His thoughts raced over the previous night's fire, then paused when it came to Olivia Howard. What a remarkable woman she was—and pretty, too.

"Are you up to mending fences today?" Dad asked.

Nate scrambled to grasp what his dad had said. "What? I'm sorry, Dad. My mind was on last night."

"I asked if you were up to mending fences."

"I can be tired doing just about anything, but I'd like to check on the woman who survived the fire last night. I was thinking of running by where she's staying late this afternoon."

"You do whatever you feel is necessary. I wonder if she has a church home?"

"I imagine so. She mentioned God and didn't object to my praying for her at Doc Matthews'. Dad, the fire took everything. She tried to be strong, but I saw she was hurtin' really bad."

"Did she live alone?"

"Yeah, a second-grade teacher."

"Single woman?"

He nodded. "Her name's Olivia Howard. I believe her parents have passed on."

"Oh yeah? I knew her folks. Fine Christian people.

They owned a feed store." Dad lifted a brow. "Now that's real interesting."

"What's real interesting?"

"Never mind, son. I'll let you find out on your own."

Nate opened his mouth to ask his dad what he meant, but thought better of it. He'd been around his dad too many years not to know that whatever was "interesting" would rise to the surface sooner or later. He put the disinfectant on a shelf in the milk house and noted his growling stomach. Being up half the night and doing chores had made him hungry enough to eat a dozen eggs and a whole side of bacon.

"Ready for breakfast?" Dad asked. "Your mom's biscuits should be done by now." He lifted the brim of his hat. "Have I told you how good it is to have you here, sleeping in the house and working alongside me?" Tears shone in his eyes, and he blinked them back.

"Yeah, but I don't mind hearing it again. All the while I was gone, I kept dreaming about you and Mom and wondering if I'd ever see you again. I wasn't afraid of going home to be with the Lord, but I wanted to see you one more time."

"God answered our prayers. Your mom and I haven't said much about this, but whenever you want to talk about what happened in the war, we're here to listen."

Nate took a deep breath. Seeing the pleased look on his folks' faces and the knowledge of the good Lord walking with him every step of his days were all he ever needed to keep the happiness level at the top—like rich cream atop a pail of milk.

"Do you want to talk about it?" His dad's shoulders

rose, and the silver of his hair symbolized the wisdom that Nate longed to grasp.

"Someday, but not today. I have to sort through things a bit first."

"I understand." His dad grasped Nate's shoulder. "Reckon a man couldn't have a finer son than you."

With those words, Nate blinked back his own tears.

At midafternoon, before the milking, Nate climbed into his truck and headed over to Olivia Howard's home— or rather, what used to be her home. He figured she was probably still at the Tanners'. She'd been on his mind off and on all day. A pretty little thing with the longest eyelashes he'd ever seen. Cow eyes. He grinned. Most likely, Olivia wouldn't be pleased about being compared to a cow, but it was true. She had big ol' brown beauties lookin' out at the world like she might miss something.

What a tragedy, losing all her belongings in the fire. But she looked like the type of woman who could bounce back and be a better person for it, so why did he need to check on her? *I want to make sure she's all right.* After all, he'd spent a lot of the night with her. It seemed appropriate to pay her a call.

Nate drove down Main Street, then turned left to stop in front of the Tanners'. His gaze swung to the charred remains of the Howard home. Olivia stood there, her back to the street, her body rigid, as though resigned to the fact that everything she treasured was destroyed. With the windows down in his truck to help deal with near ninety-degree heat, he could smell the fire.

He watched her for a minute as she stood motionless. Her shoulders rose and fell. Strength and courage weren't unknown to him. The war had thrust those who possessed it, even those who didn't know they had it, to the front lines when duty called. From what little he knew about Olivia, he thought she had the quality, too.

Olivia picked through the ashes, now and then bending to examine whatever caught her attention. She could step on something and get hurt, and her record of avoiding accidents wasn't good. The idea of rushing her to Doc Matthews with a nail in her foot didn't appeal to him.

"Olivia, let me give you a hand," Nate called through the window. He snatched up his work gloves and opened the door.

She whirled around and offered him a faint smile. Already her left hand was black with soot.

"I use gloves for that kind of thing." He waved them at her.

"You don't have to help with this." Olivia attempted to brush off her left hand with her right; her effort didn't improve things much. "I wanted to see if anything in this mess could be salvaged."

"Never can tell." He wanted to sound optimistic, but he doubted if any of her belongings would be recognizable. An image of a far-more-devastating fire in France captured his mind, but he willed it away.

"Does that happen very often? I mean, things left untouched in a fire?"

Those eyes would melt the snow off a mountaintop. "Sometimes."

She gave him a hint of a smile. "I think you're wanting me to feel better. . .and I appreciate it."

Nate took the toe of his boot and flipped over what

was left of a beam. "Were you able to rest up today?"

"A little. I needed to see my insurance man and tend to a long list of other things."

"Do you have a place to live?" Nate asked.

She pointed to the Tanners' house. "They'll let me stay for as long as I want. Right now, that's home until I find a place to rent."

"They seem like good, Christian people."

She nodded. "They've been like parents to me for the past few years. My parents were close friends of theirs."

Nate watched her nearly trip as she moved around the debris. He worried about her arm being in a sling and a leg bandaged. Falling into the charred remains didn't sound good at all. "My folks wrote me every day while I was gone in the war. There were days that I received so many letters, I couldn't read them all in one sitting. Don't know what I would have done without them."

They continued to inch their way across the ashes. Olivia pointed to the spots where rooms had been in the upstairs and downstairs. She spoke of her daddy's favorite chair and her mother's knitting basket, of his worn work boots and her mama's yellowed wedding dress. All of which she had kept to remind her of them.

"Every Thursday, Mama baked bread," Olivia said. "Didn't matter what was going on. Nothing took precedence over her bread-baking." She sighed. "I know I sound sentimental."

"Not at all. Always helps to talk."

"Thank you, Nate. I barely know you, and here I am, going on about personal matters."

"I think we became friends last night. Tragic times can

make for close friends."

"You did see me at my worst." She shook her head as if to rid her mind of all the ugliness of last night's fire.

"Why don't you tell me more about your home and your folks?"

She smiled and glanced his way for a second. A faint hint of color spread over her cheeks. He hoped she wasn't overdoing it, considering her injuries. "Even after Mama and Daddy were gone, I kept certain things out to remind me of them." She pointed to a location that would have been in the middle of the house. "Daddy loved his pipe. I kept a half-full can of Prince Albert on a table beside one of his pipes as though he were coming home."

Nate clung to each of Olivia's words. Her voice reminded him of freshly churned butter—soft and rich. He inwardly cringed. Her eyes reminded him of cow eyes and her voice of butter? The comparison didn't sound complimentary, but he meant it well.

"I suppose you heard enough sentiment during the war without me carrying on so," Olivia said.

"Grief and sorrow don't pick times or places. It hits us all, no matter where we are."

She bent to pick up the handle of what was left of an iron skillet. "Thanks again."

Nate gazed at the lovely woman beside him. "You have a black smudge on your nose."

She attempted to wipe it off with a dirty finger, spreading the soot to her right cheek. "Is that better?"

He pulled off his glove and, with a clean finger, brushed off the smudge. The moment he touched her skin, sparks flew—and it had nothing to do with the previous night's fire. *What's wrong with me? I'm fixing to make a fool of myself, acting more like a kid than a grown man.*

Olivia must have sensed the same discomfort, for her cheeks reddened even more than before. Nate slipped his glove back on and returned his attention to searching through the rubble.

He lifted up the remains of a beam and caught sight of a brown piece of leather. He threw the wood to the side and bent to take a closer look. Olivia had wandered off to his right but stopped when she saw him bend over.

"Have you found something?" she asked.

The expectancy in her voice cautioned Nate. He didn't want to raise her hopes. But when he lifted up a brown leather book with *Holy Bible* written in raised gold letters, shivers raced up his arms. "Maybe so." Once he blew off the ashes, he saw that not a spark had singed it. There was no apparent water damage, either.

"What do you have?" She made her way toward him.

"A miracle." He handed her the Bible.

Her eyes pooled. "Why, it looks like the fire didn't touch it. Thank You, Lord." She swallowed hard and took the book from his hands. "This Bible has been handed down in my mama's family since Texas became a state."

"God is showing you His love by giving His Word back to you," Nate said, not exactly sure where his statement had come from.

"Yes, like He's telling me not to worry. . .that everything will be all right."

"He's letting you know He's got you in the palm of His hand."

Her gaze locked with his, and he could not turn away.

"You're a blessing, too, Nate Forester, and God has used you to show me I can go on."

For one of the first times in his life, Nate was speechless.

Chapter 3

Olivia wanted to cry, but Nate had seen her shed enough tears. "I want to look through every page, but I can't until I wash up." She glanced up at Nate. "Join me at the Tanners', will you, Nate? After all, you found it."

"I reckon I could for a few minutes, then I need to get home."

"Chores to do? Let me come and help you. I might limp a little, but surely I can do something."

"No, thanks. I'd be afraid you'd fall, and we'd be back at the doc's. By the way, how did you break your arm?"

She laughed for the first time since the fire. She pointed to the stump of what remained of a tree. "I saw an apple higher than my ladder, so I climbed up to get it."

His eyes widened, reminding her of a particular little boy in her class. "And you fell out of the tree?"

"No, not exactly." Merriment swept through her, and she basked in the sweet flirtation. "I found my juicy apple, but on the way down, I decided to jump instead of wiggle down."

Nate closed his eyes. A grin spread across his face. "Why do I think this wasn't the first time you climbed that tree or jumped from it?"

"It wasn't." Memory Lane, as her mother called it, hit her like a summer twister. "The first time, I was six and used Daddy's ladder while he took a nap." Her musings slipped back to the afternoon when Daddy caught her up in the apple tree. "Of course, he found me sitting on a limb eating an apple."

Nate laughed. "What did he say?"

"To get myself down out of that tree before he came up after me." Olivia crossed her arm over her sling. "I was too scared to move, and he had to come after me."

"Ouch. What happened then?"

"I figured the only way to get on his good side was to offer him a bite." Olivia remembered the curve of Daddy's smile beneath his light-colored handlebar mustache. "He tried to be angry, but right in the middle of scolding me and chewing on the apple, he burst out laughing. A few moments later, he pulled his harmonica from his shirt pocket, and we made up a song about being stuck in an apple tree."

"Your dad really loved you."

"Yes." She sighed at the precious memories. "He called me his princess. You see, I was an only child, and I'd rather climb trees and fish than play dolls." Nostalgia settled into her heart and threatened to prompt a few tears, but she held them back, as before, determined that Nate Forester would not see one more drop of emotion displayed. "Are you ready to visit with Mr. and Mrs. Tanner?"

"Olivia, I need to be getting home, and reading your

Bible is a private thing."

Olivia raised a brow. "Don't be thinking you can slip away."

Nate looked startled. "Would you come chasing after me, limping down the road after my truck?"

"I might. I know farm life is busy and you have things to do, especially in helping your parents." She smiled. "But surely you can spare ten minutes for a cup of coffee and to look at my Bible."

He stuck his thumbs in his belt loops. She had noticed earlier that his pants were clean, with no hint of farm smell. His boots didn't look like work shoes, either. "I'd be honored."

Nate joined her in the slow walk to the Tanner home. She sensed his uneasiness, and she wanted him to understand her gratitude for all he'd done. She liked this stranger-friend, a gentleman who gave the impression of being one who had weathered a lot of turmoil but still managed to hold on to life.

"Would you tell me about your farm?" she asked.

He nodded. "Dairy cows. Lots of rich cream and good milk." He chuckled. "Before the war, I hated farm life, but it was all I could think about during the quiet times when we weren't fighting. Couldn't wait to get back."

"I think farms are good places to live."

"I agree. I hope to have my own herd of dairy cows someday."

"Daddy used to talk about selling his store and takin' up farming," she added. And for a brief moment, she allowed her thoughts to wander to an idyllic farm where a man such as Nate called her his own.

"How is Miss Howard faring?" Dad asked at supper.

"Better, since we found the only thing that wasn't destroyed in the fire," Nate said between mouthfuls of roast and potatoes.

"And what was that?"

"Her Bible. Actually, it was a family Bible that had been in her family since Texas became a state."

"What a miracle," Nate's mom said. "God is watching out for that young woman. I loved her mama. Not a finer woman around. Whenever anyone was feeling poorly, she was right there to help."

"Olivia's staying with the Tanners," Nate said. "I think she'll be fine, but I might check on her from time to time."

Dad cleared his throat.

Nate ignored him.

Mom handed Dad the corn bread platter and a generous helping of a disapproving look.

"Everyone likes Miss Howard." His mother reached for a cup of coffee. "I hear tell she sings at her church."

Nate recalled Olivia's story about singing in the tree with her father. "I imagine she has a fine voice."

"Are you smitten?" his mother asked.

Nate reddened.

Dad laughed. "Interesting. Very interesting."

Choosing to ignore his dad, Nate reached for the corn bread. "We didn't get finished with mending fences today. I'll take that last stretch myself after milkin' in the morning and running a quick errand."

His dad chuckled, and his mother immediately reached

for her coffee. Nate wondered what his parents had been discussing in his absence. He shot a frown to his dad, but the elderly man found the situation extremely funny.

∽❀∾

Olivia gingerly picked through the clothes spread across the sofa in the Tanners' living room. Friends from school and church had banded together to outfit her for every possible occasion. Many of the items were better than what she'd owned before the fire.

Her pastor and his wife had brought more clothing just after a friend from school delivered a box.

"Mrs. Dixon said she has an empty house you could rent," Pastor Wilkins said.

Olivia smiled and shook her head. "I need to look for something a little more affordable."

"Mrs. Dixon said you'd make a comment like that." The pastor laughed. "She wanted me to assure you the rent would be very reasonable."

"And the Coles have furniture items for you, too," Mrs. Wilkins said.

Olivia rubbed her palms together. "This is incredible. Why, I could be set up in a new place very soon. But I do have insurance money."

"I'm sure you will be fine," Mrs. Wilkins said, "but let those who care about you do their share."

"I feel a little uncomfortable—accepting charity," Olivia said.

"Nonsense," the pastor said. "The community appreciates what you're doing for our children. Can't put a dollar amount on that."

Olivia picked up a light blue shawl; it was very nice.

"I'd much rather be helping someone else."

The pastor chuckled. "By accepting these gifts, you are blessing others."

Olivia moved toward the window and the scene of her burned home. "All right. Daddy used to say the same thing." She laid the shawl across the sofa back. "I'd like everyone to know how grateful I am for their generosity." Olivia stared into the pastor's face. "Can I sing this Sunday?"

He chuckled. "Don't have to twist my arm with that request. Choose whatever song you want. We all love to hear you sing."

Mrs. Tanner stood in the doorway. She swiped at a tear with her apron. "Don't know why I'm dripping from my eyes."

"I do," Pastor Wilkins said. "It's the way everyone wants to help Olivia."

Mrs. Tanner nodded, then dabbed at her eye again. "I've a roast in the oven. Why don't both of you stay for dinner?"

Pastor Wilkins got an approving nod from his wife. "Sounds wonderful. I've been smelling dinner cooking, and it has my stomach growling something fierce."

"Wonderful." Mrs. Tanner patted the back of her hair as if her neatly pinned bun had somehow slipped below perfection. "And I have some fresh apples for a cobbler." She disappeared into the kitchen, leaving Olivia once again with the Wilkinses.

"If y'all will excuse me for a moment, I want to take these things to my room," Olivia said. "Please have a seat in the living room. I won't be but a minute."

Olivia gathered up an armful of clothes and tossed them over her sling-supported arm to take upstairs. She really wanted to spend the evening alone. Her heart was not in the mood to be sociable, even with the Wilkinses and the Tanners. Oh, she felt deeply grateful for what the church and community had displayed in response to her plight, but memories assailed her when she least expected them. She needed time to sort it all out.

A pull on her emotions signaled her tears near the curtains of her eyes. She had a right to grieve; the Bible didn't deny it. But she didn't have any desire to wail like a banshee in front of the people she cherished. They would remind her of the family Bible and of God's provision. They were right, of course, and soon she'd feel like agreeing with their every word and praying for her selfishness to slide under the bed. But not tonight.

I simply want to cry until there's nothing left inside of me.

❧

"Teaching those children is the highlight of my life," Olivia said the following morning while gathering up her belongings for school.

"They love you, that's for sure," Mrs. Tanner said. "My little Sunday school children talk about you all the time. They love it when you teach them Bible songs in school."

The words warmed Olivia's soul while a smile curved her lips. "Mama used to say that kind words spread more comfort than a world of feather beds, and a song spread honey over the soul."

"She also said a child's smile is a glimpse of heaven."

Olivia paused for a moment. "I guess if I think about it,

I don't need photographs and Mama and Daddy's things to remind me of them."

"All *I* have to do is look at you," Mrs. Tanner said, patting her arm. "You are the best of both of them. My, you look pretty this morning in green."

"Thank you. Lydia gave me the dress. She said she'd outgrown it, but I know better."

Olivia studied the older woman. She must have had fiery red hair in her youth, for she had no gray, only lighter shades of red. Her pale blue eyes sparkled, and her laugh was as infectious as that of a lively child.

"I have felt a lot of self-pity the last few days," Olivia said.

"Grief is not selfish. It's a part of life that cannot be denied. Without sorrow and grief, we have no measuring stick for true joy."

Olivia set her bag on the kitchen table and hugged the dear woman with her good arm. "You are the best medicine for what ails my heart."

A few moments later, she was walking off to school. All along the way, folks greeted her. Most of the time she took their greetings for granted, but not today. With a deep breath, she resolved to keep her chin up and put some light into someone else's life today.

Up ahead, a now familiar truck eased into the small parking area designated for parents and teachers. Nate Forester stepped out, made his way to the passenger side, and lifted a bouquet of yellow mums from inside.

"G'morning, Miss Howard," Nate said. "I brought you a little something to brighten your day."

Olivia's gaze met Nate's. In the morning light, his

nearly black hair seemed to glisten. She diverted her atten-tion to the flowers he presented to her. "They're beautiful. Thank you so much. What have I done to deserve these?"

He shifted from one foot to another. "I guess it would be teaching the town's children, when another person would want to tend to business after a fire."

The deep timbre of Nate's voice reminded her of how a knight in shining armor must have sounded to a damsel in distress. After all, he'd been Olivia's hero.

"Olivia? Are you all right?" Nate asked.

Color flooded over her body. "Oh, yes, things are much better. Thank you. Folks have been so very kind."

He smiled; every tooth must have been hand selected by the angels in charge of pearls. *What's wrong with me? My thoughts are wandering like a silly schoolgirl's.*

Nate moistened his lips. "Uh, would you like to take supper with us tomorrow evenin'?"

A sweet sensation spread over her. "Why, I'd be happy to come," Olivia said.

He grinned, and she smiled back.

"Are you courtin', Miss Howard?" a little boy asked.

Olivia swung around to see one of her students staring at her with wide-eyed curiosity—the same little boy who had reminded her of Nate. "Why, of course not." Her stomach turned a little flip. "Run along, Jimmy. I'll be there soon." She forced her gaze back to Nate. "I'm sorry. I don't know what got into him."

But Nate grinned, a very wide grin.

Chapter 4

Nate watched Olivia's face brighten to the color of a ripe tomato.

"Sometimes children speak without thinking," Olivia said.

"I'm sure that's true." Nate nodded, no longer wanting to pick fun at the young woman before him. "Can I pick you up about six o'clock?"

She nodded and turned to head toward the two-story, redbrick school building.

A twinge of regret swept through him. Maybe he wasn't ready to see a woman. Maybe loneliness and a pretty face had taken over his good senses. He expelled a heavy sigh. Too late now anyway. Olivia had already accepted his invitation to supper. He'd need to have a long talk with his parents tonight.

⁓◦⁓

Olivia hurried toward the building the best she could with a bandaged, aching leg and an arm in a sling. She wanted to get inside before Billy returned to make another comment. Maybe she should have refused the invitation to supper. But she really wanted to go.

"Miss Howard?" asked an unfamiliar male voice. "May I ask you something?"

With her heart beating faster than a hummingbird's wings, Olivia turned to meet a stranger carrying a pad of paper. "Yes."

"Are you the Olivia Howard whose home burned a few nights ago?"

She eyed the man and realized she had never seen him before. "I am. Why?"

"I'm from *Family Life Magazine*, and I'd like to do an article about the fire that destroyed your home. I'm writing a series of articles about grief. These are accountings about people who've lost everything. How do they go on? How do they manage their grief? Where is their hope and strength?"

Startled, she thought of telling the man to leave her alone. "Did you say *Family Life Magazine*?"

"Yes, ma'am."

The publication had a Christian following. "The newspaper here already did an article."

"I have it, and it's good; but I'd like to know why you're smiling after losing everything."

She nodded. School awaited her, but she could give the man five minutes. "My hope and my strength are from Jesus. Without Him, I would have walked back into the fire and let it take me, too." She took a deep breath, feeling more courageous by the moment. "My church and the community are blessing me with clothes and furnishings to replace those destroyed in the fire."

"Excellent," he said. "We're hoping other folks who have met with similar tragedies will be able to find comfort in your words."

She leaned over the man's shoulder and saw that he'd written every word she'd spoken. "One more thing," she said. "The fire ruined everything but the family Bible."

He smiled. "God is good, Miss Howard."

"Indeed, He is. So all is not lost. I have precious memories, friends who care for me, and God's promises."

And for the first time since the fire, Olivia truly believed God cared. She hurried inside to find Lydia in her first-grade room, opening the windows for a breath of the cooler fall air.

"Good morning, Lydia." Since no one was in sight, she whirled around. "I had to wear your green dress. It's so beautiful."

"I believe the dress is yours now." Her sandy-haired friend smiled.

Olivia laughed. "I don't think for a minute that you've outgrown it."

"Of course I have. Besides, I'd become tired of it."

"Nonsense." Olivia gave her friend a hug. "And I love you for your generosity."

"I must say you are faring quite well for all you've been through. Your eyes are sparkling."

Olivia thought of Nate but said nothing. She'd wait until she had something more to tell. Then she remembered what had unfolded on the school steps. "You'll never guess what just happened."

"Another blessing?"

"More like a miracle in the making." Olivia proceeded

to tell Lydia about the reporter and how God had filled her heart with happiness.

∽◦∽

"Dad, promise me you'll watch what you say in front of Olivia." Nate herded in a contrary bull that possessed about the same temperament as Nate at that moment.

"Of course, son." Dad chuckled.

Nate fumed. "And promise me you won't say anything about courtin' tomorrow night."

"I promise."

"Why don't I believe you?"

"I have no idea, son. I gave my word, didn't I?" The silver peeking out from his hat gave him a comical look.

"Too easily. Olivia and I are friends. She's a nice lady, and I'm simply making sure she's all right after what she's been through."

"Very interesting."

Those words lifted Nate's frustration level another notch. "What do you mean by 'very interesting'?"

Dad lifted his shoulder and let out a sigh. "It's interesting that you have taken a liking to this young woman when no other lady has ever caught your eye before."

"I believe in being responsible."

"My point, son. Very interesting." Without another chuckle, sigh, or comment, Nate's dad headed into the barn.

By Friday morning, Nate wished a thousand times he hadn't asked Olivia to supper. His mother was going to more trouble than with Thanksgiving dinner. He hadn't seen this much effort since the day he returned from the marines. She starched the white linen tablecloth and napkins, baked two kinds of rolls, and fussed over a sour cream–raisin pie along with a carrot cake. Nate trembled in his work boots. Something would happen that would make the comment about courting sound like good table manners. He could feel it in his bones—like those times when he waited for enemy attack. There was not a thing he could do but be ready for the worst.

❧

Friday evening came much faster than he expected, and despite his reservations, Nate had to admit that the idea of spending time with Olivia caused his stomach to turn flips. He raced through milking and hurried to get cleaned up.

"You sure are in a mighty big rush," Dad said.

"Doesn't seem proper to keep a lady waiting."

"I noticed you washed the truck."

"A lot of dirt and manure in there. Wasn't fittin' for a lady."

"I see. Don't know what's wrong with me. I thought it shone like a new penny because of Miss Howard."

Nate gritted his teeth. "You made a mistake."

"No matter anyway. If you don't get a move on, you'll be late."

Now, as Nate pulled up in front of the Tanner home, he wished he weren't alone. No need to worry about awkward conversation with someone else talking away. . . . Then again, another person might be the cause of awkward conversation. Pushing his discomfort aside, he took a deep breath and opened the truck door.

Haven't done this since before the war—

❧

Olivia caught her breath. Nate had arrived; his truck sat outside the Tanner home. All day long she'd wrestled with her decision to spend the evening with him and his family. She wanted to get to know Nate better, but every time she thought about it, butterflies took flight in her stomach.

When Nate knocked at the door, she jumped. Olivia glanced around. Thank goodness the Tanners were in the kitchen. With a deep breath and a quick glance in the hall mirror, she turned the knob.

Calm down, Olivia.

She pulled open the door. Nate stood before her, more handsome than any of the leading men at the picture show. He smiled, not wide, but big enough to cause shivers to race up her arm.

"You're right on time." She gestured for him to come inside.

"I try to be. You look real pretty in that shade of blue."

Olivia smiled. "Thank you. I'm collecting a good many nice things from folks. Well, I should tell the Tanners I'm leaving. Would you care to join me?"

"Sure."

She turned and headed toward the kitchen, expecting Nate to follow just as her second-graders would. The Tanners were washing dishes: Mrs. Tanner washed, and Mr. Tanner dried. As usual, he teased her about something, and she feigned annoyance.

"Good to see you," Nate greeted.

"I'm doing chores—again," Mr. Tanner said, holding up a bowl and dish towel. "Mark my words, Nate, this is what happens when you get married. One day you wake up and realize she has you right smack-dab in the palm of her hand." He winked at his wife. "After you get over being put out about it, you kinda enjoy it."

Oh, my. First Billy and now the Tanners. Nate will never want to see me again.

"You like helping me, and you know it," Mrs. Tanner said. She planted a kiss on his whiskered cheek.

Olivia inwardly cringed.

"I suppose if it were the right woman, I'd not mind a bit," Nate said.

This time, Olivia held her breath.

Mr. Tanner laid the soggy dish towel on the table. "I'm playing papa here tonight, so don't keep Olivia out too late."

Mercy, when will this end?

"I'll have her back early enough." Nate turned to Olivia. He seemed oblivious to what the Tanners were doing. "Ready?"

"Yes, and I'm very hungry."

After a quick good-bye, they were bouncing along in Nate's truck. The night of the fire was easier than this—when Mrs. Tanner rode with them. Olivia searched for proper conversation, but all she could think about was what had gone on at school today.

"Did you have a good week?" Nate asked. "Other than the fire?"

She nodded. "The more the calendar moves into fall, the more excited the children are about the approaching holidays."

"I remember feeling that way. Pure excitement as soon as the temperature got a little cooler." He appeared to relax, but his hands gripped the steering wheel firmly.

"Why are you so nervous?" After going through the war and all, Olivia didn't understand his uneasiness. Unless the Tanners' conversation had unsettled him.

"I haven't done anything like this since before the war. I feel like a catfish flopping on a riverbank."

"I don't do this much, either."

His shoulders lowered. "Good. I mean, that makes me feel better."

Once they pulled onto the lane leading back to the house and barns, Olivia remembered driving by the place a few times and admiring its green pastures and vast herds of brown and white Guernsey cows. All the barns and sheds fairly glistened with white paint, as did the farmhouse with its huge porch. With the sun making its trek in the west, she thought the scene looked like a picture hanging on a wall.

"You're smiling," Nate said.

She pointed to the surrounding pasture through the window. "Look at this. It's beautiful, and so peaceful."

When he turned off the engine, she listened to a couple of mockingbirds. A big, brown dog with floppy ears and a wagging tail made his way to Nate. "Hey, fella, got a lady for you to meet. Mind your manners now and don't jump on her."

"I love dogs," Olivia said. "Is he friendly?"

"Yep. No watchdog in Fred at all."

As soon as she officially met the dog, an older couple came out of the house. *Am I ready for this?* Olivia shivered and prayed for a good evening—pleasant conversation and an opportunity to get to know Nate and his parents.

"Come on in," Mrs. Forester said with a hug. "Supper's almost ready."

"Welcome, Miss Olivia. Don't know why a pretty young lady like yourself would want to spend the evening with Nate," Mr. Forester said, "but I'm glad you came." Mr. Forester chuckled and glanced at Nate. "How did you trick her into joining you tonight?" His blue eyes held more teasing than she thought the good Lord should allow.

"Now, Gus, you hush right now. No point in embarrassing them young people." Mrs. Forester shooed them all inside like a mother hen. And for the next three hours, Olivia enjoyed the Forester family—especially Nate.

"I'm sorry about my dad," Nate said, once they headed back to town. He shook his head. "I don't know where Dad comes up with things."

"I didn't mind." Olivia thought back over the way Mr. Forester had spent most of the evening talking about Nate needing "a good woman." She laughed.

"Glad you thought it was funny." He didn't sound convinced.

"Well, if it makes you feel any better, I'm sorry about what Mr. Tanner said."

"Looks like they're trying real hard to throw us together."

She sighed. "Seems that way."

Neither spoke for a few moments.

"How do you feel about obliging them?" Nate asked.

Olivia startled. "What—what do you mean?"

Nate pulled the truck to the side of the road. He said nothing for several moments, and Olivia shivered.

"Are you cold?" he asked.

"No. But I'd feel more comfortable if we'd get back on the road."

"I'm sorry. I was trying to get up enough nerve to ask you something." He turned the key in the starter, and the truck roared in response. "Sorry, didn't mean to give it so much gas."

She didn't move a muscle, but another chill raced up her arm. "What did you want to ask?" Forcing herself to breathe, Olivia willed her nerves to relax.

Nate cleared his throat. "With the Tanners suggesting things and my dad's comments that made us feel—strange, I wonder if we might—uh—try courtin'. I've been talking to God about it since the fire, and He hasn't said no."

The butterflies crowding the sides of her stomach increased in number. *Dear Lord, what do You want me to do?* Olivia swung her gaze in his direction, and a partly scary, partly thrilling sensation spread through her body. *Hot and cold?* This sweet man, her hero, with his precious family, wanted to court her? He must have felt her gaze, for his head turned in her direction. In the shadows, his handsome features—his square jaw and the memory of his intense blue eyes—caused her to catch her breath.

"I didn't mean to upset you," he said, barely a whisper.

"I'm fine. Just a little taken aback, that's all."

"I never asked if you had a man friend."

"No, not at all." *Should I have led him to believe otherwise?*

"Too soon?"

Olivia contemplated his question. For the first time in her life, a man attracted her. The sensation—besides making her feel strange—was one she welcomed. Yes, she *did* welcome this new attention wholeheartedly. What an unusual set of happenings since she'd lost her home to a horrible fire.

"Nate, I wouldn't want to take advantage of the fact you were there during the fire and took care of me."

"Believe me, I'm not. And I wouldn't want you to say yes 'cause you felt sorry for me being in the war."

Olivia started again. "The thought never crossed my mind." She smiled from her heart to her lips. "Nate, I think I'd like to try courting."

He blew out a long sigh. "Wonderful. When can I see you again?"

She laughed. "We haven't said good night yet."

"You've just seen one of my faults. Since the war, I can be impatient."

An eerie sensation tickled her awareness. This could be a mistake.

Chapter 5

Olivia thought about Nate all weekend. She shoved aside her misgivings about his impatience, in hopes he wouldn't turn out to be demanding about certain things that good girls didn't do. Then she remembered his excellent reputation and his statement about talking to God about them.

I'm overreacting. Nervous. Scared.

Sunday morning, after she sang "What a Friend We Have in Jesus" and thanked the congregation for their generosity, Olivia offered up a silent prayer for guidance with Nate. A week ago, she hadn't even met Nate Forester, and now he dominated her thoughts. A special spot grew in her heart for him. Could this be the beginnings of love? This quickly?

"You're certainly happy," Mrs. Tanner said as they walked home from church.

"Maybe it's the cooler temperatures." She shifted her Bible.

"Or the young man who took you to supper," Mr. Tanner said. "He doesn't attend our church, does he?"

"No," she said, much too quickly. "His family goes to a church in the country."

"He would have loved your song this morning." Mrs. Tanner sighed.

If Nate had been there, the song would have died in her throat. "He's a nice man."

"When you seein' him again?" Mr. Tanner asked.

Olivia took a deep breath. "Wednesday night. We're going to his church for prayer meetin'."

He nodded. "Good man. I'm still playing papa here, you know."

How well she knew, but she couldn't help but love him for his protective nature. "I'm glad you care."

"I aim to make sure Nate Forester does you right."

Nate's confession of being impatient echoed in her mind, leaving her a bit unsettled. The horrors of war could have done unspeakable things to him.

⤙ৎ⤚

Nate gave the razor one last swipe over his cheek. He turned his face from side to side and studied his reflection in the mirror to make sure he had gotten every last whisker. All of a sudden, it hit him that he was seeing Olivia in less than an hour. She'd been on his mind since the past Friday night. He'd pondered about where this courtin' thing would lead them. How different she was from any woman he'd ever known. Olivia possessed this blunt honesty that could see through a man's soul. And she had this tomboy appeal that made him want to take her fishin' and huntin'. Her large brown eyes turned his senses inside out. He smiled in the mirror. Contemplating on Olivia Howard seemed a whole lot easier on the heart than dwelling on the realities of war.

The war had threatened him physically. He ate, slept, and breathed with the demons of death nipping at his heels. He lived and breathed the game of war by holding on to the hand of God.

But Olivia threatened his heart.

He snatched up a clean shirt and buttoned it while he made his way down the stairs. Remembering he hadn't combed his hair, Nate made his way back up to his room and met his dad on the steps.

Dad held up his hands. "I'm behaving myself tonight. Your mom will kick me out of the house if I don't."

Nate chuckled. "I heard the ear chewin' she gave you."

Dad scowled. "You wait. Your time is coming."

"Don't think so. I'm learning what I'm not supposed to do by watching you."

∽⊚∾

A week later, Olivia showed Nate Mrs. Dixon's rental house. "Do you like it?" she asked. "I can move in tomorrow if I want."

"Looks like the right size for you," he said.

She walked to a living room window. "She offered to sell it, and I might be interested." She whirled around to see the expression on his face.

"It appears to be well built. I can see how it's fittin' for a single woman." He glanced up at the ceiling, then back to her. "How long has it been since we started seeing each other?"

"Three and a half weeks." Olivia smiled. "Same as the fire." She considered saying that the time spent with Nate made dealing with losing her home easier to bear, but she chose not to. Her emotions ran like a race horse with blinders. Each time they were together—a total of six times, counting the night of the fire—she better understood his personality. And she appreciated the man she was coming to know. Four of those six occasions were with his parents, whom she was becoming attached to, as well.

"When can I kiss you?"

"Nate Forester."

"I was teasin' you."

"No, you weren't." *Now I see how you take after your dad.*

He scratched his face. "Don't hide it well, do I?"

She rested her arm over her sling. "Not exactly. You remind me of a little boy in my class."

Nate raised a brow. "Do I want to hear this?"

"Probably not, but I'm stating it anyway. He brings me an apple every Monday. On Friday, when we have a spelling test, he asks if I liked the apple."

Nate moaned. The man could coax the stars out of the sky with his looks. She wondered if he practiced charm in front of a mirror or on the cows.

"Does he do good on the tests?" he asked.

"Does he do *well* on the tests?" She laughed. "Sometimes."

"So this means I won't get a kiss for a long time?"

"Maybe Christmas, if you're sweet."

"My lips will be in a permanent pucker by then."

"Nate! Someone might hear you."

He grinned. "The only one who counts is God, and I've already told Him about my feelings."

"We barely know each other. A kiss is special."

The grin disappeared from Nate's face. "I agree, Olivia, and I wouldn't want it any other way. As much as I tease, we do need to spend a lot of time getting to know each other. I have some scars from the war, some real painful memories, that need to get out. Dad said they'd eat me alive if I didn't talk about them."

"He's right. I can't imagine how awful it was for you."

Nate's lips pressed into a thin line. "I've heard you talk about your folks and the special things lost in the fire, and I've felt the urge to talk about the war, but not yet."

"You will someday. And it may not be with me. Your parents love you very much."

"I hope it is with you, Olivia. I really do. Each time we're together I want us to pray, to be certain this is God's plan for our lives."

"Would you like to pray now? I mean, is it too soon?"

"Now is perfect." He bowed his head. "Father God, Olivia and I are just getting acquainted. We want to be sure You want us to keep going on as friends with maybe something more in the future. I keep asking for a sign. Now, we're asking together. Make Your purpose plain as day to us. Amen." He lifted his head. "I think we have a beginning."

From across the room, she saw the tenderness in his eyes. "I think so, too."

∽⊗∾

In the days ahead, Nate stood back and watched Olivia transform the small house into a home. People in the community donated furniture. Some of it was in bad shape, but Olivia had a way with arranging things and using a little paint that made the worst look good. She sewed curtains and covered chairs, making him wonder if the folks who donated yard goods and furniture might want them back.

"You don't have an apple tree," Nate said as they walked around the outside perimeter of the house.

She lifted her cast-free arm. "That might be a good idea. But you have a couple of apple trees on your farm. One of them looks like a good climbing tree."

"I might have to chop it down."

"No need. I won't tell you when I plan to climb it."

He scowled. "I'll make sure Fred tails you wherever you go. That old dog is trained to come after me at the first sign of trouble."

She wiggled her shoulders. "You wouldn't dare."

Olivia's eyes danced, and he mentally added up the weeks until Christmas. One month and he was smitten. He hadn't found a single thing about Olivia Howard that he didn't like. When the idea of loving a woman scared the daylights out of him, he wished he could find something disagreeable about her. It hadn't happened yet.

"Knowing you, I'd come calling and find you repairing the roof."

"My daddy taught me how to be useful."

"He also told you to stay out of trees."

"I don't listen well."

Nate reached for her hand. "I need to make sure you're within arm's reach to keep you safe."

"What an excuse to hold my hand, Nate Forester."

"Do I need one?"

She stopped and peered into his face with a look so serious that Nate wondered if he'd upset her. "I don't think you need an excuse."

"Good, 'cause it's a long time till Christmas."

She laughed and touched his cheek. "You're a fine man, Nate. My hero."

Olivia had called him this many times. Some of his war buddies had claimed he was a hero, too. The title made him feel uncomfortable, undeserving. "When you call me that, I think about the war."

She gasped. "I never meant to upset you. What you did for me the night of the fire was incredible. I'll never forget it."

"I understand, and it's all right. War makes a man think differently about himself. What I did there came from duty and gut fear. Nothing heroic about it."

"But, Nate, heroes are made by circumstance, not by choice. You never wished for our country to go to war any more than you chose for my home to burn. God gave you a gift to see others in their time of need."

He studied the light-haired woman beside him. "I hadn't looked at it that way before." He shrugged. "But I never talked to anyone about it, either. Reading the Bible helps a lot."

"When you're ready, I'm here to listen."

He nodded. "Thanks, Olivia. You're one special lady." Peering into her sweet face with the smoothest skin and prettiest eyes this side of heaven, Nate struggled to keep from gathering her up into his arms and collecting his Christmas kiss.

Later, while driving home, a thought hit him and sent his emotions into a tailspin. Sweat broke out on his brow. What if Olivia didn't like him much at all? What if she felt sorry for him because of the war? Nate had no use for pity, no matter what the disguise.

The many times people asked him how he was doing washed over him. *Olivia's not like that. She sees me for the man I am, not for what happened in the war.* The sickening slaughter at Normandy pounded against his brain. The memories sometimes attacked him when he least expected it.

〜∞〜

Olivia reached for a sweater before walking home from school.

She stepped outside and lifted her face to a cloudless blue sky. The weather had turned decisively cooler in time for Christmas vacation. All the students had been dismissed early for the holiday right after lunch. They had sung Christmas carols and made ornaments for their parents, then shared sugar cookies. Their little hearts were so filled with joy in anticipation of the celebration of Jesus' birth. The sixth-graders acted out the first Christmas complete with angels, shepherds, and a doll that played the part of baby Jesus. The play caused Olivia to cry. This would be the first Christmas without the decorations of days gone by. Surely Mama and Daddy smiled down from heaven— their third with Jesus. How wondrous to spend Christmas with the Father of the universe and the One who died for their sins. Olivia smiled through her tears, truly a mixture of envy and love for all who had gone on before her.

Now, as she peered up at the sky and watched cottony clouds float by, her spirit soared. Did they all smile on her for the fragile love she'd found with the dark-haired, blue-eyed fireman?

Tonight she and Nate planned to attend his church. She envisioned sitting next to him on the pew, with Mr. and Mrs. Forester to the right of her.

"You're becoming a permanent fixture here," Mr. Forester had said last Wednesday. "Very interesting."

"Are you planning to give my spot to someone else?" she asked.

"Not if I have anything to do with it," Nate said.

"Do we need to be planning anything?" his dad asked. "I like to be ready for things."

"Hush," Mrs. Forester said. "You embarrass those two to death."

Olivia had grown to accept the teasing, in hopes she and Nate might be together for a long time.

Olivia's thoughts turned to the present when one of her students shouted, "Merry Christmas!" She waved and picked up her step down the street. The world looked good. Two weeks ago, she'd received her check from the house fire and deposited it in the bank. Mrs. Dixon wanted her to buy the little house Olivia now called home, but Olivia hesitated. She and Nate were growing closer, and a house might complicate things for the future. *Dare I hope for more? Am I being foolish?*

Once home, she saw a box had been delivered and blocked her way to the front door. She hadn't ordered anything. Olivia studied the sender's address: Dan and Bev Fisher from Easton, Pennsylvania. She knew no one there. Maybe the box had been sent to the wrong address. She glanced at it again and saw that there'd been no mistake.

Curiosity caused her toes to tingle as though she'd received an early Christmas gift. Olivia dragged the box inside, set it on the kitchen table, and slit the taped edges with a knife.

Inside the box, she folded back white tissue paper to reveal a quilt. Olivia lifted it from the box and immediately recognized the pattern as a Crazy Quilt, similar to one her mother had once made. She gasped. *How beautiful.* The delicate, hand-tied stitching with a heavy, gold-colored yarn had been the work of an expert seamstress. And the patches of various colors—shades of blues and purples, with gold, scarlet, and emerald scattered throughout—were perfect in every way. Her hand spread over the quilt—mostly cotton, but several squares of velveteen caressed her fingers. Why had she been sent this work of art?

Fumbling through the tissue paper, she found an envelope.

Dear Miss Howard,

My husband and I read your story in Family Life Magazine, *about how you found strength in God after a fire destroyed your home. We praise Him for the miracle of preserving your life and your family Bible.*

We feel as if we know you. You see, Dan's story once appeared in the magazine, too. My husband, daughter, and I have decided to send you the enclosed patchwork quilt. This quilt was made by my husband's first wife, Darcy, and given to him on her deathbed. She wanted it to be something that would remind Dan of her undying love, and the joy they shared in helping others during their time of need. Dan has carried on his wife's legacy by helping others like my daughter, Amy, and me. He gave the quilt to Amy for Christmas the year before Dan and I were married.

Amy, Dan, and I hope this patchwork quilt will bring you comfort and act as a reminder that there are others who care and are praying for you.

Sincerely,
Bev Fisher

Olivia wept and held the quilt to her heart. God's promises rang through each thread. This Christmas might not be like all the others, but it would still hold what was most important: God's never-ending love.

When she took the time to consider all that had happened since the fire, she marveled at the way so many people had been blessed by giving in her time of need. Even more, she wouldn't have met Nate and known the stirrings of love.

Thank You, Lord, for seeing me through these difficult

times. Nothing will stand in the way of a holy Christmas. I will give to others as Mama and Daddy did and treasure the sweetness of Nate's tender affections. This Christmas will be one I will cherish for years to come. I can just feel it.

Chapter 6

Nate knew something special had happened to Olivia the moment he saw her face all lit up like a Christmas tree. Her eyes sparkled as though the stars had taken residence within.

"Oh, Nate, wait till you see what was delivered to me today," she said as she opened the door.

"Delivered? In the mail?"

She nodded and took his hand. "Come inside and let me show you."

Nate could see that Olivia had transformed her small living room into a picture right off the cover of a quality magazine. A small tree with twinkling lights and ornaments made by her students occupied one corner. A Nativity scene sat on a table near her sofa; adjacent to it was a Bible opened to the book of Luke. Atop her piano were three miniature kings riding their camels and carrying gifts to the baby Jesus. The scent of aromatic pine swirled around the room, and everywhere, colors of red and green pointed to Christmas.

"It looks really pretty here," Nate said.

"The Tanners brought me the tree, then other folks left the decorations on my steps." She pointed to the ornaments made by her students. "These are my favorite. Little hands worked so hard to make my Christmas perfect."

"Mom's been working hard making sure our house looks good, too."

"Now that I'm out of school for the holidays, I can help her." Olivia folded her hands at her waist. She hadn't stopped smiling since he took his first glimpse of her.

"You look like you're about to burst."

"I am. See the quilt across the sofa back?"

His gaze focused on the many colors. He walked over and touched a velveteen patch, his callused fingers feeling the softness. "This is new?"

"New to me." She picked up a folded piece of paper. "It came in the mail today along with this letter. Do read it, Nate. It describes why the quilt was sent to me."

Nate read every word aloud. The thoughtfulness of the Fishers gave him renewed faith in mankind, something he often neglected to see in others in the aftermath of the war. "Good people," he said. "They know the meaning of unselfish giving."

"I think so, too. I've written them a thank-you, but it doesn't seem like enough."

He raised his head and caressed her cheek with his palm. Up to this moment, he'd hesitated to touch her for fear of offending his precious Olivia or scaring her away. "This quilt coming so close to Christmas makes me want to believe in you and me."

The smile from her lips to her eyes said she wanted to believe the same thing. She turned her cheek and kissed his hand. The featherlike softness against his work-worn hands made his knees feel like jelly and his heart like mush.

"Oh, Olivia, you mean so much to me. I never thought I'd feel this way about a woman. I—" Nate stopped himself before he revealed the love longing to be opened like a gift under a tree.

"Maybe we need to be on our way to church," she whispered.

"Reckon so."

"I'm afraid you might be collecting on your Christ-mas kiss."

His pulse quickened. "Would that be so bad?"

"Not at all." She hesitated and her cheeks reddened. "I've always enjoyed early gifts."

His fingers crept down from her cheek, throat, neck, and back to weave silky strands of lightbrown hair onto his hand. Sudden shyness came into her eyes, but he could only smile and draw her closer to him.

"Merry Christmas, my pretty lady." He bent to taste her lips. In all of his musings about her, he'd not imagined such a wonderful moment. The instant their lips parted, "I love you" rose in his throat. He'd thought about it for days and believed his subconscious had taken voice.

A tiny sob escaped from her lips, and she buried her face in his chest. "I love you, too, Nate, but I'm frightened."

He held her close and rested his head on her silky hair. "What are you afraid of?"

"Of losing you, I think. You are so good and kind—a gift from God when I needed a hero." She sniffed. "I'm afraid I'll wake up one morning and you'll be gone."

The desire to hold her and never let her go swept over him, a fierce protective instinct that seemed to drown out all of his other needs. "Don't think so. The good Lord saw me through the war, so I guess he'll see me through a whole lot more."

"Hold me awhile longer, Nate. I don't want to be late for church, but having your arms around me feels so right."

⌒◎⌒

Snuggled next to Nate, Olivia inhaled the fresh scent of soap and the outdoors. With her eyes closed ever so tightly and the sound of his heart pounding in her ears, she wondered if the angels had lifted her onto some magic carpet and carried her and Nate to heaven.

In the next breath, Olivia realized what she would give Nate for Christmas. A new pair of work gloves lay wrapped beneath the tree, but this new idea excited her. In fact, as soon as she was home from church tonight, she would begin.

The pastor's sermon was about the saintly qualities of Joseph as Jesus' father, the man who did not have a single word recorded in the Bible. Jesus' earthly father evidenced a profound faith in following through with his commitment to Mary. She had an angel visit her to reveal God's plan, but Joseph clung to God's Word after hearing from an angel who appeared in a dream. Mary's angel had a name—Gabriel—but Joseph's angel had no name. So many things were like her Nate, or maybe she wanted him to have all of Joseph's fine qualities. On the way home, Olivia's mind raced with what she wanted to do for Nate's Christmas.

"Are you all right?" Nate asked. "You sure are quiet."

She touched his hand, which gripped the steering wheel. "My mind keeps thinking about tonight's sermon and how very much you are like Joseph."

He startled. "Me?"

"Yes. The silent hero. . .always making sure I'm fine. . . and you're giving and kind."

He laughed. "But you don't know all my faults."

"I'm sure Mary found out about Joseph's faults later, too." In the darkness, she leaned over and planted a kiss on his cheek. "You're a fine man, and I'm proud to know you—even more proud to have your love."

He said nothing, but a single tear met her lips when she once more brushed a kiss across his weathered cheek.

Once home and the door latched, Olivia snapped on a lamp by the piano and sat down on the bench. *I want to write the finest song ever for him.* A smile lingered on her lips as she thought about the first song she composed in the apple tree with Daddy. Her fingers touched the keys, and a soft tune moved from her head to her fingertips. Phrases danced across her mind, but nothing seemed to be the God-given words meant for a perfect song for Nate.

"Everlasting Song" repeated in her mind. She wanted words and a melody that spoke of Christmas and also of her love in a subtle way that didn't sound like a love-struck young girl. Nate had been a gift, and she wanted him to know how much she appreciated everything about him.

She peered at the quilt and recalled the Fishers' story. It wove more images through her heart, and she jotted them down for his song.

Sometimes when she wrote a song, the melody came before the words. Other times, the words came first and their meaning became a springboard for the music. Tonight a melody floated through her mind, a tune that refused to let her go. She knew Nate preferred gospel music, those songs that gave rise to faith and living in the South. Her goal was to create something just right for him—not an ancient hymn or a classical sound, but a song about life as Nate lived it.

—— PATCHWORK HOLIDAY ——

As the clock struck one in the morning, Olivia placed the finishing touches on "Everlasting Song," what she felt was something between a ballad and a Christmas love song. The words plagued her; they didn't really say what her spirit felt during this holy celebration, nor did they fully reveal the depth of her feelings for Nate. But the song was the very best she could do.

> *The strings of time weave through my heart*
> *Back to a place where memories beckon.*
> *Like a patchwork quilt that calls me home*
> *To the love of those who know God's heaven.*
>
> *The blessings of Christmas fill me*
> *With the peace and joy of a simpler life*
> *Where love is the gift to all mankind;*
> *It overcomes a broken world's strife.*
>
> *Spoken through a wee babe's gentle cry*
> *I hear the message loud and strong.*
> *Quiet love given to a common man*
> *Give ear! An everlasting song.*

When she finally laid her head down to sleep, she was overcome by a deep sense of passion and gratitude to the Lord, who had given her a bit of creativity—and she felt an overwhelming urge to weep for allowing her to love a man as fine as Nate Forester.

On Christmas Eve, Nate couldn't sleep. A part of him said he'd never grown up, and the anticipation of Christmas denied him needed rest. He remembered past Christmases that he had spent defending his country, and the brave men with whom he'd shared the hope of peace. Some of those men had shed their blood on the battlefields. Nate took time to think about them: their names, the sound of their voices, their conversations, and the things that made them laugh and cry. He also pondered the day they had died.

His mind moved to June 6, 1944, at Normandy, France, the day he and thousands of Allied soldiers had landed on a beach to fight against the armies of Nazi Germany. His two best friends died that day. One fell on each side of him. They were both married and had children. Nate realized the legacy they'd left at the time, and for once, he'd wished he had a wife in the States. Later, he believed the thought selfish, for no woman or child should have to endure the heartache of telling a soldier good-bye and then having to wait for the war to end. Nate decided in the following days that he would never marry. If the war ever ended, he'd go home and spend his days courtin' cows. And if another war ever broke out, he'd sign up again. Now, here he was, thinking about Christmas. . . the war. . .those now dead. . .and Olivia.

He'd propose marriage tomorrow if the proper amount of time had elapsed. She'd be shocked, not understanding how quickly life could be snuffed out—like the candles at a Christmas Eve service. But he had a beautiful gift for her, an emerald ring that had belonged to his grandmother. Knowing Olivia's soft heart, she'd be pleased.

He'd bide his time and aim for Valentine's Day.

Christmas morning, just as dawn broke on the horizon, Nate drove his truck to fetch Olivia. She'd agreed to spend the entire day with him, beginning with breakfast. He had the emerald ring in his pocket and a powerful love in his heart.

"Don't be too long," his mother had said. "But I'll be expectin' you to give Olivia her gift before you return." She flashed a smile his way.

"I'll do my best. No one wants a cold breakfast," he said.

The air was chilly, but without the snow of the north country. Nate didn't think he'd enjoy that much cold. He hummed a Christmas carol and patted his jacket pocket to make sure the little black box was still there. He'd looked forward to this day for a long time. And by next Christmas, he hoped Olivia would be wearing a wedding band on her finger.

Of course, he intended to collect on his promised kiss, although he'd enjoyed a few since the day Olivia had received the quilt from the Fishers in Pennsylvania. Each time he tasted her lips, he wanted more. Nate smiled. This celebration of Jesus' birth promised to be the best he'd ever known.

Olivia met him at the door, wearing a blue dress that seemed to bring out the color in her cheeks.

"Merry Christmas." She laughed. "Didn't we say good-bye only a few hours ago?"

"I don't remember. I'm a man in love."

"Nate, the whole neighborhood will hear you."

"Doesn't bother me. They're all jealous anyway."

She gestured for him to enter. "I have coffee ready. You don't want to be late for your mother's Christmas breakfast."

He swelled so much with the tingly feeling her voice

always prompted in him. In fact, he thought he'd kiss her in front of all the neighbors. "We have a few minutes."

She closed the door behind him. "I'm ready."

Confusion threw him a curve. "To leave?"

"No." She laughed. "For my Christmas kiss."

"Crazy woman," he pretended to growl. "If my memory serves me correctly, you had one of those last night."

"I can't remember," she said and wrapped her arms around his neck. "Remind me."

Remind her he did, until she stepped back breathless, her face wearing a healthy red glow. "I love you," he said.

"And I love you," she responded. "You have made this Christmas as close to perfect as it could possibly be."

"Naw, Miss Howard, that's *my* claim about you!" He touched his lips to her nose and then pulled out the gift from his jacket pocket and handed it to her. "Merry Christmas."

Her brown eyes widened.

"Open it, sweetheart. It won't bite."

With trembling fingers, she reached for the box resting on his palm.

"This is a hint of what I want for us in the days to come," he said. "I'm fixin' to bust if you don't open it soon."

She smiled and lifted the lid of the small, hinged box. "Oh my, Nate. It's beautiful."

"Do you really like it? It was my grandma's on my mom's side."

Olivia picked it up from the box and placed it on her right-hand ring finger.

"I'd rather it was sitting atop your left hand, but I

reckon I have something to look forward to."

She met his gaze and threw her arms around his neck. "Thank you so much. The ring is beautiful." She whirled around before he had a chance to plant another kiss on her lips. "I have two things for you. One is just plain practical, and the other is a little more special."

Nate didn't need to ponder over the matter. "To me, both will be special. You choose."

Olivia made her way to the tree and lifted a package from beneath it. "Here, open this first."

Nate ripped off the paper and found new work gloves inside. "Thanks. I really needed these."

"Now, the something that's a little more special." She placed her arms behind her back.

"Don't keep me waiting." He laughed.

She walked to the piano and sat down. Her narrow shoulders lifted and fell. With her attention on the piano, she rubbed her hands together. "I wrote this for you. I call it 'Everlasting Song'."

The moment her fingers touched the keys, Nate fell under a magical spell that spoke of the wonder of Christmas. The words and Olivia's sweet voice were a perfect blend of joy. When she finished, his heart was overflowing with happiness.

" 'Quiet love given to a common man. Give ear, an everlasting song,' " he whispered. "Your song is the most beautiful I've ever heard."

She slowly stood to face him. "Thank you, but it's *your* song."

He took her hands in his and noticed her quivering body. Nate cupped her chin and kissed her lightly. Her body stilled and moved close to his. *Thank You, Lord, for Olivia. Help me to cherish her always.*

Long after the day ended and the sun sank in the west, Olivia recalled every word that had passed between her and Nate. Such a perfect day. She didn't even mind Mr. Forester's teasing; maybe so she'd come to accept it that someday Nate would propose and they'd be man and wife. How wonderful to spend every holiday with those who had grown so close to her heart. She and Nate needed time to get to know each other better, but nothing could come between her and Nate. Nothing.

Chapter 7

December swept into January, and once more, Olivia was back at school teaching her precious second-graders. This class seemed more affectionate than some she'd had. The little boys had less trouble staying in their seats, and the little girls didn't often act spiteful to each other.

Along with spending time with Nate and teaching school, letters to and from Dan and Bev Fisher flew back and forth. Olivia wrote about Nate and his love of the dairy farm. She even mentioned he wanted to own a herd and farm of his own one day.

"I have another letter from the Fishers," she said one afternoon when Nate stopped by her home after school. "Do you want to hear it?"

"Sure." Nate grinned. "I feel like I know them folks."

She glanced up after carefully slitting the envelope. "Me, too. Hope someday we can meet them." She slipped out the letter and opened it.

Dear Olivia,

Here it is the end of January, and we are into a new year. Last night, about a foot of snow fell atop a previous depth of about fifteen inches. Today the wind is so strong that I hated to send Amy to school or to step outside the house. But I knew Dan wanted to take a few pictures of the winter wonderland, so I bundled up and faced the blustery wind like a good wife.

Dan wanted me to pass on an opportunity to Nate. Well, really to both of you. A good friend from church is retiring, and his farm and dairy herd, along with all the machinery, is for sale. Dan says the price is excellent, and if we didn't already have a good business, we'd consider it. The property has about two hundred acres with a creek winding through it and good pasture. Please let us know if you'd like to come for a visit and see the farm.

Lots of love,
Bev and Dan

Olivia folded the letter and stuck it back inside the envelope. "That was nice of them to think of us. Don't you think?"

Nate nodded. "I'd like to see the farm."

She startled. "Why? This is your home."

"I live on my parents' farm. It's not mine."

She said nothing. The thought of Nate moving away frightened her. What if she never saw him again?

"I'd like to see the farm." His voice rose barely above a whisper.

Olivia stiffened. "Then you should go. I won't stand in the way of your dream."

He nodded and pulled her close. "This could be our future home, Olivia. I have to find out."

"I know." Olivia trembled. "When would you leave?"

"As soon as I can contact the Fishers and make the arrangements."

Dread washed over Olivia. Her knees weakened and her stomach churned. She could only hope Nate didn't like the farm or that the cold would be unbearable.

⌇⌇

"This is everything I ever dreamed of," Nate said to the elderly man.

"I can see it in your eyes," Mr. Lorne said. "Although, having a missus would help."

An image of Olivia flashed in Nate's mind. "Oh, I do have a lady in mind. I haven't asked her yet, but I plan to in February."

"Smart man. Is she a godly woman?" Mr. Lorne's dog wagged his tail and sniffed at Nate.

Nate bent to let him sniff his gloves, then patted the dog's head. His mind raced to inventory Olivia's good qualities and how much he loved her. "I reckon she's about as close to Jesus as a person can get."

"Couldn't ask for more than that. And if she can cook, too, why, you've got the best." Mr. Lorne laughed, reminding Nate of Dad. Nate half expected the man to say, "Interesting."

Nate nodded. His gaze swung around the barn and noted the sturdy structure. Even with the wind whistling outside, the barn was tight. The idea of owning such a fine herd of cows and all that went with it seemed too good to be true. The house needed nothing but to be lived in, and the four bedrooms gave him room for a future family.

"Let me show you where I've always planted the garden," the frail old man said. "The soil's rich there."

Outside, the wind whipped across Nate's face; it was bitter cold, but in time he'd grow used to the climate. He would just need a few more clothes to ward off the chill—and lots of Olivia's kisses.

"Right over there is the best sledding hill in the county. Folks come from all over after a good snowfall. I've never refused them." The old man chuckled. "I've thawed out a few frozen sled riders in my day, too."

Nate envisioned people laughing and having a good time in this winter wonderland. "I'd never seen snow until two days ago. I think I'd do fine once I learned how to drive in it and stay warm."

"There are good folks to teach you how to live in the north. About two miles west of here is my church. The pastor doesn't hesitate to say what's right and wrong and knows how to have a good time. He's about your age, with two children and a sweet wife. He has more energy than a dozen schoolboys."

Nate couldn't wait to get back home and tell Olivia about the farm. No doubt she'd be sad to leave her friends, but they'd make new ones here. "I'm sure this is a whole lot more than I can afford, but what are you asking for your place?"

The elderly man grinned. "How much you wanting to spend?"

∽◉∾

Olivia couldn't hide her disappointment any longer. Nate had been acting strange since he'd stopped to see her on his way home from the Pennsylvania trip. They stood in the kitchen, sipping coffee. "What's wrong? Did your meeting with the Fishers not go well?" She wanted it to have gone badly, but she refused to let her true sentiments be known.

Nate jammed his hands into his jeans pockets. "They're great people. Made me feel at home."

"Then what is it? Oh, the farm, that's it. You were disappointed?"

"Olivia, I loved the farm. The owner made me a good offer, and I took it."

A chill raced up her arms. "But, Nate, you're talking about moving so far away. When would I see you?"

"I'm getting to that."

She gasped. Did Nate want to end their relationship? But he'd said more than once that he loved her, even hinted of marriage. "What do you mean?"

He turned and moved toward the piano. She desperately needed to see his face, read the truth in his eyes. The thought of losing him. . . No, it couldn't be. She swallowed hard in an effort to gain control of her emotions. "Please talk to me, Nate. I'm confused."

"I wanted to wait until Valentine's Day to ask you this." He sighed. "And I intended for it to be all romantic-like." With a deep breath, he turned and walked back to her. He wrapped his arms around her waist. "I love you, Olivia. I believe I did the first moment I saw you. Will you marry me? Will you be my wife and move with me to Pennsylvania?"

Shock heated her where a moment before she'd been chilled. *This is not the way I dreamed he would propose.* "We've only known each other for a few months, and now you want to marry me and move to Pennsylvania?"

"Yes. That's exactly what I want." His gaze penetrated her heart.

She saw the love; he didn't try to conceal it. "I love you, but I can't leave Tomball or Texas. This is my home, where I teach school and have friends. What would I do up north? Freeze?"

"I'd keep you warm."

"That's not funny." She placed her hands on her hips. "You have no right to ask me to do this. It's too soon, Nate. I love you, but you're moving too fast. Maybe we could write, or maybe this farm won't work out, or—"

"No!"

Olivia was startled by the interruption. He'd never raised his voice at her before.

His hands dropped from her shoulders. "Life is too short to let it pass without grabbing hold of what is good. I know what I'm talking about. I lost too many friends during the war, and I understand that life is short. My two best buddies were shot down on either side of me at Normandy. We didn't have a chance to say good-bye." He paused and shook his head. "I bought the farm for us. For some reason I thought we wanted the same things, that God had given us a special gift—" He took a deep breath. "Love like ours doesn't happen often—may never happen again."

Olivia considered what he'd said about his friends at Normandy and the intensity of his plea for her to marry him and move away from all she held dear. "Can't you buy a farm here?"

Nate said nothing for several moments. "Don't you think I prayed about this? Do you honestly think I want you to be unhappy?"

Tears brimmed in her eyes. "I—I suppose not. But I can't leave here."

"Why? What are you afraid of? You can't trust God to give you friends? Or is it that you don't want to marry me?"

"I do love you, but this is too hard. First the fire and losing everything, and now you're asking more of me than I can give."

"So when I leave, you aren't going with me?"

Olivia felt like someone had landed a fist in her stomach.

Nate's face flared. "I guess I got my answer." He picked up her quilt. "Remember when you got this? You said it was a sign from God that He kept His promises. Well, you can snuggle up to it when I'm gone."

"You're not being fair." She wanted him to stop, to say he was teasing.

He lifted his chin. "Probably not, but at least I'm honest." He flung the quilt back onto the sofa and headed to the door. "Never took you for a woman who thought things were more important than dreams and being with the one you loved."

The door slammed with an explosive sound that rivaled thunder. Dishes in the kitchen cupboard rattled. Olivia sank onto the sofa while her mind echoed with what she'd lost. Nate, her hero, the man who was so much like her daddy, had hurt her far deeper than she thought possible. No more smiles or stolen kisses. No more sound of his deep chuckle or sight of his intensely blue eyes.

She'd gotten along fine without Nate Forester before; she would do the same again. Maybe.

⁓⊚⁓

Nate sealed the envelope with a letter to Olivia inside. A week had passed, and neither of them had contacted the other. He stuck the envelope in his shirt pocket and rubbed his eyes. Maybe when he got to Pennsylvania he'd be able to sleep, but his heart told him no. He hadn't hurt this bad since the war. Back then, a man lived with dying, and the notion that a friend might not make it. Losing Olivia felt like she'd stuck a knife in his heart and twisted it.

"I'm sorry, son," his dad had said. "I know you love Olivia. She loves you, too. Give her a little time and she'll come to her senses."

Nate ached all over. "Don't think so." She had made it clear about choosing between her and the farm he had bought in Pennsylvania.

Dad frowned. "I think you're both stubborn as mules."

"How else could I have handled it?" Nate sensed the anger rising like floodwater.

"Pray."

"I have been!"

"Then pray some more until you have your answer."

Nate bit his tongue to keep from spouting words he'd regret later. Tomorrow he'd be gone, and today needed to be for making good memories. "Sorry for hollerin'," he said. "This isn't your fault."

"Love is not a fifty-fifty bargain, son. It's 100 percent on both sides."

Nate wasn't sure he agreed, but to keep peace, he didn't reply.

The following morning, after leaving his parents with "Good luck" on their lips and tears in their eyes, Nate drove into town en route to his new home. He had the letter to deliver and one last time to see Olivia. She'd be getting ready to leave for school, and that was a blessing in itself—no prolonged, painful confrontation.

Pulling up in front of her house brought back all the times he'd stopped here and took her smiling face for granted. *If she ever sees things my way, I'll let her know every day of my life how much I love her.*

He lifted the letter from the truck seat and made his way to her door. Like a kid, he wanted to see her in the doorway with "I'm sorry" on her lips. He'd be glad to apologize, too, if he'd done anything wrong.

With trembling hands, he knocked on her door—not once but three times. After several long moments, he decided Olivia had either left for school early or chose not to answer. Most likely the latter. He stuck the envelope in the door and walked away, toward his future and away from her. He should feel good about a farm of his own. Instead, he felt like he had a bad case of flu.

⁓◌⁓

Olivia saw Nate sitting in the truck before getting out. He looked miserable, and she hated it; but he'd brought this all on himself by assuming she'd marry him and move up north. When he knocked, she wanted to answer, but her feet refused to move. This way was better. They'd most likely end up quarreling, and she couldn't bear another cross word passing between them.

What could it accomplish? He'll never change his mind now that he bought the farm.

Still, the thought stayed with her like her comforting quilt. Nate might very well get to Pennsylvania and realize all he'd left behind. The time came for her to leave for school, and it didn't matter at all that she wanted to stay home, climb into bed, and cover her head with blankets.

The letter was lodged in the doorjamb. She'd read it during the walk to school. Tearing open the flap, Olivia watched one tear after another drip onto the envelope.

Dear Olivia,

I hate leaving town like this, without telling you good-bye real proper, and I don't have an idea if you'll even talk to me, but I'll try one more time in delivering this.

I'm sorry about our quarreling. I guess I never dreamed you'd not marry me and move to Pennsylvania. I'm not sure where I went wrong. Maybe I should have called you before I made the owner an offer. When I think about it, you told me how you felt before I left.

If you change your mind, you'll know where to find me. I wrote the address at the bottom of this letter. I'm sorry if I hurt you. You are a special lady, and I will always love you.

Love,
Nate

Chapter 8

Weeks became a month, and Olivia hadn't heard a word from Nate. Her anger had drifted to hurt, and now she missed him terribly. On Valentine's Day, he sent her a card and simply scrawled his name across the bottom. No "I love you" or "Missing you," and no newsy letter. Nothing special.

She'd been too stubborn to send a card.

That same day, Olivia received a copy of *Family Life Magazine* with the article about herself and the fire. Memories of Nate assailed her heart. Immediately, she was transported back to the day the reporter from the magazine had approached her outside of school, asking how she dealt with grief. She'd been so proud of her answers, giving God the glory for the strength to keep going. She also realized God had given her Nate. Would those days soon be forgotten?

When the shadows of evening settled in around her, Olivia wrapped up in her quilt and remembered how Nate had foretold that she'd do that very thing. Flinging the quilt aside, she crossed her arms over her chest. Oh, how she wanted to forget

Nate Forester. A huge drop fell from an eye and splashed over her cheek, then another and another. She buried her face in her hands and willed the liquid to stop flowing, yet it didn't.

Remembrances of every moment spent with Nate scrolled through her mind. Her thoughts sped on, unbidden glimpses of him making her laugh. She recalled his woodsy scent when he came to fetch her, "all gussied up" as his dad had said. She walked with him to bring in the cows for milking. She saw his eyes sparkle with the mischievousness of a little boy just before he chased her down to tickle her. Oh, how he loved to tease. She heard the jaybirds and mockingbirds and felt his whiskered cheek before he stole a kiss. Once, he climbed to the hayloft in his dad's barn and swung down on a rope—like a hero coming to save his princess.

Nate, I miss you so much. Then why hadn't she gone with him to Pennsylvania? Why did she insist upon remaining here, miserable and living in memories? He'd become her best friend, and she was lost without him. . .and alone.

Oh, God, what am I to do? He'll never come back here. I saw the determination in his eyes and heard it in his voice. He shouldn't have deserted me.

Olivia opened her eyes and blew her nose. Her gaze rested on the quilt, and she focused on what led up to receiving it. Olivia shuddered. She'd shunned the gift her heavenly Father had so generously given—Nate Forester. Her thoughts moved on to the quilt and the very first letter from Bev Fisher. Their story had been one of faith. How many times had Olivia remarked how much she and Nate were like the Fishers?

Now, Olivia wanted to despise them. They'd taken her Nate away. They would introduce him to a woman, and Olivia would be a mere shadow of Nate's past.

"I'm feeling sorry for myself," she whispered into the darkened living room. "My place is with Nate." But she'd chased him away.

Her fingers brushed over the quilt. The softness of the velveteen reminded her of how a man so comfortable with the outdoors could be so gentle. She craved his tender ways.

God, help me. Guide me in what I should do. Am I supposed to stay here or move to Pennsylvania and marry Nate? I'm afraid of never having good friends again or not being able to teach children. But I can't seem to go on without him.

Olivia closed her eyes, and sleep finally overcame her. When she awakened with the quilt draped over her, she knew exactly what the Lord purposed for her life.

❧

Nate folded the newspaper and laid it on the kitchen table. He downed the dregs of his bitter coffee and noted the quiet. And at this very moment, he missed Olivia so much that his whole body hurt. How long would this go on? She didn't write, and he'd only sent the card at Valentine's Day. Perhaps he should have done more.

The phone rang, and he listened to make sure it was his ring and not the family down the road. Two quick rings and then a third moved him to answer it.

"Nate, how are you?"

His body warmed to his toes. *Dear Lord, thank You for the sweetness of her voice.* "Fine, Olivia. And you?"

"Better now. How's the farm?"

"As good as I could possibly ever want." He started to say it was a lonely place but stopped, the words stuck in his throat. "My herd is real fine."

"I'm happy for you."

Silence pounded through his senses. "What are you doing?"

"I'm packing."

She sounded happy, and he took a deep breath to steady himself. "Where are you going?"

"That depends on you."

Did he hear teasing? "Me? I reckon you need to explain."

"Is it cold there?"

He chuckled despite his misery. "Three degrees below zero last night. Thought I might have to thaw out the cows before I milked them this morning."

She responded with the giggle he remembered—and loved. "Do you need a comforter?"

"Now, Olivia, don't do that. Bev and Dan gave the quilt to you."

"Not that kind of comforter. A wife to keep you warm on those cold nights."

Nate sat bolt upright in his chair. "Did I hear right?"

She laughed. "If you heard I want to be your wife, your ears are telling you the truth." She paused. "If you still want me."

Nate felt a smile spread from one ear to the other. He stood, unable to sit still. "I love you. Of course I want you for my wife."

"Then I'm heading your way. I have to finish packing, but I plan to leave day after tomorrow. Is that too soon? Should I wait?"

"Don't waste a single moment, or I'll come after you."

"Would the Fishers let me stay with them a little while until we're married?"

"I'm sure they will. Oh, my sweet Olivia, I can't wait to get my arms around you."

She sniffed. "I'm so sorry for being stubborn and hurting you."

"I'm sorry for not thinking about your feelings and assumin' you'd marry me. I know God wanted me to buy the farm, but I should have asked him when."

She laughed. "God's timing is always the best. I learned the hard way."

"Oh, Olivia, wait till you see the cows. They are the prettiest black-and-white cows in the country. This house is so big, but it needs a woman's touch. And I can hardly wait for you to see the sled-riding hill—"

She giggled again, and seriousness grabbed hold of him. "Most of all I want to wrap my arms around you and kiss you until you beg me to stop."

"I'll never say stop."

"Then we'll never be cold or want for anything," he said. "For as long as we live."

DIANN MILLS

DiAnn Mills believes her readers should "Expect an Adventure" when they read her books. She is the author of fourteen books and nine novellas, as well as nonfiction, numerous short stories, articles, and devotions. She is also the contributor to several nonfiction compilations. Five additional books will be released in the next year.

She wrote from the time she could hold a pencil, but not seriously until God made it clear that she should write for Him. Five of her anthologies have appeared on the CBA Best Seller list. Two of her books have won the distinction of best historical of the year by Heartsong Presents, and she is also a favorite author of Heartsong Presents' readers.

She is a founding board member for American Christian Romance Writers and a member of Inspirational Writers Alive and Advanced Speakers and Writers Association.

DiAnn and her husband are active members of Metropolitan Baptist Church, Houston, Texas.

Web site: www.diannmills.com

REMNANTS OF FAITH

by Renee DeMarco

Dedication

For Mom. . .and all those like her
who meet life's challenges with courage,
optimism, and hope.

"And Jesus said unto them. . .
If ye have faith as a grain of mustard seed,
ye shall say unto this mountain,
Remove hence to yonder place;
and it shall remove;
and nothing shall be impossible unto you."
MATTHEW 17:20

Prologue

Boise, Idaho

The shining snow, sapphire blue sky, and dark evergreens just outside Olivia Howard Forester's apartment window were no more colorful than the pile of Christmas envelopes cluttering her quilt-draped lap. Threadbare and worn, it remained her favorite lap robe and reminded her of days long past. So many days, years, and decades! Now the world had moved into the twenty-first century. Life had been good, even though her beloved husband, Nate, had long since passed on. They had never been blessed with children of their own, but the students Olivia taught for so many years had filled the couple's lives with love.

Olivia wiped away a tear with a wrinkled hand and turned her attention to the paper remnants, printed with varied postmarks, littering the floor beside her comfortable rocking chair. Each bore witness to the far-reaching effects of her many years of teaching. She smiled and reread the scrawled personal message inside the card she had just opened.

I never forgot the advice our principal gave me when I told him I wanted to grow up and become a teacher like you, Mrs. Forester. He smiled and said, "You can do it, if you remember one thing. She isn't just in the business of teaching ABCs. She teaches children." Now, after many years in my own classroom, I understand. Thank you.

Olivia raised her head and looked out the window. The card slid to join others with similar messages that had already fallen to the carpet. What a blessing the cards were! Year after year they came, bringing joy and gladness that left her both proud and humble. "Thomas Wolfe was wrong about not being able to go home again," Olivia whispered. "These Christmas messages take me back each year."

The world outside her window faded. A wealth of memories, starting with those from her earliest recollection, gently carried her to another time.

Childish laughter mingled with the *whoosh* of sleds on snow-packed streets. Older brothers and sisters pulled siblings up hills too steep for short legs. Children made snow angels. Teen boys chased girls, threatening to wash their faces with snow. Snowballs flew between hastily constructed snow forts, and snow people dotted the landscape like winter statues. Carolers swarmed through the neighborhoods, wrapped in so many layers of clothing they could barely walk, filling the night with song.

Other images formed in her mind. Christmases during a succession of world conflicts had been hard, almost unbearable, but there had always been joy. Olivia looked at her tastefully decorated Christmas tree, relieved that those times were over. Yet looking at the envelopes, she realized days of hardship were not all in the past. Despite some of her students' brave attempts to be cheerful, pain lay between the lines. Loneliness, poverty, conflict, disaster, and tragedy invaded this era as they had in days long ago. If only she could relieve some of the distress and bring comfort!

Olivia chuckled. "Foolish old woman. What little you have wouldn't lessen the suffering of ten persons, much less a hundred." Her laughter died. "Besides, many of my former students don't need money. They need love, friendship, and to know the Lord. How can I supply that?"

All that day and evening, Olivia pondered these things in her heart. She became convinced she could do something. She would select one or two individuals from among the many, but how would she know whom to choose?

"You don't have to do this alone," a small inner voice whispered. *"Remember what you learned more than half a century ago."*

"Of course!" Olivia reached for her well-used Bible and turned to James 1:5–6: " 'If any of you lack wisdom, let him ask of God, that giveth to all men liberally, and upbraideth not; and it shall be given him. But let him ask in faith, nothing wavering. For he that wavereth is like a wave of the sea driven with the wind and tossed.' "

"Thank You, Lord, for guiding me," Olivia whispered. She caught up the stack of cards and began going through them once more. The first dozen or so she discarded. Not because she didn't sense need, but because she instinctively knew they were not the right ones. The next card contained a chatty letter. Gavin Scott, the young man in whom she once delighted and despaired, had taken the time to update his former teacher on what was happening in his life. Happiness and well-being spilled from every word. Olivia laughed when she read the postscript:

I've been so busy, I haven't had time to find a woman with whom to share my life. God willing, someday I will.

She tossed the card down with the others. Obviously, all was well with him. He had no need of her inheritance.

The next to the last card offered no news, no hint of what was going on in the sender's life, only a one-word signature, "Natalie," written in the distinctive script Olivia immediately recognized. Interesting. Her former student must not be married or she would have signed her full name.

Gavin's words, "too busy. . .a woman to share my life. . . God willing. . ." beat into Olivia's brain, followed by a daring idea. The two writers were within a few years of each other in age but not close enough to have overlapped in school. What if their teacher were to make it possible for Gavin and Natalie to meet?

Olivia chuckled. "At this moment a matchmaker is

born!" The more she thought and prayed about it, the more she was convinced it might be God's will for her to carry out her plans. First, she would sleep on it. She placed the small stack of cards on her nightstand. "I need Your confirmation, Lord. Please help me know if this is who You want me to choose." Within minutes, sleep claimed her.

More snow fell on Boise during the long night hours. A white cape blanketed the city. Fence posts and mailboxes donned jaunty ermine caps. When Olivia awakened, she sat bolt upright in bed and snatched up the cards over which she had earnestly prayed. Her fingers shook with excitement. The warm glow in her heart confirmed God's approval. Gavin and Natalie were the right two.

After breakfast, Olivia called a lawyer friend. "I want to make a new will. Can you come today?"

"Of course, if you feel it's urgent. Are you ill?" Mr. Graves asked.

"No. I'd just like to get my affairs in order before the holiday rush."

"I'll drop over around two," he promised.

Olivia cradled the phone and smiled.

❧

Long before her attorney arrived, Olivia knew exactly what she wanted in her will. The two people named would need to understand and abide by her wishes and conditions.

If Mr. Graves thought the will odd, only an amused twitch of his lips now and then betrayed him. At one point in the discussion he chuckled. "Up to your old tricks, are you? You always did have a way of getting people to do what you wanted! But love has a mind of its own."

"Sometimes it can use a little shove," she retorted. "How soon can you get copies made?"

"You are in a rush," he teased. "No problem. I'll have them prepared and bring them back for you to sign this evening." He rose. "You're up to something, Olivia Forester. I can always tell." He was still smiling when he went out. A few hours later, the new will was properly signed and witnessed. Mr. Graves wished Olivia a happy Christmas and rose to leave.

"Thank you," she replied. "I have a feeling this is going to be my best Christmas ever."

"I wouldn't be a bit surprised," her attorney agreed.

When he had gone, Olivia plugged in the lights on her Christmas tree. She thought about the man and woman she had chosen to list in her new will. Suddenly they seemed more important than all the students she had ever taught. Would her crazy scheme to help them work?

～❧～

Just before midnight on Christmas Eve, Olivia Forester sat in her comfortable rocking chair. Her worn hands lay in her quilt-clad lap, clasping two cards. The clear, steady glow from the Bethlehem star on top of her Christmas tree filled Olivia's heart with longing. "Father," she said, "more than two thousand years ago, wise men traveled a long, hard road. They followed the star until they found the Master. I've done all I can to help my chosen students on their journeys. The rest is up to You."

The mantel clock struck twelve, ushering in another Christmas and bringing peace to Olivia Forester's giving heart.

Chapter 1

Washington State, the following November

The door slammed shut, but not before the icy fingers of a Seattle November evening reached in and put a physical exclamation point on Mark Thorsett's bitter words that still lingered in the air.

"I'm finished. I can't do this any longer."

Through the night, Natalie, his petite, brunette wife, replayed the evening's events through sleep-deprived, teary eyes. How could it have gotten this bad? Only the soft breaths of her sleeping seven- and five-year-old daughters answered. Mark and her relationship hadn't always been marked by the turmoil of late. She remembered fondly the days when friends and strangers would freely approach them and ask the secret of their obviously strong relationship.

Mark would look at her with his ocean blue eyes, wink,

and jest, "No secret at all. Anyone married to Natalie would have it easy."

He'd place his arms, strong from physical labor, protectively around her, and she'd melt back into his embrace. Had someone told her back during those blissful post-honeymoon days that she'd ever have cause to question the foundation of their relationship, she would have laughed them out of the room. Natalie wasn't laughing now.

Mark's frosty farewell, though reminiscent of conversations of late, held a finality she hadn't heard before. *Would he really leave the kids and me?* The question taunted her weary mind into the predawn hours. Her writhing gut played counterpoint to her mind's adamant *no*.

The fact that she, Natalie Thorsett, poster child for mother and wife of the year, was even asking the question spoke volumes of the tumultuous past couple of years. Glancing around the barren shell of the one-room space they now called home put an exclamation point on the experience. To say life had dealt them a series of unfortunate blows was to put it lightly. A flagging economy and poor annual sales figures in his engineering firm had left Mark with a pink slip in hand. He had enough time under his belt to hold on through the first round of layoffs, but his lack of age and experience sank him in the second round. While others facing the same fate had panicked, Natalie and Mark had unified in faith, sure that another, better opportunity lay just around the corner. Neither had the slightest inkling that the corner would be over two years away. Or how incredibly treacherous those two years would be.

Natalie shivered, partly from the memories, but more

from the chill of the room that evidenced poor workmanship and lack of insulation. Oh, what she would give to be soaking in the tub she had once deemed too small in her suburban dream home. The glut of unemployed Northwest engineers and lack of jobs had turned the Thorsetts' job search from days into weeks. When those weeks turned into years, they had been forced to sell their possessions to make ends meet.

First it was the extras. The entertainment center. A newly purchased ivory and muted rose sofa and love seat set. The bedroom furniture they had given each other as a wedding gift.

Then it was cashing out their retirement accounts. Taking out credit cards. Avoiding bill collectors. Natalie had picked up part-time work where she could to help out, but her lack of a college education had relegated her to a series of minimum-wage fast-food jobs. Through it all, Mark bolstered the family with faith-based scriptures and his positive attitude.

"When life gives you lemons. . ." became Mark's mantra. It was always followed by a shouted youthful duet of "the Thorsetts make lemonade!" The girls would propel themselves across floors and over couches into Mark's waiting arms. The giggle festival that invariably followed brought a smile to Natalie's face then—and now.

The bittersweet memories rubbed raw on the night's open wounds. Banishing them from her mind, she rose from the side of the threadbare twin bed she and Mark shared to check on her sleeping girls.

Even in restless slumber, the innocence of youth permeated the area where they clung together. Seven-year-old

Amber had her arm protectively around her little sister Mollie's small frame. Amber's bravery through the last couple of years brought tears to Natalie's eyes. No matter what life served up, Amber met it with optimism. With both parents trying to make the finances work, Amber had stepped into the roll of part-time mother for her younger sister. The faith of a child.

"How will that faith hold up if Mark really leaves?" Natalie's words lingered unnaturally in the frigid room.

As much as she wanted to deny the possibility, Natalie couldn't. The Mark of late bore little resemblance to the leader who once guided and directed their home. The loss of their house and the journey into a series of increasingly more squalid dwellings had been one lemon Mark Thorsett couldn't convert into a pleasant drink. Natalie had seen the progressive toll guilt had waged on his soul. His inability to provide for his family had eaten away at his self-esteem and left a crust of a man. While some of their acquaintances in similar circumstances had sought refuge in controlled substances, Mark had refused that method of escape. Instead, his personal path had led to depression and anger.

"Anger that caused him to make rash statements he didn't mean," Natalie whispered, remembering his parting words earlier.

"Oh, Lord, please let them be statements he didn't mean." At the sound of her own prayerful words, Natalie Thorsett came face-to-face with the reality of the present. Her husband, the love of her life, the father of her children, might not be coming back.

Natalie fell to the cold floor, clutching her grieving

heart in indescribable pain. Through broken sobs she cried, "Father, I can't do this. I'm not strong enough. I don't want to be a single mom. I don't want my husband to leave. Please make this go away. Let me come stay with You for a little while where I don't have to feel this."

Her cries softened to quiet whispers. "I love him, Lord. Please bring him back. My girls and I need him." She paused and added, "And, Lord, my girls and I really need You."

After many long hours, sleep finally released Natalie Thorsett from the anguish of the night's events. In the throes of slumber the icy floor numbed her limbs and body, even as a warm heavenly embrace surrounded her heart.

Chapter 2

If someone had told Natalie Thorsett she would ever feel more discouraged than she had on the November night a month ago when Mark left, she would have called them crazy. Yet here she was, on December 10, facing the bleakest holiday she could ever remember. Mark, true to his word, had left. A couple of letters had come since, but amidst the greetings to the girls and the attempt to put an optimistic spin on his fruitless job search, were layers of pain. The postmarks told a story of travel down the I-5 corridor south, but the last letter had come with a Portland, Oregon, postmark.

"He's left the state," Natalie whispered, turning the envelope over in her shaking hands.

Hope that the letter might also contain some much-needed cash or news of a new job fled as she opened the envelope and a single sheet of paper floated to the floor. Usually he had managed to send a few dollars here and there from part-time work, which, coupled with Natalie's meager earnings, had managed to keep her head just above the water.

With Christmas just days away, things had never been worse financially.

Resigned to what she had to do, Natalie fought back her pride and sat down to write the letter she should have sent weeks ago. She carefully addressed her letter to the scrawled return address in Portland, Oregon, and then began.

Dear Mark,

    I'm sorry about our fight. I said some things I never should have said. It's just that it's been so hard to recognize you lately. I can't tell you how much I miss the man I married, the man who has carried us through the tough times with humor and optimism. I know you feel that our financial woes are somehow your fault, but they aren't. Life isn't always easy. We were never promised it would be. I don't blame you—I wish you wouldn't blame yourself. You have done your best. I just miss having you around—the real you. The girls need you, too. We could live in a tent, but if we were together as a family, that would be enough for me.

    I don't know how much longer I can make the money stretch. We are already behind on rent, but I think the landlord will give us an extension—I just don't know how much time he will give us. They turned the telephone service off yesterday, so if you decide to call, it won't go through. I'm scared, Mark.

I really wish you were here. I pray for you every day.
Whether or not you find a job, if you decide you want
us to come—we will be there in a heartbeat. I love
you and believe in you. Please forgive me. I really
want to work this out. If you want to give us another
chance, as well, please let me know.

All my love,
Natalie

Natalie slowly licked the envelope and walked down the street to the public mailbox. Pausing before depositing the letter, she whispered a prayer. "Please help this find my husband, and please wrap Your arms around him as he reads it. He needs not only my love but Yours. Give us a new start."

Ten days later the mail provided an unwelcome answer. Two envelopes arrived. The one she had sent Mark days earlier had been stamped "Addressee Unknown." Mark would not be coming home. The second came with a postmark from Idaho.

"I don't know anyone in Idaho," Natalie muttered. "I wonder if Mark has gone all the way up there?"

Opening the envelope provided a definitive no to her second question. The letter, on official-looking paper, was from a legal office: Graves and Billings, Professional Corporation.

She scanned the enclosed text with interest.

We regret to inform you of the passing of Mrs.
Olivia Howard Forester. You have been identified
as a conditional beneficiary under the terms of her

last will and testament. She has indicated that you are to receive a designated item of personal property under the conditions and terms set forth in the will. We have enclosed, for your signature, a release. Upon receipt of your signed release, we shall tender the bequest to you per the terms of her testamentary document. If you have any questions or comments, please do not hesitate to call.

Sincerely,
Bill Graves, Attorney-at-Law

Natalie's emotions raced. Olivia Forester, her beloved teacher, dead? But a bequest! "What could it be? Maybe the money we desperately need to pay the rent? Or will it be something of value that I can sell or pawn to pay bills?"

Natalie put down the letter and headed for the door. The young couple in the apartment across from them had been very good about letting her use their phone since Natalie no longer had phone service of her own. The lawyer had left a toll-free number where he could be contacted.

Once inside the walls of her neighbor's comparatively warm house, Natalie dialed the number, shaking with anticipation. Could this be the Lord's answer to her mounting financial woes?

"Law offices of Graves and Billings, may I help you?" the official-sounding voice queried.

"Um, I'm Natalie Thorsett and I received a letter about being left something in the will of Mrs. Forester."

"One moment. I'll transfer you to Mr. Graves."

A deep, warm older voice resonated from the line. "Ms. Thorsett? How are you? I assume you are calling about Olivia's will."

"Yes, I am." Natalie's voice trembled. "What was I left, if you don't mind my asking?"

"Not at all, dear." Mr. Graves chuckled. "You know that Olivia; she always did things a little outside of the box. She left you what she deemed her most prized possession—her heirloom quilt. But there is a condition. At the end of one year, you must deliver it to another individual whom she has named. She has provided in the will the financial arrangements for you to take such a journey to deliver the quilt."

Mr. Graves's words rolled off Natalie like water off a rock. After the word "quilt," she found herself unable to hear much else, awash in a sea of dashed hopes.

"Anything you ask," she managed to force out. "I'll send you the release. Thank you."

It was only later, in her home, after Amber and Mollie were tucked securely into the twin bed she and Mark once shared, that Natalie allowed herself to think of the day's events.

"Mrs. Forester. . .gone?" Even speaking the words didn't make them any more believable.

Mrs. Forester had been Natalie's safe place when, during her third-grade year, Natalie's own mom had succumbed to cancer. Olivia had seen through the shy girl's rapidly constructed facade and had invited her into the home she and her husband, Nate, infused with warmth. Never having grandparents of her own, Natalie was informally adopted by Olivia and Nate Forester, grandparents-in-training.

They had embraced the little girl with love and friendship. After school each night, she had been invited into the Foresters' home until her dad could pick her up after he got off work. Those afternoon hours had been among the best of Natalie's life. Baking cookies, learning to knit, sitting and reading stories with Olivia, fishing and whittling with Nate. Natalie's days had been filled beyond measure.

Remembering the sweet days of the past infused Natalie with a warm longing. The Foresters' home had been such a sweet refuge from her childhood storms, much like Mark's arms had been for many years of her adult life. Now, when she needed it the most, neither harbor was available to her. Shaking off the thought that threatened to plunge her into a well of pity, Natalie once again looked over the letter from the attorney's office.

"Why would Olivia leave me a quilt? Why would the quilt be her most prized possession? And who is this person I'm supposed to be giving it to?"

Knowing none of the questions could be answered without the passage of considerable time, Natalie shivered up to the children in the bed thats only warmth came from the three huddled bodies beneath its thin cover.

"Well, my inheritance may not be money, but right now a warm blanket would be a real blessing. I hope it comes quickly." Tired beyond measure, Natalie punctuated the last sentiment with a soft snore.

Chapter 3

Natalie Thorsett closed her eyes and willed a few extra moments in the blissful dream world she had been so abruptly thrust from. So clear were her imaginings, she could almost touch the dark-haired, blue-eyed, smiling Mark. It had been the Christmas morning after they were married. Memories mingled with the sweet leftovers from her dreams. Neither she nor Mark had experienced the joy of firmly established Christmas traditions when they were children. Her father had found Christmas memories without his beloved wife too painful, and Mark's parents had figured that their once-yearly Christmas Eve trek to church was more than enough tradition for them.

Not Mark or Natalie. They had vowed early in their relationship to instill sweet, warm traditions throughout the Christmas holidays. Celebrating Christ's birth in the Thorsett family was going to be something special.

It had started the year they were married. Mark had

awakened her at 12:01 a.m. Christmas Day.

"Talie," Mark began tenderly, using the special name only he used. "Time to get up. It's our first Thorsett Christmas."

Natalie, never one for early mornings—especially not this early—had groggily protested, until the smell of fresh bacon had serenaded her senses. She shuffled the short distance between their apartment bedroom and kitchen. There, a full-fledged breakfast extravaganza greeted her. Not only had Mark prepared bacon, it was bent to look like candy canes. The pancakes were slightly misshapen snowmen, the fruit cut into Christmas trees, and the eggs molded into ornaments.

"What is this?" Natalie asked, unsuccessfully hiding her bemused smile.

Mark's ear-to-ear grin had said it all. "You said you wanted Christmas tradition, Mrs. Natalie Thorsett. You got it."

Mark had been true to his word. The Thorsetts did Christmas like no other family Natalie knew. Amidst all the fun, though, her favorite tradition had not changed. At that first midnight breakfast, Mark had pulled out his Bible and began to read.

" 'And it came to pass in those days, that there went out a decree from Caesar Augustus, that all the world should be taxed.' " In his gentle, emotion-tinged voice, Mark read the Christmas story.

Once again, before retiring to bed, Mark had gathered with Natalie and read from the Bible the passages concerning Christ's birth. Even as some of the holiday traditions had been replaced with others as the girls got older, each year Mark had continued to insist that the day start, and end, the way it should—remembering the Savior's birth. Not a present was touched, not a morsel eaten, until Dad, often flannel-pajama-clad, welcomed the day with the heralding words of the angels: " 'Glory to God in the highest, and on earth peace, good will toward men.' "

Like Natalie, the girls came to love this tradition more than any other. This year, while it appeared most of their traditions would have to be put on hold, the girls had only asked about one. Their recent questions had revolved around how Dad would read them the Christmas story this year. Natalie had attempted to sidestep the questions, not sure of the answers herself.

Thoughts of unanswered questions propelled Natalie unwillingly to the present. Getting out of bed and gathering a thin blanket around her, she dejectedly slumped against the barren, drafty wall. Her gaze fell on the tilting branch in the corner, trying to pass itself off as a Christmas tree. Who ever heard of decorating a pine limb? When informed there would be no tree this year, Amber and Mollie had dragged the downed branch from a local ditch, stood it upright in a plastic bucket half full of rocks, and christened it "The Thorsett Family Tree." The hanging snowflakes, cut from old newspapers collected along the road, didn't help the image.

Glancing across the room at her two sleeping children huddled together in thin blankets, Natalie's frustration mounted. *They sleep on an old mattress. They eat whatever meager rations I can scrounge for them. It's been over a year since I could even buy them a new pair of shoes. Haven't we all been through enough?*

Natalie looked at the two presents beneath the tree. She shuddered, thinking how disappointed the children would be to find two-liter soda bottles under the newspaper wrapping. Probably not as disappointed as finding out there wouldn't be Mark's traditional Christmas turkey. Somehow, she didn't think boxed macaroni and cheese would get the same reception. Natalie's biggest concern, though, had nothing to do with the food or the gifts. How would the girls get through Christmas without the man who was the center of their existence? Needless to say, it would be a far cry from Christmases past—Christmases when Mark was with them.

Natalie's musings were interrupted by Amber's quiet voice. "Mom, are you thinking about Dad?"

Natalie looked at the mussed dark brown hair of her oldest child. "Yes, honey, I am."

"It's okay, Mom. I miss him, too." Amber's eyes contained a knowing look befitting one far older than she. "I sure hope he can make it home. We have each other. He doesn't have anyone. Who will he read the Christmas story to?"

Natalie had to turn away so Amber wouldn't see the tears her daughter's selflessness had triggered. *Here I've been thinking only about the girls and myself and how awful this Christmas will be. How lonely it will be for Mark.*

At her silence, Amber continued. "You know what I think we should do? We should draw him pictures and write him stories of all our favorite Christmas memories. That way, he can tape them on his wall and look around all Christmas Day and feel like he's doing all the things with us."

Natalie rose and put her arms around Amber. "That's a wonderful idea. I'm not sure how we will get them to him, but we'll try."

"Mom, he'll get them." Assurance resonated from Amber's voice. "You are the one who tells us that all things are possible through Christ."

"Yes, honey, you're right." Even as Natalie said the words, she wasn't sure exactly how much she believed them right now.

If she had cause to question the scripture when Amber quoted it, her questions only increased as the day went on.

❧

December 21 was not a red-letter day for Natalie Thorsett. It was, however, a red-notice day. A THREE-DAY NOTICE TO PAY RENT OR VACATE day. Natalie stared at the piece of red paper taped hastily to their door. Handwritten on the bottom of the note was a scribbled, "I'll give you till December 26 as a Christmas present."

"The creep." Even with the pit of terror in her stomach growing, Natalie still felt anger at the spiteful, unfriendly old man who deemed evicting a family on the day after Christmas instead of Christmas Day his charitable deed for the year. She crumpled the notice into her pocket, determined that her girls would not learn this news until after they had celebrated Christmas.

Once within the walls of the apartment, which suddenly looked pretty good, Natalie fell to her knees in prayer. "Dear heavenly Father, please help us. I don't know what to do. I'm scared. I used to think I could do anything through You, but I'm just not sure anymore. Please strengthen my feeble knees. If it were only me affected by this, I'd be okay, but my daughters are just little girls. They belong in nice warm beds, not living on the streets. You love little children. I know You do. Please protect mine. In Jesus' name, amen."

Natalie's hope that a last-minute reprieve might come through a large sum of cash in the mail or a knock on her door telling her she'd won a sweepstakes did not play out. The mail, however, did bring two items that sent the girls into a frenzy of excitement.

"Two packages, Mom." Mollie's freckles stood out on her pale cheeks like stars in the winter night sky. "What could they be?"

Knowing the next few days would not hold much happiness for her dear children, Natalie wanted to prolong these moments. "I don't know. Why don't you open them?"

"Can we really, Mom? You are the best." The unison response brought a slight smile to Natalie's troubled countenance.

The girls ripped into the packages with the wild abandon of Christmases long past. The first bore a letter, which Amber opened and began to read.

Dear Family,

My job search has not been as successful as I hoped. Since I won't be with you this year, I wanted to send you my Bible.

Amber, I have marked the special passages that I read each year. If you will wake everyone up one minute after midnight and read the marked verses, I will wake up here at that time and think about you reading them.

I know this Christmas isn't the way any of us wanted it to be. Certainly not me. Just remember—Christmas is not about us. It's about Jesus.

I love you girls. Merry Christmas.

Dad

As the girls turned to the other package, Natalie carefully cradled the worn Bible that stirred so many memories of better days and years. Would she ever again know the joy of those long-lost times? The gleeful voices of her girls caused her to focus on the other package. Amber and Mollie were in the process of lifting a quilt out of a box. As they gave one final tug, the folds dwarfed the two of them as they collapsed on the floor. Looking at her girls wrapped like Christmas packages, Natalie was caught by the beauty of the old handcrafted masterpiece. In the dismal, undecorated apartment, its still-vivid colors seemed alive with light.

"Oh, Mom. It's the warmest, softest blanket I've ever felt. And it's big enough for all of us—even Dad. Isn't it the bestest present you've ever seen? God must have told someone we needed a warm blanket." Mollie, the more reserved of her daughters, gushed with enthusiasm.

Mollie's exuberance was catching. Natalie burst into laughter and joined the girls in the embrace of the woolen remnants stitched with love. She knew the piece of paper in the bottom of the paper carton must shed light on the origin of the priceless possession, but she set the paper aside for another day. She was going to capture the joy of this moment. Snuggled beneath the generous cover with her precious daughters, Natalie allowed herself to dream of better times to come. In the arms of the quilt, she quietly hoped. She touched each lovingly stitched square as the girls glued their little bodies to her. Fabric swatches, which individually bespoke little glory, blended together into a magnificent creation. The person who had created it must have had vision.

Like my little seeds of faith, Natalie thought. *Not much on their own, but perhaps together they'll make something beautiful.*

Glancing back down at the heirloom quilt, Natalie whispered, "Remnants of faith. Perhaps Olivia has sent us remnants of faith."

Chapter 4

I f Mark Thorsett believed life would get better when he walked out of his Seattle apartment a few weeks ago, he had another think coming. As miserable as being jobless, depressed, angry, and poor was, it wasn't as bad as being jobless, depressed, angry, poor, *and* lonely. His last exchange with Natalie sent him into fits of guilt during those rare moments he was able to pull himself out of his self-pitying reverie, to boot.

He was having one of those treasured "kick me in the stomach" moments now. Watching mothers and children shop for the Christmas holidays in downtown Eugene, Oregon, conjured up thoughts of his girls at home. Boy, he really missed them. Ever since he and Natalie married, Christmas had been the pinnacle of his year.

Feeling the sudden chill of the winter wind, Mark bundled his threadbare coat around his bonier-than-usual shoulders and muttered, "Christmas certainly won't be the highlight of this year."

He had sent his well-worn Bible home to Amber so that she could read the Christmas story. Their Christmas would be better without him home anyway.

After moving progressively southward in search of work, he had just secured a temporary part-time construction job in Eugene. Of course, December was not the busiest of construction times in the Northwest, but he was making more than the Golden Arches had offered. At this point he would have dredged sewers to garnish enough coins to provide himself lodging and send some home. Turning the corner from his new employer's office, Mark was heralded by the familiar ringing of bells. Natalie was always giving to the bell ringers. Mark couldn't recollect a time she had passed one by, even in the poorest times, without depositing some offering.

"Well, Talie," Mark whispered, searching his pockets for orphan change, "this is for you."

His meager deposit sounded puny as it joined few other coins in the holly berry red Salvation Army can.

"God bless." The ringer's soft-spoken voice was a perfect match for his snow-white hair and gently worn face.

"I sure wish He would." Mark's spoken response surprised even him.

The edges of the man's blue eyes wrinkled at the corners. Placing his hand on Mark's arm, he spoke. "Son, I believe He has sent you plenty of blessings. You just have to open your eyes to see them."

Mark stammered a few socially polite responses and then uncomfortably hurried on his way. The last thing he needed was advice from a stranger.

What does he know? How can he say I've been blessed? I've lost everything. I lost my job. I have no money. I can't support my family financially, and now, when they need me the most, I'm not there. I have no friends. I'm a terrible husband and father. I'm sleeping on a flea-infested mattress in an old building with a bunch of strangers in a town I've never set foot in before. I may be a lot of things, but blessed is not one of them. Mark's thoughts became a bitter avalanche as he angrily strode down the concrete sidewalks to the shelter where he was bedding down on a cot.

"I loved God. I served Him. I don't know what I've done to anger Him, but it must have been something terrible. I haven't seen a blessing in months. Maybe even years!"

With that, Mark ran a hand through his dark, curly hair and stamped his foot with a finality that would have convinced even the most apathetic onlooker, had there been one.

Late into the night Mark's words floated through the land between sleep and awake. Visions of his girls. Midnight Christmas breakfasts. Natalie running on the beach. After hours of restless slumber, Mark Thorsett had to admit he once had been incredibly blessed. He longed for those days— the days when he had found favor with God and men. But, as in his dreams, they were too far away to reach.

The days leading up to Christmas were almost unbearable for the man who had become the guru of Christmas traditions. On his hours off, he took to walking the Willamette River. Swollen from heavy rain, the waters took on an almost brown cast. Beside the rushing torrent, he could almost forget the memories. Almost.

"If I hadn't been so good at creating them, I wouldn't have so many memories tormenting me right now," Mark wryly admitted to himself.

Slouching down on a bench, Mark stared at the angry river.

Suddenly, a slightly familiar voice made him look up.

"Mind if I join you?"

Mark's ocean blue gaze met that of the Salvation Army bell ringer.

"Jack Pace." The man's smile seemed to stretch all the way down to his hand, which he extended for a shake.

Mark obliged. "I'm Mark Thorsett."

"Well, Mark, I must say I've seen a lot of heartbreak this holiday season. You know, ringing bells all day, you get a chance to watch people very closely. You see the arguers and the criers. The exhausted mothers and the fathers who want very much to be anywhere else. You see the lonely. You see those who have lost companions and those who are longing for them. You see those who are remembering the real reason for the Christmas celebration and those who don't have a clue what it is all about."

Jack paused and then looked up at Mark. "But you know, son, of all the folks I've seen this year, I haven't seen one as lost or as sad as you. Don't suppose you want to talk about it?"

Mark looked at the kindness emanating from the older gentleman's well-lined face and suddenly felt as though he did want to talk. As he opened up, years of pent-up frustration, depression, self-doubt, and pain poured out like the torrential Willamette, whose clamorous flow kept his story company.

After a steady hour, Mark was spent. He slumped against the weathered bench, waiting for the disgust, condemnation, and judgment he was sure were coming from this obviously good man. To his surprise, Jack remained peacefully silent.

When he finally did open his mouth, it was not to condemn. "I can see why you are so sad, my boy. I can tell you love your wife and children very much, maybe as much as I loved my Marjorie. It's nearly five years she's been gone, but I still wake up every day expecting to see her gentle face next to mine. Every minute I lived with that woman was joyous. Memories of those wonderful moments are blessings that keep me company every day until my Lord sees fit that I join her." Jack's lip quivered. Regaining his composure, he continued.

"Son, we lived through the Depression. There were times we didn't know where the next meal would come from. Sometimes it didn't come. I'd stand in long lines waiting for a chance to work for one day at a place. We didn't know how, but we knew that even without food or shelter, God would provide. They were happy times because we had each other.

"We lived through the war. Separated. Never knowing which letter would be the last. But they, too, were happy days because we knew our love would last beyond this life, and each moment became precious.

"I'm sure we had some of the same issues that face all couples today, but I vowed when I married her that I would do as much for my sweet companion as I could." Jack paused and placed his arm on Mark's shoulder.

"Selflessness, repentance, and inviting your heavenly Father into your life on a daily basis. The Key Three, I like to call them."

Mark looked at the old man. "Do you think there is still hope for me? For us?"

Jack winked and then rose to leave. "Do you think I'd be sitting here if I didn't? Let your wife know you still love her. Then come see me tomorrow. I'll be ringing on my street corner, and we'll start the process of taking care of you."

Walking back to the shelter, Mark felt a small ray of hope

pierce his bitter and wounded heart.

"Selflessness, repentance, and You." Inwardly measuring his standing in each category, Mark shook his head. "Well, I guess everyone has to start building somewhere. Even if it is ground zero."

With his declaration of intent, Mark Thorsett took out a pen and began to write the letter he had wanted to write for a long time. A letter claiming responsibility—and telling Natalie how much she was loved. Most of all, it would be a letter expressing his remorse. It was a letter long in the works, but if Jack Pace were right—and Mark sure hoped he was— Mark had just taken the first step along a road to healing.

Chapter 5

"Homeless." The word sounded as foreign and strange as Natalie Thorsett felt. This was the stuff of other people's nightmares, not hers.

"Funny, I feel the same as I did yesterday, when I had a place to come home to," Natalie mused. "Yet nothing is the same."

January 2 was not one of the Thorsetts' better days. Natalie was grateful the girls were back in school; Amber was doing well in second grade, and Mollie loved her all-day kindergarten class. Natalie hadn't yet found the courage or words to inform the principal of their plight. In fact, she was still debating whether she would have to. "As long as I have them to the bus stop every morning, no one will be the wiser." Even as she said the words, however, she knew they didn't ring true.

Natalie needed help. This was one secret that needed as many people working on it as possible. She had managed to secure the next two weeks at a local women and children's shelter, but the head of the facility had been clear: Winter was busy. Too busy. Demand outstripped supply by leaps and bounds. Each bed had a waiting list with multiple names. People were waiting, hoping for a night's sleep away from damp freeway underpasses and makeshift tarps.

Gingerly making her way down the pavement layered with ice, Natalie clutched her jacket around her shoulders. Shopkeepers were diligently removing seasonal decorations and boxing them up for storage. Post-Christmas return-laden shoppers brushed by her, hurrying to take care of unfinished business.

Natalie and the girls wouldn't be returning any packages this year. Other than the two brightly wrapped bottles of sparkly soda, there hadn't been any presents under the Thorsett limb. Despite the obvious contrasts with Christmases past, the girls had dutifully followed Mark's directive, rising at midnight to read the story of Christ's birth. Somehow this year, the young Mary and Joseph trying to find shelter when the inn was full struck a painfully familiar chord with Natalie. There had been no room for them anywhere, either.

Natalie had known only too well, when she had hurriedly tucked the THREE-DAY NOTICE TO PAY RENT OR VACATE into a drawer, that it foreshadowed a not-too-far-distant time when she also would be searching for a place for her sweet family to lay down and rest.

Now the time was upon her. Natalie shook her head. With the gesture, the memories from last week fled like the foraging pigeons she startled. There had been no further word from Mark, even after her plea for help and forgiveness. Natalie reconciled herself to the idea that he must have decided to move on. Sadness gripped her heart more piercingly than the bitter cold. She banished the feelings. Right now she couldn't afford to think of anything but getting food on her girls' plates and a place for them to have refuge from the cold.

She plopped down onto a well-used bench, relieved to find rest from lugging around the bag that almost equaled her in size. The process of deciding what to take had been more difficult than she expected, given how little they had. Clothes and blankets took up the lion's share of the space. A few precious keepsakes, including Mark's Bible, had filled the remaining space. Looking out over Puget Sound, Natalie lifted the largest quilt from the bag. Olivia Forester's quilt. As she opened its folds, an envelope fell to the ground. Funny, she hadn't seen it since the day the quilt had arrived. Her icy fingers fumbled to manipulate the paper. Once opened, a familiar handwritten script greeted Natalie.

My dearest Natalie,

I am sitting here, rocking in my chair, remembering a time when we used to sit together and read stories. When you get to be my age, memories become your best friends. You have given me plenty of fond ones. For some reason I feel compelled to send you this quilt and to tell you the story of where it came from.

When I was a young woman, a raging fire just before Christmas took my ancestral home and everything I owned, except for the family Bible. Insurance replaced my material things, but I really struggled. Not long after that, a reporter did an article on my loss. Soon afterward, a large package arrived. A Pennsylvania family named Fisher had read the article. They felt God wanted them to send me the patchwork quilt the first Mrs. Fisher had made during her last days on earth. It was a reminder to her husband of her love—and God's. Every time I touched the beautiful covering, it helped bring comfort and healing. I feel sometimes as if God's own arms wrap around me in its folds.

I am nearing the end of my earthly journey. I look forward to meeting the Master Quilter. May my most priceless earthly possession be a reminder: God uses the tattered bits and pieces of our lives to create something beautiful and lasting.

I am not sure how this quilt will touch your life, but I can promise you this: It will.

With love,
Olivia Forester

Natalie wiped the tears that rolled down her cheeks and pressed the letter to her breast. Memories of times spent with Olivia infused the letter with warmth. Natalie wasn't sure how the quilt would make a difference in her life, but she knew that even in the short time since its arrival, the generous folds had warmed and healed and comforted her small family. *Even now,* she thought, *though its fabric is not nearly thick enough to stave off today's frigid temperatures, I feel no chill.*

After gazing out across the whitecapped waves tossed by the whim of the bitter wind, Natalie rose to her feet. Tucking the quilt and letter securely back in the bag that literally held all of her earthly possessions, Natalie hefted the heavy load onto her thin shoulders and turned to leave.

"Excuse me, lovely lady." The thin masculine voice sent an unexplainable chill down Natalie's spine. She turned to face its owner.

A gentleman overdressed in leather and fur finery leered down at her. His jet-black hair sharply set off an unnaturally pale face. Despite the fact that he was obviously approaching middle age, his face showed no lines. It was as if an eraser had removed any trace of emotion or experience from the man's countenance.

Natalie was grateful her coat covered the back of her neck, where each hair stood at attention. "May I help you?" she mustered, surprised her voice was much more assertive than she felt.

"I noticed you sitting over here all by your lonesome, and I am always on the lookout for a damsel in distress." His beady eyes surveyed her like an X ray. "Especially a fine-looking one. Now, why don't you let ol' Kinsey help you."

The silky smooth voice wrapped its way around Natalie's confidence the way a boa constrictor encircles its prey before the final, deadly squeeze. She stretched herself to her full five-feet-two-inch height, hoping the layers of clothing might make her seem more substantial. "I'm not in distress, and the last person I need help from is you. Good day, Mr. Kinsey—or should I say have a good life, since I am sure we will not meet again."

Kinsey looked at the bag slung over Natalie's shoulder, and with a chuckle that raised goose bumps that Natalie didn't even know she had, he responded, "Oh, my little beauty, to the contrary. I'm sure we will meet again." He bowed stiffly at the waist, and with a lift of his leather beret, he turned and headed down the street, serenading himself with strains of "Some Enchanted Evening."

Natalie shook her fingers, hoping to restore the blood that had drained from them. Adrenaline pumping, she half-walked, half-ran in the opposite direction the man had strolled. Natalie had always taught her children not to judge others, but for the first time in her life, she was trashing her own advice. She didn't need any further conversation to determine that this man was one she truly never wanted to see again. The evil aura around him rivaled nothing she had previously encountered.

She worriedly glanced backward a dozen times on the way to pick her children up at the bus stop. She did not want to be followed. After quickly hugging the girls, she set off with them for the shelter. Darkness set in and cast an ominous air over the Seattle streets. Natalie drew the girls closer as she passed each alleyway. She tried to stay close to the well-dressed masses leaving workplaces to head home.

After blocks of walking, Natalie spotted the shelter. The brick walls of the building welcomed the small family from the icy cold that was not generated solely by the weather. Heat poured into the street when Natalie opened the door to the entryway.

Before the girls could set their belongings down, huge black arms surrounded them. "Oh, let's get these babies in out of that cold. Get them some blankets and warm chocolate."

For the next five minutes, the Thorsett clan stood speechless as they were wrapped, warmed, and otherwise cared for by a dozen hands. Only after they were secure in front of a raging fireplace were introductions made.

"I am LouEllen." The two-hundred-plus-pound African American woman extended one of the large hands that had initially encircled the family. "I'm what they call the boss around here."

She looked down at the two wide-eyed girls and plopped down between them. Arms encircling their shoulders, she continued, "You two babies. You can call me Mama El. That's what I let my favorites call me. Now, you two want to help me with supper while your mama gets your stuff upstairs?"

Natalie watched in amazement as her two smiling girls clamored behind Mama El into the kitchen. She took her bag up to two empty cots that had been reserved for the girls and her. She pushed the cots together and then fished in the bag for the quilt. It covered both beds welcomingly. Glancing out the window before heading downstairs, she caught the shadow of a man gazing at the shelter. Fear gripped her as she recognized the leather cap adorning his head. She drew the curtain and moved quickly from the window. Grabbing the quilt off the bed, she wrapped it securely around her and closed her eyes. In a few moments, the welcoming spirit of the shelter and the folds of the blanket had worked its wonder. Peace filled Natalie's soul. It was, as Olivia Forester had put it, like the arms of God Himself had wrapped themselves around her. Natalie knelt and offered thanks. She knew that no matter what evil lurked outside, tonight she and her girls were safe in the watchful care of their heavenly Father.

Chapter 6

Mark Thorsett stared at the envelope in his clenched hand and tried to stem the mounting frustration that threatened to overflow. The red-stamped words, "Addressee Unknown. Return to Sender," taunted him. For the third time in as many weeks, Mark's letter to Natalie and the girls had been returned. His numerous daily phone calls had been equally unsuccessful. The operator's monotonous recorded message, "I'm sorry. The number you are trying to reach is no longer in service," kept him company throughout each waking hour.

"Where is my family?" The question hung unnaturally in the gray Eugene fog.

Calls to the landlord had gone unreturned. Mark knew his family was in desperate need of the money he was trying to send. He also wanted to tell them what had happened to him over the last month. The job offer. His new friend, Jack. The church he had been attending. He had so much to say, if only he could find Natalie and the girls to say it to.

"You look like a man in need of a friend." Jack Pace's warm voice pierced Mark's worried musings. Glancing at the envelope in Mark's hand, Jack shook his head. "Still no luck finding them? Maybe you should go up there and see what you can find out."

"I'm still a probationary employee at Whitneys. I've been looking for an engineering job for longer than I can tell you. How would it look if I took off after two weeks on the job? No." Mark vehemently shook his head. "I can't risk losing this opportunity. Besides, they've got me working around the clock."

"Son, you don't know they would fire you. Maybe if you explained your situation, they'd give you some time off."

Mark refused to even consider the notion. "No way. If you had been through what I have the last couple of years, you wouldn't risk losing your position, either. I am not going to make waves."

Jack shook his head, obviously concerned. "I know how important this job is to you, but what about your family?"

Mark looked him square in the eye, jaw set and voice raised. "This is about my family. Keeping this job is going to put food on their table and clothes on their backs. It is all about my family."

The silence that followed hung as dense as the fog that surrounded the two men. When Mark spoke again, his voice had lowered in volume and intensity. "Can you imagine if I did go? What would I tell Natalie? 'Yes, honey, I had a great job but lost it coming up to Seattle. In other words, we're right back where we started before I left.' No, thanks." The laugh that followed was forced and humorless.

Jack responded gently. "Mark, I don't have all the answers,

but I know the Lord does. Maybe He can help you decide what to do." Jack glanced up at the ornate wooden church doors in front of them and then down at his watch. "In the meantime, if we don't get moving, we're going to miss out on serving dinner at the soup kitchen."

Despite his worries and frustrations about his own family, Mark had found that volunteering to serve meals to Eugene's homeless community brought him a peace that defied his circumstances. The church had started the program years before, and it had progressively grown from a few families fed in the church kitchen to more than one hundred people who filled a newly built cultural hall. Every evening, scores of volunteers amassed, cooking for and serving the ever-increasing number of hungry from the community. Recently, the halls had been filled with an inordinate number of elderly who had been forced to choose between much-needed medications and food. Even when the food bank couldn't keep up with the demand, the church always managed to.

"Soup kitchen" hardly described the spread that was furnished each evening. Jack's pet name for the feast, "the loaves and fishes dinner," had stuck, much to the congregation's delight. Even those in the community who had never cracked open a Bible knew that, often, the food at the Community Church's table had been stretched far beyond what could be explained in earthly terms.

Tonight, scanning the large crowd he was serving, Mark's gaze fell upon a young man holding a small baby. Two little girls clamored about his legs. Sudden longing pierced Mark's heart. What he would give for the embrace of his two sweet children.

After wrapping up his serving duties, Mark approached

the man. Extending his hand, he warmly smiled. "Mark Thorsett."

The man gently returned the grin. "Evan Strong. I'd take your hand, but as you can see, mine are both in use."

Mark laughed aloud, looking down at the two girls hanging on the arm the baby was not in. "I've been there. I have two girls of my own."

The smallest child released her dad's arm and grabbed Mark's hand. Staring at him with bright blue eyes, she asked, "Are your girls here?"

"No. They aren't with me tonight." Mark shifted uncomfortably, not sure where the questions were headed.

"Are they at the shelter?" Innocence infused the question.

"No, honey. They are in Seattle."

If the child thought it strange that the children and dad were not together, she gave no indication. "We live at the shelter."

Mark managed to hide his shock. "You live at a shelter?"

"Yes. We used to have a house with just our family, but now we get to live with a lot of people. It's not too bad, except when they let the really noisy snorers in. They wake up the baby." The small girl rolled her eyes at Mark.

Mark caught Evan's gaze, who smiled back at him. "After my wife died a couple of months ago, I went into a deep depression. I missed a couple of shifts and lost my job. I suppose for most people that isn't a big deal, but when you're living paycheck to paycheck, one missed check can put you under."

Evan paused to muss his eldest girl's hair, who still silently clung to his leg. "The girls and I don't mind, though. Getting evicted gave me the wake-up call I needed. It kicked me out of the depression. I realized how much I still have to be grateful for." Evan's voice caught, emotions brimming. "These girls are the most incredible gifts from heaven, and I am the most blessed man on the earth."

Mark and Evan talked for another few minutes before the Strong girls hugged Mark and announced it was time to go. Watching the departing family, Mark was subdued. Even Jack's normal banter couldn't draw Mark out of his contemplative state. How could the homeless man be so upbeat? How could he be so peaceful? The man's words reverberated in Mark's head all night long. "I am the most blessed man on earth."

His brief spurts of slumber were restless at best. Self-posed questions reverberated in his head. No matter how many times they spun around, they remained unanswered. Had his wife grown so disgusted with his attitude and inability to provide that she'd deserted him? He wouldn't blame her. He had been a royal pill, but something deep inside told him that wasn't the case. Unfortunately, that same voice also told him things weren't well with his three Thorsett gals.

After hours of fighting a losing battle with the sandman, Mark rolled out of bed and knelt down. "Father, I know I've kind of fallen off the faith wagon, but I'm trying to get back on. I can't be home to watch over my family. I don't even know where they are. I know my kids desperately need a father. Right now I can't be there. Will you do double duty as their Father for me, until I can make it home? Please. And Father, could You maybe point me to the answers Evan Strong found? I think I could use them. In Jesus' name, amen."

Mark's prayer didn't bring closure to the reverberating questions, but peace, like a warm blanket, drew him into sleep.

Chapter 7

Natalie awakened early Saturday morning to the sounds of giggling children. Prying her eyes open, she spied pajama-clad Mollie and Amber laughing with two other children on the floor. As she sat up, she could see they were playing with handmade paper dolls. Some of the dolls were covered in colored advertising newsprint and junk-mail clothes, but the girls were obviously enjoying themselves. As Natalie observed the children, she realized they were as happy with the "fake" dolls as they had been with the plethora of store-bought dolls that had resided in the Thorsett home in the past.

"I wish we adults were as adaptable as those kids," Natalie muttered to herself.

"You got that right, sister."

Natalie turned abruptly, startled by the voice that came from her side. From the cot next to her, a six-foot-tall black woman unfolded herself from the makeshift covers. Natalie smiled at her neighbor and then made a mental note. *Do not speak thoughts here that I intend to keep private.*

Her lesson learned was confirmed as the line of women emerging from cots and preparing for the day soon were engaged in animated conversation about the adaptability of children.

Her bunkmate laughed a deep belly laugh before verbally reiterating the lesson. "First thing you learn around here is that in close quarters, anything you say becomes fodder for conversation." She extended her hand. "Name's Sue. I'm on loan here from the domestic violence center down the road. They were full booked up last time Lloyd did a number on me. Dear El opened her doors and told me to stay until I could get my wounds healed and senses together." She looked at Natalie and then the girls. "What's your story?"

"Evicted." Natalie wasn't sure how open she wanted to be with the details of her life.

"Got a man?"

"Yes." Once again, Natalie provided only the most minimal response required.

"What's he like?"

Natalie turned and caught a glimpse of the wounded spirit in the eyes of the tough-looking woman next to her. She took a deep breath, then responded. "Mark's a good man. He's a great father. He's got the gentlest hands I've ever seen. I used to look at them and wonder if perhaps Jesus' hands were a little like his. Sometimes he's like a little boy—his excitement at Christmas. His play with the girls." Natalie had to stop as an incredible longing for her dear husband filled her and threatened to overflow.

Silence hung as Sue stared down at the cot. "I wish my man had gentle hands." The woman's body shook with the kind of grief that left no tear unshed.

Natalie searched for words but came up empty. Suddenly, she knew exactly what she should do. Taking the heirloom quilt off the bed, she took it over and wrapped it around the thin arms of the woman next to her. Before long, the shaking subsided.

Sue began to speak, blanket still held tightly around her shoulders. "El says I just need to use the courage and sense I have. Sometimes I don't feel like I have enough. Funny thing, though. Right now, I feel like maybe there's more down there than I know. Maybe there is some reserves in me."

Natalie uncharacteristically reached over and grabbed the woman's hand. "You know, if there is one thing I have learned lately, it's that when my strength falters, the Lord will fill in. 'I can do all things through Christ which strengtheneth me.' He's filled in for me, and I absolutely know He can strengthen you." Natalie was shocked by her own words. While she was definitely a believer in Christ, a Bible-quoting, testifying witness she was not. Had she gone over the line and offended this woman?

Sue lifted the blanket from around her and placed it gently back in Natalie's lap. She gazed at Natalie, tears brimming in eyes that bespoke years of pain. "I never been much of a church nut, but I think you are onto something. When you said those things, I knew you weren't just all talk." Pointing to her heart, Sue continued. "I felt something here."

"That's Him," Natalie whispered. "And He will never leave you or forsake you. I promise."

The women were interrupted by Amber's and Mollie's voices begging for breakfast.

Embracing both girls, Natalie kissed them and directed

them to layer their clothes for the day. At El's directive, she loaded their belongings into the bag to haul along with her.

"Desperate times will drive even the purest heart to temptation, child," El had warned with a wink. "Hold on to what you have."

After Sue declined to join them, the three Thorsett girls headed for the dining area and the waiting oatmeal.

El approached Mollie and Amber, white teeth glowing. "Are you guys going to be my ladies-in-waiting today while your mama goes and tries to find herself a good job?"

Excited affirmations followed. As the girls finished their sugar-laden porridge, El took Natalie aside. Handing her a piece of paper, she cautioned, "Now when they ask you for an address on an application, you are going to have to put down something. Putting no address is an invitation for denial. I've given you my home address. You just put that down." Looking at the large sack of belongings on the floor, she winked and added, "And I'll keep those in my office. It wouldn't do you any good announcing to the world you are carrying your earthly wealth on your shoulders."

Natalie shook her head. "El, you've done so much for us already. You don't have to do this."

"Child, this is nothing. I just wish I could do more. Now, you take as long as you need. Little Miss Mollie and Miss Amber will be in good hands here." El's brows furrowed a bit when she added, "And Natalie, be careful. There are some awfully mean critters out there on the street. Watch your step."

Natalie hugged El and the girls, bundled into her coat, and set out for the central Pike Place Market area. The post-Christmas season was not the friendliest for any job seeker, especially a homeless woman with two children. Day care was out of the question—far too costly to support on close to minimum wage—so flexible hours were a must. By the end of her search, however, Natalie had ceased to mention anything about children, hours, or place of residence, hopeful for any employment. Discouragement nipped at her, as did the frosty late-afternoon air. *One day of this and I'm already feeling like a failure. No wonder Mark struggled after doing this for two years.* Understanding filled her, but the guilt that accompanied it only weighed more heavily on her burdened soul. *Why wasn't I more supportive? Why did I nag?*

Caught up in her own thoughts, Natalie failed to notice she had wandered past the street the shelter was on. Glancing around, she suddenly felt a sense of foreboding. The feeling turned to outright terror when a hand gripped her arm.

"Well, pretty lady, what a coincidence—and you thought we'd never meet again." The chillingly familiar voice gripped her intestines like a vice. "It must be destiny."

Natalie twisted around, desperately looking for an avenue of escape. Unfamiliar streets taunted her, and the industrial buildings about her seemed to have no entryways or people inside. She uttered an internal prayer for help and then faced Kinsey square on. "Kindly take your hand off me."

The expressionless face that stared back twisted into a sardonic grin. "Why, of course, my lady. Your wish is my command." His handgrip on her arm only tightened, however.

Once again, Natalie closed her eyes and prayed for help.

"Nobody's gonna hear those prayers down here, little lady. This ain't His territory." Kinsey laughed maniacally.

Suddenly, from around the corner, a yellow lab ran toward the two of them.

"Oh, look, a dog in shining armor," Kinsey joked, his eyes showing no humor.

Natalie watched in surprise as the seemingly tame, gentle creature, tongue lolling, approached them, then forcefully lunged at Kinsey. Grabbing the man's arm in his great jaws, the dog broke the connection between Kinsey's hand and Natalie's arm. Freed, Natalie took off for the shelter as fast as her legs would carry her. Only after she was safely inside its doors did she pause to send a word of thanks upward.

Between labored breaths, she whispered, "Father, thank You. Thank You for all the things I took for granted and should have thanked You for long ago. A warm bed. A roof over our heads. Knowing You. My family. Safety. Mark. And thank You for all the recent times You've been there for me and with me. I love You, Lord. Oh, and I especially thank You for quilts and dogs."

Her prayer was interrupted when Amber and Mollie came around the corner and peppered her with questions. "How was your day?" "Did you get a job?" "Did you know we got to help stir the soup and press the biscuits for dinner?" Busy answering the girls, Natalie was left with little time to worry about the events of the day. If El felt something was out of the ordinary, she kept her mouth shut.

Before bed that night, Natalie cozied up under the covers with the girls. The bed Sue had occupied the night before was vacant. Natalie silently sent her off. *God bless you, Sue. . .and all the many others like you out there who have never known the warm, loving arms of a husband, or of a heavenly Father. May you find your way home soon.*

Late into the night the girls whispered stories of those they had met that day. A blind woman who played the accordion on the corner each day with her dog, hoping for enough money to pay for food and shelter. A family who had been burned out of their home and had not had adequate insurance. A mother and son who had been forced onto the streets after medical bills for a terminally ill child had mounted.

Amber reached over and gently stroked her mother's cheek. "You know, Mom, I never realized how lucky we are. I think we should have a family prayer to thank God."

Natalie nodded and softly whispered to her daughter to go ahead. The sweet words of the seven-year-old brought silent tears to her mom's eyes. She thanked the Lord for sight, for health, for their "new home" and Mama El, and for her family. She prayed for each person she had met that day and for those who weren't as lucky as Amber's family, having no nice, warm place to sleep that night. She concluded her prayer, "And Father, please bless my mom, that she might be safe and find a job. And bless my dad. Bring him home to be with us. We need him." Natalie and the girls fell asleep wrapped in the heirloom quilt that held their tattered lives and remnants of faith together.

Chapter 8

Mark Thorsett bolted out of bed, his heart pounding like a jackhammer. Sweat drenched his brow and trickled down his neck. He shook his head, trying to banish the visions that lingered from the all-too-real nightmare. Natalie was in danger. He rose and headed for the fridge, hoping a snack and glass of milk might counter the adrenaline coursing through his veins.

"Dreams are not reality," he said out loud, but the sound of the words failed to convince the rest of his body of the statement's truthfulness.

Shaking, he closed his eyes. Natalie was in a dark alley. She was looking around, terror etched on her face. Something was in the alley with her. Mark couldn't see what or who it was, but he could feel something. Whatever was on the brick-lined street with his sweet wife did not have good intentions. A sense of foreboding weighed on Mark like damp fog. Dream or not, he could tangibly feel the evil that had spurred him abruptly awake.

"What did I eat for dinner last night?" Mark shook his head, trying to figure out what gastronomic misstep had landed him in the world of indigestion that generated bad dreams.

One by one, he analyzed his food choices. "Ham sandwich, milk, bowl of tomato soup, salad, large piece of chocolate cake." At the cake, Mark paused. "That's it. It must have been the double-layer devil's food."

Swearing off pre-twilight sweets, Mark chalked up the unpleasant night as a lesson well learned and began his morning preparations for the day ahead.

Even with his concerns allayed, Mark still added a precautionary postscript to his early morning prayers. "Heavenly Father, be with Talie. I can't. She needs You. I know I certainly do. Keep her safe and protect her from evil. In Jesus' name, amen."

After finalizing his prework ritual, Mark sat down for a hurried breakfast. Despite finding the explanation for his early morning terror, he was having difficulty shaking the images and the uneasy feeling that lingered.

"Paranoia. That's what a large slice of chocolate cake, coupled with a bit of worry about finding where Natalie and the girls have gone, will do to your imagination." He added, "Besides, now she is in our heavenly Father's hands—she's better off there than in mine." Even as Mark said the words, however, he was not entirely convinced.

Throughout the day, images from his predawn visions kept him unwelcome company. Pictures of Natalie's terror-stricken face danced across his computer whenever he had any downtime. Mark threw himself into his work, determined to drive out any space for unwanted images.

At the end of a long, exhausting day, Mark dragged himself down to Community's Soup Kitchen. Rushing to his serving place before the hungry hordes amassed for what would be the day's only meal for many of them, Mark only had time to quickly nod in Jack Pace's direction.

The line tonight seemed much longer than usual. As Mark dolled out large clumps of mashed potatoes, he was particularly drawn to the faces of the women and children. Had they always looked so gaunt? How had he missed the fear and concern etched in the mothers' countenances? Wherever his wife and children were, he was glad they had not fallen prey to the streets that aged these young souls far beyond their years.

One young woman approached him with two little boys. She appeared to have barely made it into adulthood. How old could she be? Nineteen? Twenty? And that was being generous. As he went to place the potatoes on her plate, his gaze met hers. The raw pain her emerald green eyes contained caught Mark's breath.

"Please, sir. Don't mind me. Could you give my portion to the boys?"

Her pleading tone and selfless gesture touched Mark's heart. "Ma'am, we have plenty here for everyone."

The woman shook her head. "But if I give my boys mine, they can have more, right?"

Mark gently placed his free arm on the woman's. The bone he felt seemed to be covered by little more than a layer of skin. "There is enough for all. You need your strength, too." Mark paused, then felt compelled to continue. Words flowed from a source seemingly outside of him. "It doesn't matter what has brought you here. It doesn't matter what you have done or how low you have sunk. You are loved. Your Father in heaven is intimately aware of you and Devon and Charlie. Katie, He loves you. He wants you to come home."

Tears flowed down the young woman's cheeks like floodwaters. "How did you know our names?" she stammered through sobs.

Mark, for the first time, realized he had used their names. Not quite sure himself what had happened, he simply shook his head in wonder. "Our Father knows everything. Go home, Katie. Go home to your family. You will be welcome."

Reaching across the vat of potatoes, the teenager gave Mark a tearful, bony hug. "Thank you. You have no idea how hard it has been."

Mark nodded quietly, knowing she was right. Piling huge mounds of spuds on the plates of the small family, Mark heard his own words reverberating in his head. "Doesn't matter what you have done. . .how low you've sunk. . . . He wants you to come home. . . . Go home to your family."

Were those words designed for someone besides Katie? Was God sending him a message, as well? Why else would He have chosen someone as imperfect and tainted as Mark to deliver His message to the young girl? Mark didn't know the answers, but he knew someone who would have them.

Long after every person in line had been fed and the last dishes were done, Mark and Jack Pace sat down to their own meals. Mark reviewed the evening's events with Jack, then waited for his interpretation. To his disappointment, Jack declined.

"Mark, I've made my share of mistakes. I have learned over this long life, however, that when God communicates with someone, He is talking to that person alone. I can tell you what I think, but what good would that do? He didn't talk to me; He talked to you. If you have questions, ask Him." Jack's eyes twinkled as he winked at Mark. "Not that

I don't love to put my two cents in every chance I get, but this is one I don't have the answers for."

Mark's frustration mounted. How could Jack not know? He was the most spiritually grounded person Mark knew. Having struck out in his attempt to get help with his experience earlier in the evening, Mark debated not bringing up his dreams at all. Curiosity won the debate, though, and Mark cleared his throat.

"Well, since you're not giving advice in the miraculous-communication-from-God department, how would you like to try the bad-food-induced-dream department?" Mark chuckled, hoping to lighten the memories of the morning's musings.

Jack raised an eyebrow. "Dreams and promptings from God. Wow, He must really be trying to tell you something." He smiled. "Go ahead, son."

"Well, I had this large piece of chocolate cake a couple hours before I went to bed, and—"

Jack interrupted. "Get to the dream, boy. I don't need to hear how you blew your diet."

"It was Natalie. She was in trouble. Scared. Alone. Something really bad was after her. That's it. I don't know what it was or anything else. I don't even know where she was."

"What do you think it meant?" Jack said, flipping the question back to Mark as quickly as a short Ping-Pong rally.

"I've thought about it all day. I think my bad food choices and my inability to contact my family the last few weeks collided and produced a monstrosity of a dream." Mark looked at Jack, hoping for validation.

"You recall the story of Samuel?" Jack queried.

"Not sure. You want to give me the CliffsNotes version?"

"Samuel was a young man placed in Eli's charge at the tabernacle. One night he awakened, hearing a voice calling his name. He went to Eli to inquire what he desired, but Eli said it wasn't him calling. Twice more the voice came. Twice more he went to Eli. Eli finally perceived it might be the Lord and told Samuel that when the voice came again, to say, 'Speak, Lord; for thy servant heareth.' On the fourth occasion, Samuel did as he was told, and the Lord called him to be His servant and gave him a message."

Mark looked at Jack incredulously. "You can't be saying what I think you are. God spoke to Samuel. I didn't hear any voices."

"Son, God speaks in a multitude of ways. Some people see visions. Some dream dreams. Some hear voices. Some feel a warm feeling in their bosoms." Jack looked at Mark gently. "I'd say between what happened this morning and what happened this evening, you ought to ask Him what He would have you do."

"But if He wants me to go back up to Seattle, what will happen with my engineering job? I'm still on probation." Mark knew his face displayed intense fear. Letting go of the job he had searched years to find was unthinkable.

Jack placed his hand on Mark's shoulder. "If God asks you to go, He will provide a way."

Mark prayed long into the night. His evening pleadings began with the caveat, "I will go if You will find a way for me to keep my job." The peace that settled on Mark during his heavenly communications wrought a mighty change in his heart. By midnight, Mark had eliminated any conditions and changed his plea: "I will go if You want me to. Just keep my family safe. I can't bear the thought of something happening to them."

A repeat of the former night's performance left Mark with no doubt where he needed to be. Drenched in sweat once again, his beloved Natalie's terrified expression lingered in his mind.

He sat bolt upright, adrenaline pulsing. Clearly and decisively, Mark blurted, "I will go. Immediately. But where is she? And will I be there in time?"

Chapter 9

El shook her black curls and stared down at "her" sweet babies, Mollie and Amber, then back up at their mom. "Natalie, I am so sorry, child. I've tried everything I can to buck the red tape and get you an extension here. Nothing doing." Disgust emanated from her large body. "Those fancy-dancy office-bound decision makers haven't had a night out in the cold their entire lives. What do they know about anything?"

Natalie sat silently as the words sank in. After three weeks, their time at the shelter was up. El had managed to buy them an extra week by burying their paperwork, but the powers that be had found it and were insisting the Thorsett family be tossed out. El's crescendoing voice caught Natalie's attention.

"Imagine a bunch of bureaucrats thinking they can tell me what I can do with my own home. They said taking you all into my place was some sort of conflict of interest. They don't know nothing about interest, except maybe a lack of it. And here you are not having no job yet, and these sweet babies need protection and warmth. It's criminal." El's stomped foot punctuated her feelings and reverberated across the wood floor.

"How long do we have?" Natalie's voice sounded thin and frail, even to her.

"Tomorrow, honey. Tonight will have to be your last night." El lowered her voice and looked around. "And you'll have to spend it in my office. They don't exactly know you're gonna be here. They are sending their inspector goons over first thing in the morning."

Even in the midst of her fear, Natalie felt gratitude for the woman whose heart matched her massive body in size. "Thank you so much for what you've done for us. I understand. There are a lot of homeless women and children needing the beds here. We've already had more time than we should have."

"Until they provide enough shelters to meet the demand, they ought not be coming in here and spouting off about building codes and capacities," El stormed. "Who cares about some building code when babies are dying on the streets from exposure?"

"Oh, Mama El, we'll be okay." Amber stretched her arms around part of El's middle. "Don't you worry. We won't be cold. We have each other and our special quilt. It will keep us warm and safe."

Amber's words triggered El's tear ducts. Large round drops coursed down her cheeks. Gathering the two girls in her arms, she gently rocked and nodded. "I reckon you're right, child. I reckon you're right."

Later, after the girls had been set to the task of preparing supper, Natalie had a chance to talk privately with El.

"So, what are our options?" Natalie queried.

"I checked with the local tent city. It's moved again, way up north. Too far for you to track down a job. All the other shelters are full. The domestic violence homes are full up, too. I've got my feelers out, but nothing's coming back good." El placed her arm around Natalie's shoulders before heading to the kitchen to help the girls. "Something will work out. Don't you worry."

Natalie closed her eyes, hoping inspiration would hit her. The three weeks had flown by. Days of fruitless job searching followed by nights of restless sleep. The staff at the shelter had adopted Amber and Mollie. Each morning one of them would faithfully take the girls to the bus stop, and each afternoon the girls would be picked up as Natalie tried to find employment. Despite the hardship and fear, the last three weeks had also opened Natalie's eyes to her many blessings. The revolving shelter door had brought her in contact with scores of women and children whose lives had been far more tumultuous and difficult than she could have imagined.

Some stories brought her to open tears as she tried to comfort wounded hearts and souls. The magnitude of sorrow and suffering in the world astonished her. She hadn't purposefully turned a blind eye to it. She had been involved with charities and had donated their family's used clothes. They had all volunteered for community work. And Natalie had been involved in her church. But she had no clue, not an inkling of understanding, how widespread and deep were the wounds that affected so many.

Despite having fewer temporal blessings than at any

other time in her life, Natalie found herself more thankful for what she did have. Each night found the girls and Natalie on their knees in gratitude for all their blessings.

Natalie had been especially grateful for her relationship with her heavenly Father over the last few weeks. She had come to rely heavily on His direction and still, small voice when looking for a job. Almost daily she had been directed down a certain street or away from a certain area. Such direction had saved her from any further encounters with Kinsey.

"Perhaps he's moved on," she hoped fervently.

The last couple of weeks had also provided key insight into her husband's world. Nothing in her life had prepared her for the feelings of inadequacy and dread that came from not being able to provide basic needs for her children. The fear hung over her head like a vulture and constantly threatened to send her into an emotional abyss of guilt and depression. She knew only too clearly how such feelings ate away at one's self-esteem.

I've only been at this a few weeks, she thought. *Mark's been dealing with it for years.* Gratitude for her husband's strength coursed through her. If only he were here.

Natalie went to join the girls in the kitchen, hoping the culinary work would take her mind off the looming deadline.

Entering the small space, Natalie saw her two girls, elbow deep in bread dough. "Hey, Mom. We're kneading." Amber's smile spread dimple to dimple.

"I can see that. Any room for another set of hands?" The girls' positive response reflected how long it had been since their mom had been available to join them in activities. Her tireless dawn-to-dusk job search had taken her away from the girls, as well. Side by side with them at the kitchen counter, Natalie caught up with their lives. It almost felt like old times, when the three of them would bake fresh bread to welcome Mark home from a long day of work.

After the discussion had touched on a wide variety of subjects, Amber spoke. "Mom, we'll be okay, won't we?"

Natalie took Amber's face in her flour-dusted, dough-covered hands. "Sweetheart, we will be just fine."

Amber gazed thoughtfully back into her mother's eyes, while Mollie watched attentively. "Maybe Dad will come back and find a place for us."

The statement caught Natalie off guard. "We'll see, honey." Despite her ambiguous answer, Natalie knew the likelihood of that happening was close to none.

That evening as the girls prepared to sleep in El's office, Natalie thanked God they had been able to stay in the shelter for as long as they had, then said a silent prayer that they would have a place to stay the next night. Despite being pitched to and fro in a sea of unknowns, the heirloom quilt guided the three Thorsetts safely into the dream world.

The next morning dawned bright, cold, and far too early for Natalie's liking. A small group of staff gathered to bid the Thorsett family a tearful good-bye. Offers to stop by for lunch and dinner were extended by El out of earshot of the arriving officials. She pressed an address into Natalie's hand. "I've got a friend who owns a restaurant downtown. He's got a large storage area in the alley off the back of the shop. It's not heated, but it's covered and has four walls. He said you guys can camp there for a couple of days." She wiped a tear away. "I wish I could do more. I'll keep my ear to the ground."

She grabbed the girls in a tearful embrace as they were drawn into the soft folds of her body. "You take care of your mommy, Miss Amber and Miss Mollie, you hear me? Or Mama El will come and give you what-for."

She handed each girl a package loaded with food and treats before she turned to Natalie. "Let me help you get this." El lugged Natalie's belongings up and onto her back. Poking out the top were bags of food and items El had clumsily shoved in.

"Thanks, El. For everything." Natalie gave the large woman a hug, and the three Thorsett girls walked out onto the chilly street.

The day was spent hanging around shops in the downtown corridor. Pike Place offered some indoor areas where the family walked as unobtrusively as possible, trying to stay warm. Natalie was amazed at how many other people she recognized from the shelter. *I've been to Pike Place dozens of times before. Why didn't I see all of these homeless people?*

Occasionally a shopkeeper would ask them to leave, but by and large they welcomed the little girls and their mother. Aromas assaulted them almost cruelly, tempting of goodies and treats out of reach. French baked goods. Russian filled pastries. Stuffed pork humbow. Natalie tried to steer the girls away from the vendors, but both Amber and Mollie begged. "Oh, Mom—even if we can't eat them, we can smell them and dream."

As evening approached, Natalie was reluctant to leave

the crowded but safe market for the address that lay buried in her pocket. She bundled the girls around her and headed in the direction El had indicated. After blocks of walking, they approached the marked alleyway. Darkness cast shadows across the bricks. Even the usually cheerful girls looked at the black corridor with concern.

"Are you sure we have the right place?" Mollie asked timidly.

Natalie attempted to put on a happy face, hesitant to step from the relative protection of the streetlights into the unknown. "Remember, girls, as soon as we get safely inside, we have the flashlight El gave us and the book she sent along. We also have Daddy's Bible. We'll read together. I think she may even have thrown in some cookies."

With the promise of cookies, the girls tentatively followed Natalie into the alleyway. Passing three closed metal doorways and a Dumpster, Natalie came to a large metal door with the numbers 6064 scrawled in black paint. Graffiti lined the walls with symbols and letters unfamiliar to her. She reached the door and turned the knob; the door opened into a pitch-black room. Grabbing the flashlight from her bag, she shone it around the small space. The concrete floor had not been cleaned in some time, and the plywood walls were lined with cardboard boxes. It was not pretty, but it was better than the street. Natalie herded the girls in, then quickly shut the door behind them.

She reached to lock the door but fumbled trying to find it. Shining the light on the door, she came to an extremely unpleasant realization; it had no lock. She struggled to put on a brave face for the girls, hoping they weren't aware of what she'd learned. "So, who's up for some story time and cookies?" She layered the girls in all their clothes and then wrapped the quilt around all three sets of shoulders. In the darkness, illuminated only by the small flashlight, the quilt brought a measure of peace as they read from the picture book and Bible.

Tired from their long day at the market and exposure to the elements, the girls fell asleep immediately. Natalie was glad. Seattle was not a calm place at night. Loud voices and laughter filled the small room as people cut through the alley. Some seemed to be coming home from dinner or parties. Others sounded more ominous. The threats and obscene language of gangs. The clatter of other homeless people, searching through the Dumpster for food. Even within the folds of the quilt, Natalie couldn't sleep; she was only too aware of the girls by her side.

Finally she drifted into a fitful rest, giving in to the effects of the physically and emotionally exhausting day. In the early morning hours Natalie was awakened by a sound she hadn't heard before—a slow shuffling. Someone was searching the alley. *But what could they be looking for?* Terror gripped Natalie as the footsteps stopped outside the door. Despite the thin metal barrier separating her from the alleyway, Natalie could feel a presence on the other side. She didn't need to see what was out there to know its intentions. The evil that permeated the small room where she and the girls lay was palpable. She silently reached out and placed a hand on the Bible. Her other hand stroked the quilt. After what seemed like hours, the steps moved on down the alley.

Natalie breathed a sigh of relief. She and the girls had dodged a bullet tonight, but how many more nights would they have? "Oh, Father, send help," she whispered. "And please send it soon."

Chapter 10

Light stretched slender fingers under the door and gently awakened the Thorsett girls. Amber yawned and sat up. "Boy, Mom. I thought the bed at the old apartment was hard. This floor is hard as concrete!"

Natalie smiled. "That's because it is concrete." Both girls laughed. In the daylight their surroundings didn't seem nearly as ominous as they had the night before.

Still, Natalie quickly set about gathering their possessions and loading them into her bag. They would sleep here out of necessity, but she wasn't going to stick around during the day. Home sweet home this was not. She scouted the alley before leaving the room. Lessons from last night lingered. She would make every effort to enter and exit their sleeping quarters in as inconspicuous a manner as possible. No need to call unwanted attention to themselves. It seemed unnatural to have the weight of her children's safety resting solely on her shoulders. How she longed for her husband's much broader shoulders to help carry the load. In fact, right now there was no place she would rather be than in the safe and loving embrace of his arms. "Regrets won't get me anywhere this morning," she muttered before heading down the corridor back to the main street.

While normally not a supporter of Sunday shopping, Natalie was glad the stores were open this day. They offered needed warmth from the chilly winds. Ducking in and out with the girls, she managed to keep them semiwarm until they reached the shelter.

El had directed them to use the back door, in case any "official mucky mucks," as she termed them, were hanging around.

Natalie knocked three times and waited for an answer. El's curly mop poked out of the door. Eyes opened wide with pleasure and surprise, she corralled the clan into the small kitchen. "Land sakes, let's get you all out of that freezing cold." She met Natalie's gaze above the girls' heads.

"How was your night?"

"Okay." Natalie shook her head silently, conveying that the rest of the story would have to be out of earshot of the girls.

El obviously understood, as she put the girls to work making the bread for lunch. The promise of a warm afternoon spent in the shelter's kitchen, coupled with seeing El, made the girls almost giddy. Their laughter followed El and Natalie when they left the children under the watchful supervision of the shelter's cook.

Safe and alone in El's tiny office, she turned her piercing brown gaze on Natalie. "How was it?"

Natalie set forth the night's events, only this time she left nothing out.

El shook her head, worry clearly etched upon her face.

"Most of this I've heard before. Gangs, transients looking for food. I knew you might see those things. But the person hanging around looking—that worries me. Did anyone see you go down the alley?"

Natalie shook her head, trying to remember. "I don't think so. I tried to be careful."

"I don't get it. What would somebody want in that alley? You had any problems like this before?"

Natalie dropped her gaze. "Well, I did have this one guy following me."

El's eyebrows shot up. "And who might that be?"

"Some guy named Kinsey." Natalie's tongue almost spit the name out.

El's face bore an expression Natalie had never seen. "Oh, no, child. He's the worst of the worst. Bottom of the pile. Even the baddest down here stay clear away from him. How on earth did you get hooked up with him?"

Natalie relayed the story.

El pursed her lips. "I am coming down and staying with you-all tonight." Her tone offered no opportunity for argument.

The Thorsetts stayed as late into the evening as safety would allow, and then El, Natalie, and the children set out. El kept a careful eye peeled for those who might be following. Finally satisfied they had made the trip alone and unobserved, they opened the metal door and entered. The night was uneventful as they went through their story-and-cookie ritual and then wrapped up in the quilt. It managed to stretch to cover even El's oversized body. Kneeling, they each prayed. Mollie went last.

"And Lord, please keep us safe. And help Daddy find us.

We need him." The chorus of amens was heartfelt and loud. Long after the girls and El had been overtaken by sleep, Natalie was repeating the words of her youngest daughter's prayers.

Natalie couldn't be sure what time it was when something outside disturbed her sleep. The hair on her neck rose as if sleepwalking. Someone was in the alley. She didn't need anyone to tell her that this was a repeat performance of the night before. She gazed down at the sleeping trio on the floor, thankful that none of them were snorers.

As the steps moved down the alley away from her, Natalie braved a peek out the door. A tall, lean figure clad in black, its back to Natalie, made its way down the alley toward the Dumpster. It bent and stooped, searching every square inch. Then, turning his attention away from the Dumpster to the building behind it, the creature rattled each door and began working his way back down the alley. Doors with no locks were opened. Realization hit Natalie like a freight train. The person was determined to find what he was unable to learn last night and was methodically going through the alley to do it. It wouldn't be long until he reached the door that hid the Thorsett family and El.

Natalie glanced down at her small children wrapped safely in the patchwork quilt and knew what she had to do. If the figure continued, he would find them all. Natalie had to distract him. Quietly, she kissed each girl on the cheek and wrapped the quilt more tightly around them. She silently slid out the door and clicked it behind her. Praying for her safety and theirs, she took off running in the opposite direction, knowing full well her footsteps would notify the evil searcher of her presence.

She was right. She hadn't taken but a few strides when she heard the footsteps behind her give chase. Running for her life, she balanced her terror with the knowledge that the farther she could get away from door 6064, the farther this evil was from her sweet daughters. Twenty yards. Fifty yards. Then the street.

Terror pierced Natalie's soul when she found the street empty. What had she expected? It was the middle of the night. She knew she didn't have much longer before the odious footsteps caught up with her. She headed for the streetlight; if she were going to die, perhaps someone would see it happen.

Knowing he was close behind her did not prepare Natalie for the terror she experienced at the brutal grasp of the man's hand on her shoulder. Natalie knew the grip. She had felt it before.

Kinsey's panting voice rang with victory. "Don't suppose you have a dog handy tonight, do you?"

Without turning around, Natalie glanced at the hand gripping her shoulder. The dog had left deep marks in his hand, not yet fully healed. Natalie silently cheered.

With strength she didn't know she possessed, she turned and faced the gloating villain. "Who knows what my God has in store for you? Could be a dog. Could be an alligator. But rest assured, it will be something."

Kinsey's laugh reverberated down the empty street. "Oh yes. I can see, my beauty. He has a whole army here tonight to protect you." Grabbing her roughly, he pressed his lips to her ear and hissed, "It's just a shame He is going to be a little too late tonight." He underscored his statement by eerily whistling the familiar refrain from "Some Enchanted Evening."

Natalie struggled to break his grasp but couldn't. In a last-ditch effort, she looked up the sloping street and boldly announced, " 'I will lift up mine eyes unto the hills, from whence cometh my help. My help cometh from the Lord.'"

As if on cue, she saw a vision more beautiful than any dog she had ever seen. Cresting the hill and running at an all-out sprint was her husband, Mark Thorsett. Seeing the love of her life gave her power she didn't know she possessed. She sharply elbowed Kinsey in the solar plexus. The man's explosive exhale of air told her she had found her mark. As his grip relaxed, she jerked away and ran up the hill toward her husband.

"How did you find us?" she gasped.

"Later, Talie." The smile he gave her spoke more than any words as he hurled past her toward the waiting man. When he was finished with the man, Kinsey's face was expressionless no longer. Pain had replaced the evil intent that had filled Kinsey's eyes just moments earlier. The welcome wail of police sirens, followed by the arrival of the patrol unit, strobe lights flashing, allowed Mark to get off the man he had been sitting on. As they carted Kinsey off to jail, Mark looked down at his wife. Taking her in his arms, he lifted her chin to allow him to gaze fully into her eyes. "Fancy meeting you here, Mrs. Thorsett."

Natalie threw her arms around his neck and kissed him. Tears flowed down their cheeks as the two found themselves, by God's gentle grace, where they belonged—together.

"I have so much to tell you," Natalie blubbered.

Mark placed his finger gently on her lips, then said, "The same here. But later. Right now I just want to look at you. If you only knew how I've longed to see you. I am so sorry for not appreciating you when I had you, and for so many of the things I said and did."

It was Natalie's turn to quiet Mark. "It doesn't matter. None of it does. I realized it didn't matter where we were or what we had. As long as we were together as a family, it was enough. Job or no job, Mark Thorsett, we are going to follow you wherever you go."

The joyful reunion was interrupted by the sounds of young children. Propelling themselves down the alley under El's watchful eye were Amber and Mollie. "Daddy! Daddy!"

Mark lifted the girls in one motion. Holding them for what seemed an eternity, he reluctantly bent to put them back on the ground. Eyes full of merriment, he queried, "Isn't it past your bedtime?" The girls responded with giggles, obviously as much amused by the fact that their dad hadn't said anything about them being in the middle of the street in the wee dawn hours as they were by his comment.

"Oh, Daddy." Mollie wrapped herself around his leg semi-permanently. "Don't ever leave us again."

Mark tenderly knelt by both girls, under the tearful scrutiny of both Natalie and a blubbering El. "I won't. I promise." He took the girls' smallest fingers and wrapped them around his own. "Pinkie swear."

Mollie looked deep into her daddy's eyes, then asked, "How did you find us?"

Amber answered quietly. "Our heavenly Father told him where we were. I know He did. We prayed and He led Daddy to us."

Mark took Amber in his arms, noticing for the first time that his Bible was clutched firmly in her hands. "Amen to that, little girl. Amen to that."

Mollie added, "And we had faith you'd come back." She looked to her mom for reassurance that she had used the words correctly.

Natalie nodded, glancing at the quilt that El had wrapped around her shoulders. "We did have faith. Remnants of faith."

Chapter 11

Natalie Thorsett leaned her head against the window and let the sweet, warm rays of the morning sun stretch across her face. She kept her eyes shut, basking in the gentle snoring sounds that serenaded her from the adjacent hotel bed. The peaceful scene was a marked contrast to the tumultuous events of the preceding night. Natalie gazed at Mark, willing him to awaken so that she could obtain answers to her many questions. Last night she had been too caught up in the emotion of the events to question him, but today all the unasked questions begged a response.

Mark stirred, as if feeling her gaze upon him. His eyes opened. Catching sight of Natalie, a grin spread across his face. He leaped from the bed and vigorously embraced her. His joy was contagious.

Natalie waited for him to sit in the chair she had pulled to the window, then leaned back into his lap. Safe in his embrace, the questions came faster than the answers.

"How on earth did you find us? How did you manage to

show up right when I needed you? Where have you been? Why didn't you respond to my letters?"

Mark interrupted Natalie's series of questions with a heartfelt laugh. Hands raised in defeat, he joked, "One at a time, one at a time. The way I see it, we have a whole lifetime ahead of us for me to answer all the questions you want to ask, so go easy on me."

"I guess I should start with the question about the letters," he continued. "I'm not sure what letters you are talking about, but my guess is I missed them. I moved so quickly from city to city in the beginning, I left no forwarding address. I wasn't sure where the letters needed to wind up. I'm sorry. I thought that even if you didn't know where I was, I knew where you would be when I sorted things out." He shook his head. "Boy, was I wrong."

"When I finally ended up in Eugene, Oregon, I wore out my phone lines and the lock on my post office box trying to find you." Taking her hands in his, Mark turned her around to face him and gazed deep into her eyes. "I am so sorry. I had no idea what you and the girls were going through. I was terribly wrong to leave. Can you ever forgive me?"

Natalie felt her eyes fill. "It's all right. I've learned to let it go. Now you need to." Gaining her composure, she squeezed his hand. "Eugene? What's in Eugene?"

"An engineering job. . .I think. At least there was a job until I came to Seattle to look for you guys." Mark smiled wryly.

Natalie couldn't believe her ears. "A job? You found a job?" She wrapped her arms around Mark's waist. "We're going to Eugene!"

"Yes, we are. But first you need to hear the rest of the story. I left Eugene a week ago. I went first to our old apartment. The new tenants knew nothing about you, and, as I'm sure you can guess, our dear old landlord wouldn't give me the time of day." Mark's face twisted in anger at mention of the man. "Finally, I camped out on his front porch for an entire day and threatened to stay there indefinitely if he didn't tell me everything he knew about where you were."

Mark smiled. "Let's just say he found me very persuasive. He told me about your three-day notice and how, as a Christmas present, he hadn't evicted you on the holiday. Other than that, he knew nothing."

Mark looked at his attentive listener. "If you had any idea what it did to me to think of you girls out there with no place to go. . ." Mark's voice choked with emotion as he continued. "I didn't know what to do. I just knew I needed to find you. After exhausting every other avenue I could think of—shelters, low-income housing, food banks, hospitals, even police stations, I finally went to the girls' school. After getting past all the red tape, I was able to talk to the principal, to their teachers, and finally to the bus driver who picked up the girls. She's the one who directed me to the stop last night. She told me which direction she normally saw the girls head and described the woman who sometimes would meet them."

He paused and grinned at Natalie. "I knew it had been awhile since I saw you, but it didn't take a rocket scientist to figure out the two-hundred-plus-pound African American woman who was picking them up was not you."

Natalie laughed at the loose description of El, then waited for Mark to continue. "Armed with her description, I spent last evening canvassing the streets trying to figure out who she might be. I felt a sense of urgency, an inner voice spurring me forward. I knew I couldn't wait until morning."

Natalie nodded. "I've become acquainted with that voice myself recently."

Mark and Natalie shared a moment of silent understanding; then Mark went on. "Close to midnight, I ran into a woman who thought she knew who I was talking about. She led me to the shelter. I must have awakened all the residents pounding on the door, but they didn't seem to care. They told me El had taken off with you guys for the night but would be back in the morning. I just knew I couldn't wait until then."

Natalie shivered. "Thank goodness you listened to the voice."

"You don't even know the half of it. I took off in the direction the lady indicated you had headed but didn't have a clue where you might be. Every intersection, every corner, I felt a hand propelling me forward and the voice in my head telling me which direction to go. Street after street. Each time I had to make a decision, I knew where to turn. At the end I was running as fast as my legs could carry me." Mark's eyes flowed freely at the memory. "It was the most miraculous experience I have ever had. It's funny, but when I crested the hill and headed down the street toward you, I felt no surprise you were there. I wasn't sure which street you would be on, but I knew the owner of the voice that was leading me did know."

Natalie opened her mouth but couldn't speak. She knew exactly who had led Mark to her. It was the One whose arms had encircled and protected her little family out on the cold streets and whose voice had whispered words of forgiveness and encouragement to her heart. And the One who had divinely directed a loving teacher to make a gift of a warm, protective quilt. Natalie buried her head in Mark's shoulder, thankful most of all that He had also healed her family's brokenness.

PATCHWORK HOLIDAY

❧

The rest of the year flew quickly by as the Thorsett family started anew. The move to Eugene was filled with great joy and anticipation. The happiness was magnified when they learned that Mark's job was securely his. Jack Pace became an adopted member of the family. Activities soon filled their lives. None, however, could compete with their once-a-week journey downtown to help feed Eugene's homeless population. Through the spring, summer, and fall, the Thorsetts became a symbol of hope to the people who came to receive physical nourishment, but often left spiritually and emotionally nourished, as well.

On Thanksgiving Day the Thorsett family once again headed for Community Church's familiar building. Amber had insisted on taking with them something she had secretly secured in a large plastic bag. Despite repeated questions from her parents, she refused to tell what was hidden inside. She and Mollie shared furtive glances and giggles over the obviously jointly hatched plan. Finally, after the meal had been served and grownups and children broke off into little conversational groups, the secret was revealed. Natalie watched as her daughters gathered the other children around them and pulled the heirloom quilt out of the bag. As each child touched the quilt, Natalie moved closer to hear what Amber was saying.

"Last year we were just like you. We didn't have our house or bed or anything. But when we were the saddest and most scared, that's when God sent us this quilt. Every time we felt bad or cold or afraid, we'd just put this around us and we could feel His arms holding us tight. He loves little children. I know He loves me, and I know He loves you guys, too. Even if you don't have anything else, you do have something to be thankful for—God.

And His Son, Jesus. And maybe if you ask Him, He'll put His arms around you, too."

"Can we put the quilt around us?" The frail girl who spoke looked as if her own voice frightened her.

Amber and Mollie both gave her big smiles. "Yes," they responded in unison. Then Amber continued, "It won't be long until we have to give this quilt to someone else who needs it. The lady who sent it to us wanted us to give it to someone else, a man. Next week we're flying to Alaska to give it to him. But tonight, we wanted you guys to feel God's arms around you."

One by one, the motley group of children wrapped the folds of the quilt securely around their shoulders. Some closed their eyes when they pulled it around themselves. Others covered their heads in the warm cover. As the quilt passed by and everyone had a turn with it, each small child's face wore a peaceful smile. Though no longer in the quilt's embrace, its message clearly remained in the young hearts: You are loved.

RENEE DEMARCO

Renee DeMarco is an award-winning, multi-published author and a practicing attorney. She has authored many beloved titles. Renee resides in Washington State with her husband and three daughters.

SILVER
LINING

by Colleen L. Reece

Dedication

To Eric, Kelly, and all those who serve at home
and overseas, with special thanks to Ron Wanttaja
for additional resource material.

When I consider thy heavens, the work of thy fingers,
the moon and the stars, which thou hast ordained;
What is man, that thou art mindful of him? . . .
[Thou] hast crowned him with glory and honour.

PSALM 8:3–5

Chapter 1

Middle Eastern skies

That's it for this time, Burgess Benjamin." Major Gavin Scott, U.S. Air Force Raven reconnaissance pilot, grinned broadly, anticipating his wiry, red-haired RSO's usual explosive response.

It wasn't long in coming. Captain Sharp bristled like a porcupine. "Once more with the Burgess and you'll be minus one RSO," he threatened. "I can claim mental anguish as grounds for a transfer." He grimaced. "Why anyone would hang a name like Burgess on an unsuspecting kid is beyond me. It took a dozen black eyes given and received before people got the message that I'm Ben."

Gavin wasn't through heckling his reconnaissance systems operator. Ignoring the oft-heard account of his best friend's woes, he shifted in his seat and accused,

"Transfer? You? Fat chance. According to your bragging, I couldn't fly my way out of a paper bag without you." Laughter blossomed like a fully opened parachute.

"You couldn't," Ben retorted, but a grin spoiled his mock indignation.

Gavin felt his lips twitch. "Yeah, right. I do have to admit, though, you're as faithful as Patsy Ann."

"Patsy Ann?" Ben looked suspicious. "Who's she? An old girlfriend?" He brightened. "Hey, now that you're engaged to the foxy Christa Jensen Bishop, how about introducing me to your Patsy Ann? I don't like to talk about myself, but. . ." He threw out his chest and grinned again.

It was all Gavin could do to control his mirth. "No introductions. First, she's too old for you. Second, she's not your type. Third, the city of Juneau would declare war if you tried to take Patsy Ann away from them."

"Is this another one of your Alaskan tall tales? Like the one about the midair collision between a B-727 and a salmon?"

Temporarily distracted from his Patsy Ann story, Gavin shook his dark head. "According to the tour guides in Juneau, that really happened. I wasn't there, but they swear it's a matter of historical record. An eagle swooped down and caught a huge salmon. Frightened by the noise, the eagle dropped it. Result: wing damage from the salmon—to the plane, not the eagle."

Ben smirked. "Sounds fishy to me."

Gavin groaned. "Do you want to hear about Patsy Ann or not?"

"Sure."

"Patsy Ann lived in Juneau in the 1930s."

Ben snorted. "A 70-something-year-old woman? Just my luck."

Gavin ignored him. "She died in 1942. She was so respected, a huge crowd came to say their farewells when her coffin was lowered into the Gastineau Channel." He paused. "I was really impressed the first time I saw Patsy Ann and heard her story."

"What do you mean, saw her? You weren't born until the mid-70s."

"A bronze statue was erected in Marine Park. Patsy Ann greets guests arriving in Juneau by sea, just as she did for so many years."

Ben shrugged. "What was she? The town hostess? Why did you say I was as faithful as she was?"

"You are. I'll tell you what I'm talking about." Gavin cleared his throat. "Dad was career military but retired after twenty years. We came back to Alaska after I finished second grade in Boise, Idaho. Dad didn't want me yanked in and out of different schools every time he got transferred." He fell silent. Homesickness for Alaska and the MacJean Flight Service owned and operated by his parents, Mackenzie and Jean Scott, assailed him. Anger followed. If it weren't for those driven by hatred and lust for power, he'd be home now. Yet fanatics must be stopped, even when it meant tearing men and women from their homes to defend their countries against terrorism.

"What does your dad's career have to do with Patsy Ann?" Ben asked.

"Everything. When Dad wasn't busy with charter flights, he took Mom and me all over Alaska. The first trip was to Juneau. I remember how beautiful it was, built against green mountains, with the Gastineau Channel between it and Douglas Island with its snowcapped mountains. The statue of Patsy Ann sat on the dock, looking out at the harbor. A plaque told her story, but Dad had already filled me in." He paused, feeling the same awe he had experienced as a child clinging to his father's strong hand.

Ben sighed. "It would be nice if you'd tell me, preferably sometime before I have a long white beard."

Gavin pulled out of his reverie. "Okay, Burgess Benjamin. Patsy Ann was a bull terrier—"

"And I remind you of her? Thanks a lot." Ben's voice dripped with sarcasm.

Gavin grinned. "She was actually deaf and mute, unlike some people I know."

"So?" Ben bristled. "Is that supposed to make me feel better?"

"Wait till you hear the rest of the story, okay?" Gavin didn't wait for a reply. "No one knew how, but Patsy Ann could sense when a steamship was coming into the harbor. She always raced to meet it. Perhaps because return visitors brought her scraps from the ships' dining rooms—unlike today, when you can't take food off the ships. Whatever the reason, Patsy Ann never missed meeting a steamship."

"That's incredible." Ben sounded properly impressed.

A familiar tingling went through Gavin. He felt the same small-boy wonder that always accompanied the telling of the story. "It was incredible, but not so much as what happened later. A steamship was unable to dock at the usual place and time. It's not clear whether the reason was a storm or trouble aboard. Anyway, when the ship docked at a different place, long after expected, Patsy Ann was there to meet it."

"How do you explain that?"

Gavin shook his head. "No one can. It just happened. There are lots of things we can't explain. Only God understands the workings of His creation, including the intuition He placed in a deaf and mute dog's mind and heart."

"Not many people are as faithful as Patsy Ann." Ben sounded sad.

Gavin shot a quick look at his RSO, but Ben was staring straight ahead. No wonder. He had been a wishbone child, pulled between two sets of parents after a messy divorce. Sympathy softened Gavin's voice. "We can be glad God is faithful."

"Yeah." Ben hunched his shoulders. "Wonder what the flight schedules during the holidays will be? I'd sure like to be in the good old U.S. of A. for Christmas this year. Or at least for Thanksgiving." His voice turned somber. "I never knew how much I had to be thankful for until I came over here."

"You've got that right," Gavin agreed. Another wave of rage rose within him. Yet as long as wicked men chose evil over good and attempted to annihilate all those who disagreed with them, there would be conflict.

Gavin forced himself to quell his anger and concentrate on his flying. A combat aircraft was no place for negative emotions. They could lessen a pilot's vigilance and lead to disaster.

Flying. How he loved it! His mind ran double track, split between the job at hand and his earliest memories. . . .

⌇⌇⌇

"Daddy, why can't I fly like the birds?" he asked one afternoon when they stood watching a pair of hawks lazily circling in the blue, blue sky. He flapped his arms, ran across the grassy yard of their home on a hillside just outside of Anchorage, and leaped in the air, only to come down in a hurry.

Strong arms caught him up and perched him on a muscular shoulder. Gray eyes like his own twinkled when Mackenzie Scott replied, "We have to be content to fly in airplanes, son. Someday, when you're old enough, I'll teach you. Your mother and I chose the Welsh name Gavin because it means 'white hawk.' "

Gavin squinted. "But, Daddy, our hawks aren't white."

His father laughed. "No, they aren't. White hawks live far, far away in places like southern Mexico and Central and South America. I'll show you those countries on the world map when we go inside."

"Do our hawks ever go visit the white ones?" Gavin inquired.

Mackenzie Scott shook his head. "It is much too far for them to fly."

"Someday I'll go where the white hawks are," the boy vowed. "I'll tell them our hawks are sorry they can't come see them."

"I won't be surprised." His father set him down. "Run and wash your hands. It's almost time for supper."

Late that night, father, mother, and son took a walk

under the northern stars. On the way home, Gavin stood on tiptoe and stretched his arms into the air. "Mommy, if my arms were longer, I could pick a star for you," he announced.

Jean Scott's laughter rippled like a happy brook tumbling over stones on its way to the sea. "Which one would you pick?"

"Polaris. The North Star." A chubby finger unerringly pointed to the star located almost directly over the North Pole. "Daddy says it's 'portant to know how to find it, in case we get lost. First we find the Big Dipper." He moved his hand. "Then we draw a straight line from the 'pointer stars' to the end of the Little Dipper's handle."

"What if clouds cover the sky and you can't see the North Star?" Jean teased.

Gavin looked at her with wide eyes, thinking with all his might. A confident smile broke across his face. "Then you ask God to tell you which way to go." With a whoop of pure joy, he raced ahead of them toward the lighted windows that meant home and security. But he never forgot that night.

⁓◌⁓

Shortly after Gavin and Ben completed their run and headed toward home base, disaster struck. One moment, the Raven steadily pursued its course. The next, the two men were surrounded with flashing lights and blaring warning horns. Gavin's lightning-quick glance at Ben's pale face and his fervent "God help us!" confirmed the problem—a major fire in the left engine compartment. A pilot's worst nightmare, especially when flying Middle Eastern skies.

Please God, not here, not now, Gavin silently pleaded.

Summoning all his self-control, he turned off the fuel to the left engine and activated the fire-suppression system. No effect. The horns and lights doubled as fire spread to the right engine compartment. The metallic taste of fear filled his mouth. While Ben prayed and smoke started filling the cockpit, Gavin tried to stop the second fire. Yet despite prayer and Gavin's efforts, nothing worked. The plane started to gyrate as hydraulic lines to the control surfaces burned away. He felt the thud of a small explosion just behind the cockpit.

A taunting voice hammered a message into Gavin's brain: *You are going to die. You'll never see Christa, your parents, or Alaska again.* A heartbeat later, a sharp blow to his head brought darkness, as complete and total as if every trace of light had been snatched from the earth by a giant, malevolent hand. The last thing he heard before sinking into its smothering depths was Ben's loud cry, "God, have mercy! Eject, eject, eject!"

❧

Hours or centuries later, Gavin awoke to a world blacker than a starless, moonless night at sea. Dazed and disoriented, he felt a steady pressure on his head and something wet running down his face. He called out, "Dad? Did we have to ditch?" but no answer came.

"Gavin."

He struggled against the dizziness that held him against his will and finally managed to whisper, "Dad?"

"No, not your dad, Gavin. It's Ben. Wake up, Sleeping Beauty." The lightly chosen words didn't hide the gravity of his RSO's voice. "I did something to my ankle when we crashed. It isn't broken—torn ligaments, maybe. I can hobble, but I need your help. Do you hear me, Gavin? I need you. Now. We have to get out of here and find cover before unwelcome visitors come sniffing around the ejection capsule."

The urgency in Ben's voice, more than his words, brought Gavin fully alert. He reached up to his aching head but contacted Ben's hand.

"Don't touch your head—something struck you. Hard. I put a compress on the wound. Thank God it has stopped bleeding. We need to get going."

Gavin's tongue felt thick. "How can we find cover in this pitch-black darkness?" he snapped. A moment later, suspicion mingled with a stream of cold fear and raced up his spine.

"What do you mean, darkness?" Ben demanded.

The shock in his friend's voice turned suspicion to certainty. Gavin fought nausea, gritted his teeth, and ground out, "You're going to have to pilot this expedition, Ben." He hesitated, then hoarsely added, "I can't see."

Chapter 2

Anchorage, Alaska

Halfway around the world, twenty-six-year-old nurse-practitioner Christa Jensen Bishop finished the last-minute check of her well-stocked Ford Explorer, in preparation for another day's work. She paused to sniff the breeze ruffling the soft brown hair that had escaped from the hood of her scarlet parka. It was her favorite time of year—crisp, cold October. Brilliant sunlight. How she loved the snowcapped mountains. Their lofty, magnificent heads jutted thousands of feet into the cloudless sky behind Anchorage, and the sun-kissed water of Cook Inlet shimmered with a million golden motes.

Christa saluted the life-sized statue of British Captain James Cook nearby, where he had first anchored in 1778. What had he thought when he saw the site of what became a proud city? The municipality of Anchorage was one of only seven cities nationwide to have won the prestigious All-American City Award four or more times.

Christa's heart filled with gratitude. *Thank You, God. If it weren't for Susan. . .* She expertly switched her train of thought to the day ahead. The 150 miles that lay between her and the town of Soldotna offered plenty of time for reflection. Travel time was a blessing and offered the solitude she needed between cases.

A reminding nose nudged her mittened hand.

Christa laughed and patted her beautifully marked Alaskan malamute. "Sorry, Aurora. With God and you, I'm never alone." She opened the driver's door. "In, girl." Aurora barked, leaped into the Explorer, and crossed to the "copilot" seat. She looked at her owner as if to say, "C'mon, slowpoke. What are we waiting for?"

Christa slid behind the wheel. Closing the door and fastening her seat belt, she accused, "You're a faker. Before we're halfway to Soldotna, you'll be curled up and asleep, with that gorgeous tail of yours covering your nose, as usual."

Aurora cocked her head, looking as though she were smiling. Blue eyes that matched Christa's in color but were considered a disqualifying fault by the AKC—the American Kennel Club—suggested near-human intelligence. She sat back on her haunches and relaxed. A week in a kennel had obviously not been to her liking.

"My sentiments exactly." Christa started the engine and put the Explorer into gear. "It's good to be off that last case. Why I ever agreed to care for a pampered, wealthy woman is beyond me. She must never have heard of the Emancipation Proclamation. She treated me more like a slave than a professional. Imagine, refusing to let a nice dog like you on her property.

As if you'd hurt her precious yard or flowers." Christa felt an unrepentant grin form. "She doesn't have any flowers now. What few escaped frostbite became a late-night snack for a roving moose. Good thing I like the critters. They are all over the place up here."

Christa sighed with contentment. "No unpleasant, cloying atmosphere for us today, Aurora. Just fresh air and people who appreciate my services."

A sharp bark brought a rise in Christa's already-high spirits. "Okay, our services. You're part of this team, except when I have fussbudget patients." She ruffled Aurora's thick fur. How many times had she taken her medical skills on the road in the past two years? When she added helicopter calls to remote areas beyond her trusty four-wheel-drive SUV's capabilities, the total was staggering.

Happiness rode with Christa and Aurora on this day of days. Having faced and conquered a multitude of obstacles, they were well prepared with food, blankets, medical supplies, cell phone, and extra batteries. Christa's course in minor vehicle repair, her nurse's and nurse-practitioner's training, and a supply of common sense, were supplemented by an unwavering faith in the God she met as a child and had worshiped ever since.

"Aurora, if anyone had told me two years ago I'd be here with you. . ."

A loud snore showed that her copilot had succumbed to sleep, leaving Christa to again reflect on how blessed she really was. For the second time that morning, she prayed, *Thank You, God. If it weren't for Susan. . .* This time she mentally drifted into the past, although eyes and hands remained alert to her present surroundings. . . .

Susan. Flaxen-haired with laughing eyes the unusual

blue found only in the heart of a glacier. Susan. Three inches shorter and fifteen pounds lighter than Christa's graceful five-feet-eight-inch height and 140 pounds. Susan, who adored her big sister and was dearly loved in return. Christa laughed in pure delight. One of her favorite memories of her sister was the day she pouted and demanded, "How come I couldn't be adopted like Christa? You picked her, but you just had me. You couldn't send me back."

Ron Bishop had laughed. "You were both miracles, Susan. You know the story."

A look of wonder replaced Susan's pout, and words tumbled out. "You and Mommy thought I'd never come. When Christa was born and her mommy died, you took care of Christa 'cause her daddy was sick. He never got better, so you kept Christa."

"That's right," Leigh Bishop said. "We believe God sent us to help Mr. Jensen and gave Christa to us. Her daddy wanted her to have his name as was well as ours—"

"That's why she's Christa Jensen Bishop," Susan interrupted. She clapped her hands, her face wreathed in smiles. "And when she was two, God sent another miracle. Me." She had beamed at them all. "Christa was really, really happy to have a little sister!"

I still am, Christa thought, her gaze intent on the highway. There was always the danger of animals straying onto the road. *Thank You, God, for two sets of wonderful parents, even though I only know my birth mother and father through the Bishops.* A kaleidoscope of memories swirled through her mind: school; church; the good smell of leather in the Bishops' sporting goods store; the two-story home on Queen Anne Hill, furnished with love and good taste rather than an abundance of money. College and training to fulfill Christa's dream of becoming first a nurse, then a nurse-practitioner. Susan had chosen to attend business college and became an administrative assistant at the Seattle Veterans' Hospital, but all she really wanted was to marry a good man and raise happy, healthy children.

"What about your childhood dream of being a missionary?" Christa teased.

"There are probably just as many or more heathens right here in Seattle. I'll be a home-front missionary," was Susan's saucy reply, typical of the happy-go-lucky personality that sometimes hid the depth of her love for God. Her devotion equaled Christa's and bonded them in a sisterhood of friendship so strong it even prevented Christa from laughing at some of Susan's wild schemes. Like writing jingles and entering "Complete this sentence in twenty-five words or less and win the vacation (or furniture, or wardrobe) of your dreams" contests!

Susan met "Mr. Right" just after her twenty-second birthday. She confessed to Christa, who was too busy with her career to allow herself to fall in love, "It's everything they say. Stars in your eyes. Walking on clouds. Waiting for the phone to ring." She hugged her sister fiercely. "But we'll never let anything come between us. You'll always be there for me if I need you, won't you?"

"Of course." Yet even as she promised, Christa had the strange feeling all was not well. It proved true. "Mr. Right" dumped Susan a few weeks later. On a day when the heavens had opened and rivers of rain poured down on the city, his engagement announcement to a former girlfriend appeared in the *Seattle Times*.

"I can take being jilted," Susan spat out. "But to have someone I trusted do it this way is rotten." Her eyes flashed blue fire. "I'm just glad to know what he's really like!" She raised her chin. "It *would* happen on a day like today. What's that old poem?" She ran to a nearby bookcase and snatched up a worn poetry book. "Here it is. 'The Rainy Day,' by Henry Wadsworth Longfellow. Wadsworth. What a name!"

Christa gave a sigh of relief. Susan's pride was more hurt than her heart, or she wouldn't be able to sound so normal. "Read it aloud."

"Okay." Susan deepened her voice to fit the contents of the quotation.

> *"The day is cold, and dark, and dreary;*
> *It rains, and the wind is never weary;*
> *The vine still clings to the moldering wall,*
> *But at every gust the dead leaves fall,*
> *And the day is dark and dreary.*
>
> *"My life is cold, and dark, and dreary;*
> *It rains, and the wind is never weary;*
> *My thoughts still cling to the moldering Past,*
> *But the hopes of youth fall thick in the blast*
> *And the days are dark and dreary."*

Susan tossed the book down. "Rats! I'd forgotten how mournful this is! If it doesn't get better, I'm outta here." She made a face, grabbed the book, and read in a voice that softened with each line:

> *"Be still, sad heart! and cease repining;*
> *Behind the clouds is the sun still shining;*
> *Thy fate is the common fate of all,*

Into each life some rain must fall,
Some days must be dark and dreary."

For a long time, neither spoke. Then Susan shrugged. "If you subscribe to the misery-loves-company theory, I guess this helps. Look, the rain's stopping. Let's go for a walk." How like her! Impulsive, yet with flashes of wisdom that often made Christa marvel.

Susan made no more mention of "Mr. Right." Then one day, she danced into the blue and white dining room where Christa and their parents were already at the dinner table. Her soft green dress made her look like a wood sprite in spring. "Guess what!"

Christa's heart leaped to her throat. *Please, God, don't let her say Mr. Right-Turned-Wrong broke his engagement and wants her back.*

Susan didn't wait for an answer. She said in a mysterious voice, "Big sister, remember when you said you'd always be there for me? Now's your chance. Pack your clothes. Tell Mom and Dad good-bye. We're going to Alaska."

"We're what?"

"You are what?" her parents had chorused.

A brilliant smile spread across Susan's animated face. "Christa and I are going to Alaska. I told you entering all those contests would pay off."

Ron Bishop just stared. Leigh gasped. "You actually won?"

Susan smirked. "Trust me. I won an all-expenses-paid cruise for two. The contest was sponsored by a new travel agency that just opened up downtown. The promotion was a way to attract customers. All you had to do was stop by and write where you wanted to go to get away from it all and why in twenty-five words or less. So I did."

Her father chuckled and looked curious. "What did you write?"

Susan's pink and white complexion darkened until she had looked like a full-blown rose. "It's kind of embarrassing."

"Susan Bishop, exactly what did you say?" Leigh demanded.

"Uh, I was still in a bad mood over the engagement, so I wrote, 'I want to cruise to Alaska. My boyfriend dumped me. There are more men than women in the Last Frontier. Maybe I'll meet "Mr. Right." ' Exactly twenty-five words."

Ron Bishop had tilted his chair back and roared. Leigh stared at her daughter, appalled. Christa blurted out, "Are you mad? Contests publish winning essays, if you can call them that. Everyone in Seattle is going to know what you wrote!"

Susan's eyes widened; then she shrugged. "Who cares? We're going to see the land of the midnight sun, aurora borealis, whales, and icebergs. You'll go, won't you?"

"Traveling with you may be taking my life in my hands," Christa said. "But of course I'll go."

A few weeks later, she and Susan left Seattle behind and began their journey. To their dismay, instead of sailing up the Inside Passage as expected, they headed out to sea—and into a storm. Susan didn't feel well, so she took a pill and went to bed.

Christa felt fine physically but was terrified. She'd always been afraid of water; now she lay trying to sleep in a bed that felt like a bucking bronco. *What am I doing here, Lord?* she prayed. *I am so scared. Please give me peace.* She closed her eyes. A picture formed: Jesus, walking on the troubled waters of the

Sea of Galilee. "This would be a good place for You to walk," she whispered. Some of her nervousness subsided. For the next hour or so, she drowsed; then another roll of the ship brought a fresh wave of fear. "Are you still out there?" she asked, glad God had a sense of humor.

The next morning had brought gray skies, but by the time they reached Juneau, the day was glorious. So was the rest of the cruise. Both Susan and Christa fell wholeheartedly, unreservedly in love with Alaska.

Shortly after their return, Susan announced she was applying for a job at the VA hospital in Anchorage. "Dad and Mom are talking about taking a year off and traveling," she said. "Home won't be home without them. I hear Alaska calling, and your nursing skills are in demand everywhere. This may be our last chance to strike out on our own before we marry and settle down, Christa. Will you come with me?" She grinned. "Who knows? We may even be swept off our feet by a couple of strong Alaskan men!"

Christa couldn't deny the prospect tantalized her. After intense prayer, she agreed to go, hoping Susan was right when she said they wouldn't regret it.

Susan was *right*. Three days after reaching Anchorage, Christa met Major Gavin Scott, a pilot in the U.S. Air Force.

Chapter 3

Gavin. The mere thought of her fiancé sent joy flowing through Christa like warm honey. "Please, God, keep him safe and bring him home," she murmured. Aurora stirred, licked Christa's hand, then settled back into sleep, leaving her mistress to relive the weeks and months after she met the tall, dark-haired pilot. Once more her present surroundings melted into a montage of memories, beginning with the moment she and Susan reached Anchorage and first saw their new home away from home. . . .

"This can't be where we're going to live," Susan had exclaimed. Her eyes opened so wide, they looked like twin aquamarines. "It's a fairy-tale cottage!"

"Try your keys," their taxi driver remarked. "If they fit, this is the place!" He guffawed.

Christa laughed. "You're right about that." With Susan at her heels, she walked up the stepping-stone pathway that divided the lawn into two plush green carpets bordered by flowers. Tall evergreens on both sides of the small white house with dark green roof, shutters, and front door promised privacy from their neighbors.

"Hurry, Christa," Susan ordered.

Heart pounding, fingers trembling, Christa crossed the covered porch with its white wicker chairs and table. Before she could insert the key in the lock, the door swung inward. A robust, pleasant-faced woman in denim shirt and jeans appeared—along with a sweet and spicy fragrance that re-minded Christa she hadn't had lunch.

Susan's gasp of disappointment echoed her sister's sense of loss, but Christa managed to stammer, "I–I'm terribly sorry. We must have the wrong house."

The woman chuckled. "Not if you're the Bishop sisters. Welcome to Anchorage. I'm Molly Hunter. I live next door. The Hagensons said you'd be here today, so I brought over an apple pie. My, but they're glad to know you'll be taking care of their home while—"

"Hey, ladies, the meter's running," the taxi driver called. "You can flap your jaws after we unload your luggage."

Well, Christa thought, *there are colorful characters in Alaska, too.*

After the taxi disappeared down the quiet, tree-lined street, Molly led the way inside. "Like I was saying, the Hagensons feel you two are an answer to prayer."

"We're the ones who believe that," Susan burst out. "We were worried we couldn't afford a nice place. Then a church friend said he knew a couple who had volunteered for an overseas humanitarian mission that would last a year or two." She shook her head. "We still don't feel it's right that the Hagensons only want us to pay the utilities and for any repairs that might be necessary."

Molly shook her head. "Don't let that bother you. If God hadn't sent you, the Hagensons would have had to hire a house sitter. Don't worry about repairs, either. The place is in excellent shape. Besides, my husband is real handy and enjoys helping folks." She glanced at her watch. "I need to be running along, but would you like to go to church with Richard and me this Sunday? It's a real Bible-based church and not far away. You can have dinner with us afterward."

"We would love to," Christa said from a full heart. She voiced her thoughts to Susan after Molly left. "Any doubts we may have had about coming here are certainly dwindling," she said. "God is so good. A storybook cottage and a couple of earthly angels for neighbors! What more could we want?"

Susan grinned. "Just two strong Alaskan men to sweep us off our feet."

"You're hopeless," Christa told her. "Now, let's dive into that apple pie, then check out our new home." She led the way to the cheerful kitchen—and discovered well-stocked cupboards, refrigerator, and freezer, courtesy of the Hunters.

❧

Sunday morning dawned bright, clear, and cold. Christa and Susan decided to walk to church and meet the Hunters there. They started early so they could enjoy the residential neighborhood in which they now lived, giving a moose—which showed no signs of yielding the right-of-way—a wide berth. They arrived at church rosy-cheeked and excited. "Look!" Susan clutched her sister's arm. "There's another moose!"

"Where?" Christa turned her head to see. *Thud*. The next moment, she was sitting on the sidewalk feeling stupid and staring up into a pair of concerned gray eyes. It didn't help to hear Susan giggling behind her.

A strong, uniformed arm reached down and helped her to her feet. "Are you hurt? I am so sorry."

Susan giggled louder.

Christa was torn between wanting to squash her sister and answer honestly. She rubbed one elbow. "The only thing hurt is my dignity." Suddenly the humor of the situation hit her. The tall, dark-haired man she had plowed into while moose-gazing could have stepped from an Air Force recruiting ad. In spite of his recent impact with a mortified nurse-practitioner, there wasn't a wrinkle in his perfect-fitting uniform. Sunlight turned the wings—indicating he was a pilot—to gleaming silver.

"I'm Gavin Scott," her victim said. "Glad to hear the damage is minimal." His eyes twinkled and his mouth twitched. "Do I dare say 'nice running into you'?"

"Not unless you intend to beat a strategic retreat. I'm Christa Jensen Bishop. It's nice to meet you." She cast a withering glance at her companion. "This is my sister, Susan, although right now I'm not sure I want to claim her."

"Is this your first time at our church?" he asked with a nod toward Susan.

"Yes." Christa liked the way he said "our church." It made her feel welcome, at home. It also established a rapport with the handsome officer.

"Oh, here you are." Molly Hunter bustled up. "Have you met Gavin?"

"Yes," Susan demurely said. "He has been most helpful, hasn't he, Christa?"

Molly evidently didn't catch the undertones in the seemingly innocent remark. "Christa and Susan are my new neighbors, now that the Hagensons are gone. Christa is a nurse-practitioner and will be on the road a lot. Susan has a job at the veterans' hospital. By the way, Gavin, what about coming for dinner, since your folks are out of town for a few days? The girls will be there."

Gavin raised one dark eyebrow. "If it's all right with them," he politely said.

Major, you'll never know just how all right it is. Appalled at the thought, Christa hesitated a split second before answering, just long enough for doubt to darken Gavin's watching eyes and rob them of the fun that had sparkled in their depths.

Susan, who could always read her sister like an open magazine, more than made up for Christa's lapse in manners. "We would both be delighted," she said firmly.

"Good." Molly shepherded her little flock up the steps and through the church door. "Richard's already inside. We can all sit together."

Susan Bishop had the cunning of Machiavelli when it came to furthering her schemes. Christa had to admire the way she maneuvered the five of them into the pew so that Susan ended up on the far side of the Hunters with Gavin in the center aisle seat next to Christa. He didn't seem to mind. They shared a hymnal, and his rich, deep voice blended with her softer one. At several points in the service, Gavin glanced down at her and smiled, as if expressing agreement with what the minister was saying.

That Sunday had been just the beginning. When their limited free time coincided, Gavin showed Christa the many faces of Alaska. Susan and whatever young man she happened to fancy at the time accompanied them. The bonds of friendship ripened. With the future uncertain, it was enough to experience the simple joy of being together.

~ళ∕~

One particularly memorable excursion began on a day all blue and green, white and gold. Gavin had arranged a surprise for the sisters. "Wear layers of clothing," he advised. "It can be both cold and warm—and where we are going is one of the most beautiful, historical places in Alaska." His smile made Christa's heart soar like the eagles she watched gliding in the sky. "We're off to Skagway, which means 'Home of the North Wind,' to take the White Pass and Yukon Route. It was built in 1898 during the Klondike Gold Rush and is something you'll never forget."

Though familiar with the rugged mountains of Washington State, Christa and Susan had never seen such grandeur. The narrow-gauge railway hugged slopes on its ten-foot-wide roadbed blasted out of sheer rock, a feat said to be impossible. Waterfalls and streams cascaded from towering glaciers thousands of feet to the bottom of Dead Horse Gulch, where the bleached bones of pack animals, driven to their deaths by those in search of gold, remained. The train chugged through a 250-foot tunnel, midnight black and scary.

Yet of everything they had seen, one thing stood out:

a grim reminder that the evil in the hearts of men never ceases. Christa would never forget the look on Gavin's face when he pointed out the remains of a huge wooden trestle. "There was a great deal of fear during World War II that the Japanese might invade Alaska. Military personnel guarded the trestle twenty-four hours a day. In spite of their vigilance, a bomb was found at its base. Thank God it was unexploded." His lips set in a grim line. "The saboteur was never found."

"The same sort of thing is going on today," Susan blazed. Great tears dimmed her eyes. "Blowing up bridges is bad enough, but what is happening now is worse. People all over the world are being killed by those who are taught it is honorable and glorious to murder the innocent." She buried her face in her hands.

Christa clutched her sister's hand, too moved to speak.

Gavin laid one hand over hers. "I pray for the day when bloodshed will cease. Until then, I am called to fight evil wherever it is found. Dad and Mom raised me to believe in God, family, and country. I'll do whatever Uncle Sam asks of me."

A blanket of dread descended on Christa. There was something in his voice. . .

"Gavin, have you received new orders?" she whispered, hating her inability to keep her voice from shaking.

"Yes. I've been fortunate enough to have been stationed at Elmendorf until now, but it's been decided I'm needed elsewhere."

Christa's throat dried. "Do you know where?" How could she stand for him to go away? She hadn't realized how much she would miss him until the threat of his leaving surfaced. Winter loomed and Anchorage would be bleak without him.

Gavin shook his head. An expression of regret and something more flickered in his somber eyes. Something that quickened Christa's heartbeat, even though she felt she was being suffocated with fear. "Destination unknown at this point. It's going to be hard to go." He tightened his grip on her hand, then gently released it. "Let's talk about something pleasant—like getting the best ice cream cones in Skagway."

Christa hadn't been able to speak, but Susan valiantly rose to the occasion. She freed her hand, dug in her jacket pocket for a tissue, and blew her nose. "Sounds good to me."

"Great. I know a place downtown where. . ."

❧

Aurora roused and gave a short bark. Christa's thoughts returned to the present. "Smart dog, always waking up just before we get to our patient. Now to find him." The medical group for which she worked always obtained directions. Following them often wasn't easy! However, today Christa drove straight to the home of a stubborn old man she had attended after he suffered a heart attack while visiting a friend who lived in the mountains near Anchorage. Christa had been caring for a sick family nearby.

The man's heart was simply worn out. When he learned his condition, he said, "Well, the Good Lord's kept it ticking for almost ninety years. Can I go home?"

"Yes, with medicine and a nurse to visit you. Who is your doctor?"

He cackled. "Ain't got one. Don't want a nurse, either, unless it's you."

Christa grinned. "If you'll agree to let me contact someone in Soldotna to look after you for a few days, I'll come as soon as I can. Okay if I bring my dog?"

He frowned. "It ain't some itty-bitty, ratty critter, is it? Can't stand 'em."

"Neither can I," she confessed. "Aurora is an Alaskan malamute."

"Okay. You and A-Roarer come soon." He cackled again. "Don't wait too long."

Christa didn't. As soon as she got back to home base, she arranged to spend a few days with the man, hoping she might talk him into accepting help from a local nurse.

Now she pulled into the yard of a modest house, noting with satisfaction the lazy drift of smoke curling from the chimney. "Come on, 'A-Roarer.' Time to go to work."

Chapter 4

The Middle East

Of all the instructions given to Gavin Scott, Ben Sharp, and their fellow pilots before they were allowed to go on reconnaissance missions, nothing was stressed as much or as often as what to do in case of emergencies. Gavin would never forget his introduction to the hard-bitten officer in charge of orientation. He drilled procedure into the fliers' heads with the zeal of a dedicated Sunday school teacher implanting the Ten Commandments in his students' brains.

"First, remember that the EF-111's ejection capsule has an automatic distress beacon," he said. "The bad guys will hear it just like we will. When you hit dirt, grab your survival gear and run as if your life depends on it. It may." He paused to let the warning sink in. "Activate your personal radios and wait for the choppers to call."

Gavin felt ice worms crawl up and down his spine. The fear of coming down in the wilds of Alaska had never affected him like this. He squared his shoulders, knowing that every word of the lecture was being indelibly branded on his very soul.

"God forbid any of you will ever be forced down," the instructor fervently said. "In the event it happens, follow procedure—to the letter. Do not, I repeat, *do not* stay with your aircraft. Get to the nearest cover, if you have to crawl on hands and knees. Or on your belly! Once there, don't budge until help comes."

A wintry smile briefly lightened his hatchet face. "Help will come. Our helicopter crews make bloodhounds look like amateurs when it comes to rescuing our own." His smile faded into a steely gaze that traveled from face to face. It left Gavin feeling he had been stripped and searched. "Any questions?"

Paralyzing silence followed.

"Very well. Dismissed." The officer saluted and strode quickly away from the training area.

Gavin turned to Ben. His friend looked like Gavin felt— as if they'd just survived an enemy attack. Ben's brown eyes had darkened to almost black. "He made things pretty clear, didn't he?" Gavin asked.

"Yeah. That's good, though. It should discourage anyone dumb enough to try hotdogging." Ben lowered his voice. "I just pray we never have to use the information."

"So do I."

∽◈∾

Now it was time. Time to put into practice what they had been taught. Time to survive by following the procedures they had reviewed again and again during the months they had been flying overseas. After the first stunned moment when Gavin confessed he couldn't see, Ben took command.

"We could be a lot worse off," he pointed out. "I can see. You can help support me. We'll make it."

Gavin responded to the studied cheerfulness in his RSO's voice. "Of course. Between us we have everything we need—three good legs; two good eyes. Let's get out of here."

"Sure, as soon as I gather up stuff to take care of that head of yours. These limestone hills and sand dunes don't offer much in the way of hospitals and clinics!"

They don't offer much in the way of cover, either. Gavin bit down hard on the thought. Not being able to see their surroundings left his imagination wide open. He could picture unfriendly eyes watching them from behind the hills and dunes Ben had mentioned. *Stop it,* he silently ordered himself. *That kind of thinking is dangerous.*

God, we need You. I need You. Panic is not an option. Neither is fear. Are You there?

Encouragement came to mind and soothed him like a glass of ice water on a scorching day. Psalm 46:1: *"God is our refuge and strength, a very present help in trouble."* It was closely followed by Psalm 121:1–2: *"I will lift up mine eyes unto the hills, from whence cometh my help. My help cometh from the Lord, which made heaven and earth."*

Despite his heaviness of heart, Gavin grinned. He'd always associated the scripture with his beloved Alaskan mountains. Yet the God of towering peaks was the God of limestone hills. He was just as able to protect His children from danger lurking behind them as from the ravening Alaskan wolves that traveled in packs and wreaked havoc.

"Ready?"

Gavin ignored his throbbing head. "Ready, Burgess Benjamin."

"Did you or did you not put me in charge of this little expedition?" Ben demanded.

Gavin fought his pain. "I did."

"Then that temporarily makes me your superior. Let's have a little respect."

It was too much effort to think up a suitable reply. Besides, Gavin knew he'd need every ounce of energy he possessed to make it to cover.

"This little hike is going to test us as we've never before been tested," Ben warned. "It would be harrowing under normal circumstances. Now. . ."

" 'By the grace of God and a lot of grit,' as Dad used to say, 'we'll do it.' " Gavin didn't add the obvious. They had to—for each other's sake even more than their own.

"You've got that right. Here. Give me your right arm. It's my left leg that's busted up. We'll do our own version of a three-legged race."

Wounded and in pain, they started their journey. The distance that lay between them and cover loomed endlessly in their minds. The best they could do was plod. Sheer willpower kept them going. With each painful step, Ben leaned harder on Gavin, who could hear his friend's harsh breathing from the effort. Then Ben staggered and crumpled to the ground, pulling Gavin with him.

Gavin rolled away from his friend. "This isn't working. I'll carry you."

For once Ben didn't argue. "You're going to have to, at least until this crazy leg of mine is rested. I'll navigate."

"More like playing guide dog," Gavin said as he hoisted his friend into a fireman's carry position. "Concentrate on what's just ahead. It will only take one hummock to fell us. If I go down again, I don't know if I'll be able to get up and continue."

Step by shuffling step, they crossed the unfriendly land. The loss of blood from Gavin's head wound steadily took its toll on his considerable strength. So did Ben's weight. He lost track of time and place. All he could think of was putting one foot in front of the other. Left. Right. Left. Right. Strange. When had he deserted the Air Force and become part of the infantry? Left. Right. Left. Right. Would the march never cease? Where were they going? Why? It was hot. So hot.

Something warm and wet slid down his face. The next instant, he tasted blood.

It brought him to his senses. He stumbled, regained his balance, and said, "I'm bleeding again, Ben. Better put another compress on the wound."

"It's time to stop and rest anyway," Ben said. "We won't go on until we get the bleeding under control."

"Good." Gavin slid to the ground. "I'll catch a few z's, and—"

"No!" Ben grabbed him by the shoulders and forced him to sit up. "You know the drill. No sleeping when you have a head wound."

Gavin knew he was right. He had to keep going, no matter how slowly.

When Gavin's wound stopped seeping, he wearily

got to his feet. Ben insisted on walking as much as he could, which helped. Two lone souls in a country far from home—both desperately prayed that their strength would hold out long enough for them to travel the remaining distance to a safe place.

Hours that felt like centuries later, Gavin and Ben found cover. Now all they could do was wait and pray, knowing full well the danger wasn't over. God grant that help would come before they were discovered by unfriendly forces and taken captive—or worse.

Gradually they relaxed, although they didn't let down their vigilance against possible threat. Gavin's mind cleared. He told Ben, who never tired of hearing about Alaska, more stories. They talked of home. Of Christa. And of why they were there, far away from those they loved.

"If I had to put it in a few words, it would be something Christa said shortly after we met," Gavin flatly stated. He struggled to recall her exact words and the way she looked during their conversation. "Something really special happened when she and her sister, Susan, were on their Alaskan cruise, and—"

"I hope Susan is still single when we get back to America," Ben interrupted. "She sounds like my kind of woman. What are the chances of an invite to Anchorage?"

Gavin laughed, the first time since they started their arduous journey. "You're welcome anytime. You might be just what Susan needs. She's been playing the field ever since she got to Alaska. I have the feeling she just may not have met the right guy yet." He laughed again, even though it made his head hurt. "If Christa had already been taken, I'd be pitching a tent at Susan's doorstep! By the way, both of the sisters are strong Christians."

"They sound like keepers," Ben said. After a long moment, he ran a grimy hand over his matted curls and added, "I hope she goes for redheads! In the meantime, what were you saying about their cruise?"

"The dinner stewards and room attendants came from all over the world. They represented more than fifty countries, many of them under the rule of cruel dictators. Christa said the young men reminded her of little boys, homesick for their families. They were so eager and appreciative of the chance to talk with Americans! Many expressed how people in their homelands loved America and what we are doing for them."

Ben grunted. "Different from what you hear in the media, huh?"

"Right. It was also interesting to hear what the ship's employees had to say about the way they were treated. They love having American tourists because most are friendly. They take time to visit, to ask those who serve them if they have wives and kids, and so on. Evidently it isn't that way with everyone." Gavin sighed.

"One morning after Susan left the dining room, Christa lingered to finish a conversation with a young man from a South American country. He confirmed what others had said: Many European tourists are much more formal. They consider the stewards and room attendants servants and ignore them as human beings.

" 'How does that make you feel?' Christa said. 'I'd hate being treated that way.'

"The young man sadly shook his head. 'Only in America can you be somebody.'

"Christa could barely hold back the tears until she got out of the dining room. It reminded her how important it is for America to help those who are oppressed, whether by cruel rulers or caste systems. It also shows that millions of people around the world still appreciate us and the God-given freedom we want to share—even when it sometimes means giving our lives to help others."

"Like Christ gave His life to free us from sin," Ben said. "Bringing light into a lost, dark world."

"Yes." Something he needed to tell Ben hovered on the edge of Gavin's consciousness. Something to do with the darkness in which he was now trapped. There. He had it.

"Before help comes, I need to tell you something. From the time I was a kid, I knew what to do if I got lost. Find the North Star and take my bearings from it. If clouds covered the sky and I couldn't see the North Star, I should ask God what to do." He cleared his throat. "I can't see the North Star or anything else, Ben. The future looks black. Unless my sight returns on its own, this 'white hawk' is grounded. Even if surgery restores my vision, I can never fly for the Air Force again. It's policy."

"I know."

Gavin knew the pain in Ben's voice did not come from his injuries. Before he could respond, a welcome noise sounded in his ears: the *whup-whup* of a rescue helicopter, sweeter to the downed fliers' ears than the swish of angels' wings.

PATCHWORK HOLIDAY

Exhausted by the ordeal, Gavin let himself relax. His last conscious memory was of lifting off, accompanied by Ben's taunt to the crew.

"What took you so long? Where have you been? Out chasing camels?"

Chapter 5

An Air Force hospital in Texas

H ang in there, Major. We'll take care of you." The voice with a hint of Southern drawl penetrated the murk that clouded Gavin Scott's brain. Where was he? He tried to turn toward the unknown speaker, but his body felt like someone had clamped it in a vise. Too weary to figure it out, Gavin drifted into a never-never land somewhere between consciousness and reality. . . .

Scene after sunlit scene replayed in his tired mind, elusive as a dancing butterfly hovering over a hillside adorned by fireweed. Its hue was no brighter than the face of the young woman laughing at him from behind a great armful of rose purple flowers. It was Christa Jensen Bishop, who had fallen at his feet while moose-gazing.

It was so good to be back in Alaska! Back in the country he loved, with the woman he believed God had chosen as a mate for the "white hawk." For years Gavin had strived to become worthy of the love of a good woman. If or when God sent someone to Gavin, he would devote his life to being a godly husband and father.

He basked in the warmth of Christa's smile, a smile that remained as steady and true as the first time he had seen her. Gavin had never discounted love at first sight but believed people needed to take a second look before jumping into a commitment. Yet during their short time together, Gavin became convinced he and Christa were meant to spend the rest of their lives together. The wistful look in her blue eyes shouted that she was learning to care for him.

Gavin said nothing to Christa of his growing love. "It wouldn't be fair," he told his father one night when the aurora borealis put on a show worthy of a standing ovation.

"Why not? Will it be any easier if you go without telling her?" Mac Scott grunted and placed a strong hand on his son's shoulder. "I felt the same until your mother said she loved me and asked me what I was going to do about it!" He fell silent. "I married her and let her traipse along with me whenever possible."

Gavin's heartbeat quickened at the prospect of having Christa with him, but he shook his head. "It's too soon. Marriage isn't an option right now."

Mac's grip tightened. "So who said anything about marriage? You can at least get engaged." He pointed at the dancing lights in the sky. "Go buy your girl a ring with a stone that shoots sparkles like that. It will give her something to hang on to while you're away."

Gavin turned to face his father. "And if I don't come back?"

"Then you and she will at least have had the joy of today." With a convulsive grip of his son's shoulder, Mac marched away, leaving Gavin to ponder.

The next day he enlisted Susan Bishop's help in choosing a diamond ring that made her eyes widen. "It's perfect," she exclaimed, holding it up to the light. The full spectrum of colors shone from the depths of the clear white stone. "If Christa doesn't want it, I'll take it," she roguishly added. "Well, not really. I'm not ready to settle down." She moved the ring back and forth. "This reminds me of Christa's and my cruise. One night just before midnight, she looked out our window to say good night to the ocean. 'Quick, come and see,' she called. 'Hurry!'

"I ran to the window. Shimmering golden light filled the sky above the snowcapped mountains. We threw sweats and parkas over our night wear and raced up to the top deck. It was windy and freezing cold, but for the next fifteen minutes, we saw the northern lights. They weren't colored like the ones here but white and gorgeous." Susan blinked. "Neither of us will ever forget it."

Gavin's heart warmed to her appreciation of beauty. "I never had a sister," he told her. "But if Christa says yes, I will."

Susan's eyes glistened. "She'd better say yes. As has been said before, a good man is hard to find." She sighed. "Trust me. I know."

She sounded so sad, it made Gavin wonder, *Was there a lost love in Susan's past?* If so, it would explain why she never dated even the most charming, persistent suitor more than a few times before switching to someone else.

The night before Gavin left Anchorage, he picked up Christa and drove to a spot where they could see Cook Inlet, the frosted white mountains, and the city. "Are you dressed warm enough for a short walk?" he asked.

"Toasty." She snuggled deeper into her scarlet parka and pulled the hood up. "Where are we going?"

"Not far." Gavin led her to a huge rock nearby. All the pretty speeches he'd secretly practiced deserted him. He took both her mittened hands and looked deep into her moonlit face. "I love you, Christa. I always will. If God brings me safely home from wherever I'm sent, will you marry me?"

Her eyes filled with tears. She slipped from his grasp and stepped back.

Gavin's spirits plummeted to earth like a paratrooper whose parachute had failed to open. *Dad was wrong,* he thought. *It's too soon.*

The next moment, she clasped her mittened hands in front of her. "I love you, Gavin. I'll marry you anytime, anywhere you say."

When her answer sank in, Gavin felt like the white hawk for which he was named—the white hawk that soared to great heights. A beloved psalm sang in his heart: *"When I consider thy heavens, the work of thy fingers, the moon and the stars, which thou hast ordained; what is man, that thou art mindful of him? . . . [Thou] hast crowned him with glory and honour."*

The final words fit the wondrous night as no others could have done. Gavin pulled Christa close. His silent prayer ascended to the heavens. *Thank You, Lord. May our lives always bring You glory.*

For a time it was enough to simply hold Christa. Her head rested just above his heart. Could she hear its quickened cadence? The love that coursed through him with every beat? Yes, for her arms slid around his waist and her face turned toward his as a sunflower turns toward the sun.

"Is it real, Gavin?" she whispered. "Or is it all a dream? Will I wake up back in Seattle, never having come to Alaska, never having met you? I couldn't bear it."

His blood raced. He laughed so loudly, it seemed the heavens rang. "It's real, sweetheart." He freed one hand and took a small, velvet-covered case from his pocket. Unwilling to release her, he unsuccessfully struggled with one hand to open the case. "Here. You do it."

Christa laughed and took off her mittens. The case popped open. The diamond glittered bright as the twinkling stars above. "It–it's beautiful. So pure."

"It reminds me of you." Gavin reluctantly loosed her from his encircling arms, slipped the ring on her finger, and kissed it. "Someday we will stand in church and take our marriage vows before God, our family, and our friends. I look forward to seeing you walk down the aisle in your wedding dress and knowing you are mine. But I don't want to wait that long to exchange vows. Christa Jensen Bishop, I promise you here and now: I will love and cherish you. I will guard your happiness with all that is within me, as long as we both shall live."

With a little cry that Gavin knew came from joy, she flew back into his embrace like a homing pigeon.

⤜⤐

"Wake up, Major. It's all over."

Christa vanished. The night did not, except neither moon nor stars pierced the darkness surrounding Gavin. He struggled to understand. After what felt like centuries, he managed to croak, "What's all over?"

"The surgery on your eyes. We got you back to the good ol' U.S.A. posthaste after you went down in the Middle East, so you could get the finest medical help possible. We take care of our own."

Where had he heard that before? Gavin wondered. Oh, yes, the instructor who gave preflight instructions on emergency procedures. "Help will come. Our helicopter crews make bloodhounds look like amateurs when it comes to rescuing our own."

Gavin involuntarily raised his hand.

"Don't touch your head!"

Memory of the disaster returned in a rush. The fire. His futile attempts to extinguish it. Ejecting from the Raven. The endless trek to cover. Ben's forcing him to stay awake when all Gavin wanted to do was lie down and sleep, hoping that when he awakened, it would turn out to have been a nightmare. And finally, the sweet *whup-whup* sound that announced help had come, with Ben mouthing off to the helicopter crew about taking so long to get there.

"Captain Sharp?" Gavin hoarsely asked.

"He's fine. Some torn ligaments will keep him grounded for a while, but he'll be good as new in time. So will you, Major. There's every indication the surgery was a complete success and your sight will be normal."

Normal? When, as far as the U.S. Air Force was concerned, he was a has-been? Ben would heal and fly reconnaissance again. Major Gavin Scott would—what? Well, at least they would be home for Thanksgiving and Christmas, as Ben had hoped.

No use thinking about it now. He had the rest of his life to figure out why God had allowed this to happen. Or more accurately, why He hadn't prevented it. God didn't cause aircraft fires, but why hadn't He protected the men who served Him? Why hadn't He healed Gavin's eyes spontaneously so surgery wouldn't have been necessary?

God, this is more than I can bear. You know my dream of following in Dad's footsteps. It began the first time he strapped me into the seat of a plane.

Suddenly Gavin wanted to go home. Home to Mom and Dad, to everything he knew and loved. Most of all, to Christa. He clung to the thought while waiting to be cleared to return to Alaska. Yet troubled minds and hurting souls offer fertile soil for seeds of doubt. So it was with Gavin. The girl he left behind had fallen in love with a dashing pilot who soared far above the earth. How would she respond to a fallen "white hawk"?

Gavin fell into a deep depression. Did he have the right to hold Christa to a promise made under far different circumstances? Again and again he told himself, "Don't jump to conclusions. Christa is true. Christa is loyal. She will stick by her man."

Unfortunately, those very traits magnified the problem in Gavin's worried mind and brought a dozen more. Perhaps he and Christa had been so caught up in the danger that went with Gavin's job, they had convinced themselves the love they shared was God's will. What if He was trying to show them they had been mistaken? Even though Gavin knew such misgivings were normal under the circumstances, they fed on his weakened condition and haunted him more each day.

The emotional battle inevitably took its toll. Gavin worked himself into such a state that he developed a fever. "What have you been doing to yourself?" the physician in charge barked. "You should have been out of here by now and on your way home."

"I don't want to go home." Gavin was appalled at his terse reply. When had dread of returning to Anchorage begun gnawing at him like a husky with a bone? What did it matter? The statement was true, although he hadn't realized it until he spoke.

Shaggy brows beetled over the doctor's keen eyes. "Why not?"

The question stabbed into Gavin with the sharpness of a scalpel. He didn't reply. How could he confess that the thought of facing Christa was more than he could handle? Did his inner struggle show in his face? Perhaps, for the doctor—who was known more for his medical skill than his bedside manner—grunted.

"I can send you to a military convalescent center for a time, if you like."

"Thanks." Gavin's sense of relief was out of proportion to the simple offer. When he was alone, he fell into a deep sleep, the best he'd had since awakening to discover his career had been shot down.

⁓⑨⁓

Gavin continued to be troubled by the feeling that there was something urgent he had to do. Until he could settle things in his own mind, he didn't want to see Christa. "Wrong," he muttered. "I do want to see her. I want her here in my arms. I want to hear nothing has changed, and that as soon as I get back to Anchorage, we'll be married."

At that moment, Gavin Scott entered his own Garden of Gethsemane. He raised a mental wall to shut out the image of the woman he loved floating down the aisle of the church back home. The desire to ignore his qualms and go ahead with the wedding—as he and Christa had planned so long ago—left great drops of sweat on his forehead. In the end, he overcame temptation. He obtained pen and paper and began a task even harder than staggering through the desert in order to reach a safe place.

Chapter 6

Alaska

The high beams on Christa Jensen Bishop's Ford Explorer cut through the darkness like twin sabers. For the past few weeks, night had sneaked up and enveloped the land earlier each evening. Christa didn't mind. Warm and snug with Aurora for company, she actually enjoyed the dying end of day. She watched a lopsided moon peer over the top of a nearby mountain, accompanied by a lady-in-waiting star. What a gorgeous night! How many more such autumn evenings would there be before winter gobbled up even more daylight?

Christa's growling stomach reminded her of how long it had been since she'd eaten. "Wonder what Susan will have ready for us when we get home?" she asked Aurora. Her furry companion's ears perked up and Christa laughed. "I'm glad Susan and I have a standing rule: Whoever gets home first starts supper."

Home. The same thrill Christa experienced each time she reached the "fairy-tale cottage" ran through her. Its lighted windows never failed to awaken a matching glow in her heart. Every time she stepped through the door, she paused and gave thanks to God for allowing Susan and her to live there. Christa always felt the cottage held out welcoming arms to those who entered. Of course, much of the house's appeal came from the Hagensons' carefully chosen decor. The "home sitters," as Susan facetiously dubbed herself and her sister, had fallen in love with the place as it was. They put out photos of Don and Leigh Bishop and other cherished bits and pieces but left everything else the same, subscribing to the "if it ain't broke, don't fix it" theory.

Christa pressed down on the accelerator. She had always loved coming home at the end of a busy day. Yet the challenges she now faced made time spent with Susan—and dreaming of the future—special. They often ate supper off trays in front of the living room fireplace. It had become the center of their home. Crackling flames highlighted the polished wood floors. They cast shadows on the natural wood paneling and intensified the colors in the woven Indian blankets on couch and love seat. They also enriched the carpeted staircase leading to the two tastefully furnished upstairs bedrooms, each with a small but perfectly appointed bath.

"We were strangers in a strange land," Christa mused. A laugh spilled out and Aurora perked up her ears. "Not for long, Lord. Between having the Hunters for neighbors and meeting a certain Major Scott, we didn't have time to be homesick!"

An image of her fiancé's smiling face danced in her mind. Where was he right now? What was he doing? When would he get enough leave for a quick visit home? They'd had far too little time together before duty called Gavin overseas. Much of the time, she didn't have a clue where he was.

Christa sighed and Aurora woofed. "I know. You miss him, too," she told her dog. "Phone calls and e-mail help, but it's still hard. Well, as the saying goes, 'This too shall pass.' " She dropped one hand to the malamute's thick fur. "Too bad the rest of the quote isn't, 'and the sooner the better!' Wonder if I'll have a message when I get home?"

Anticipation spilled into the timeless words of Thomas Chisholm's song "Great Is Thy Faithfulness." How she loved the tribute to the steadfastness and provision of God! Now, as Christa sang one of the world's most beloved hymns, her heart filled with gratefulness. How well she understood the things Chisholm loved! Summer, winter, springtime, harvest. Sun, moon, stars. Peace. Pardon for sin. Strength for whatever each day might bring and an abiding hope for all the tomorrows. All were precious gifts God gave to His children.

The lights of Anchorage appeared and grew brighter. The moon reflecting on the snowcapped peaks and Cook Inlet reminded Christa of the night she had promised to marry Gavin. A wave of love and longing swept through her. Was any woman ever more blessed than she? "Thank You, Lord," she whispered. A moment later she added, "I just pray that someday you'll send Susan a man as wonderful as Gavin—if there is one!"

Smiling at her prejudiced point of view, Christa swung into the driveway next to the cottage. As expected, light streamed from the shining windows, bidding her come in and rest. Too hungry to unpack the Explorer, she got out, summoned Aurora, and hurried up the stepping-stone walkway. "Stop pushing," she told her dog, who had nearly crowded her off the porch. "You're no hungrier than I am."

She stepped inside. "I'm home. So is Aurora. You won't believe what happened to me today." She shrugged out of her parka and hung it on a peg by the door.

Susan popped out of the kitchen like a clown from a jack-in-the-box. Light from the kitchen streamed after her, turning her hair to spun gold. The aroma of good cooking followed. "Can't it wait until we dish up? I made spaghetti pie and salad and baked apples. I'm starving."

"So am I, but this is too good to keep to myself. It's the funniest thing that's happened to me since I got here. Don't you want to hear it?" A giggle escaped, followed by another.

Susan looked toward heaven as if pleading for patience. "Go ahead and tell me before you explode."

"I drove a hundred miles each way today, some of it on rough roads, to check out a woman who called in saying her husband had developed a mysterious rash. He was feeling 'too poorly' to drive. Besides, the truck was 'broke down,' but she 'allowed as how' someone had better look at her man. All the way there, I hoped and prayed it wouldn't be something contagious." Christa grimaced. "That family has more children than the old woman who lived in a shoe."

"So what happened?"

"I got lost twice but finally found the place." Christa felt mirth bubbling up inside her but kept a straight face. "Sure enough, the man was itching and scratching like crazy."

"Well?" Susan planted her hands on her hips. "What was it?"

Christa couldn't hold laughter in even one more minute. "Long johns."

Susan's mouth dropped open. "Long John's what? Is that some kind of disease native to Alaska? I've never heard of it. What did you do?"

Christa doubled over and laughed until tears came. "I gave him some ointment to help stop the itching and ordered him to either replace his wool underwear with cotton or at least wear something cotton next to his skin." She wiped her streaming eyes with the back of her hand. "Case closed."

Susan almost cracked up. "Why don't we write a story called *Long John's Complaint*? We could print a pamphlet, sell it to tourists, and make a fortune. Now if you can stop laughing, go get washed up and we'll eat."

"Gladly. Will you put Aurora out and feed her, please?" She started upstairs.

"Sure." Susan opened the front door and pushed Aurora onto the porch. Her scolding voice floated up the stairs. "You're a malamute, not a lapdog. Remember?"

Christa heard Aurora's reproachful bark and grinned. When Mac and Jean Scott had discovered Aurora was allowed inside, they immediately told the Bishop sisters to correct the situation. Malamutes didn't sleep in houses. Period. That's why God created them with such heavy fur. However, the damage had already been done. Aurora obviously felt she deserved preferential treatment. The nightly routine of convincing her otherwise always ended with a disapproving stare and that same reproachful bark.

Susan's supper was delicious and left Christa content enough to purr. The "Shoe" family, as Susan persisted in calling them, had invited Christa to eat with them, but she suspected there was barely enough food to go around without her partaking. She made a mental note to report the need. She hoped the family wouldn't be too proud to accept help. Alaskans were an independent lot, for the most part. It often took the patience of Job and the wisdom of Solomon to make patients see that the social services available were not handouts but were funded in large part by taxes. When put that way, most reluctantly agreed to accept at least temporary help. The other way was to point out that the sooner family members were better nourished, the sooner they would have the energy to fend for themselves.

Christa sighed. The scope of her nurse-practitioner duties was wider than the treeless tundra. It involved deal-ing with every aspect of human need: physical, mental, emotional, and spiritual. It required caring and sympathy, plus the stability to cope with human suffering, emergencies, and other stresses. She had to be able to communicate with a wide variety of peo-ple, obtain medical histories, perform physical examinations, and diagnose and treat acute health problems—including inju-ries and infections. In addition, she must order, perform, and interpret lab work and X rays. Eight-hour days were rare.

"Yet there's nothing I'd rather do," she confessed to Susan when they settled down in front of the fire. "By the way, thanks for doing the dishes." She yawned. "You didn't have to, since you cooked."

"You needed to unpack your gear," Susan reminded. "One thing about my job is that I don't have to bring it home with me."

"Really. What about all those patients you encounter at the VA?"

Her sister's eyes darkened, a sure sign Christa was on target. "About those. . ."

The ring of the doorbell, followed by Aurora's sharp bark from the porch, drowned out the rest of the sentence. Susan got up from her seat on the couch and crossed into the hall. "Are we expecting company?"

"Not that I know about." Christa stood and followed Susan. "Who's there?" she called, wondering why she felt apprehensive.

"It's Molly. Shush, Aurora. If you don't know me by now, you never will."

Susan opened the door. "Come in. We're 'home and peaceful,' as Dad says."

Their robust, pleasant-faced neighbor shook her head. "Thanks, but no. Richard and I just got home from taking a friend to the airport." She held a letter out to Christa. "This was mixed in with our mail. Your lights were still on, so I figured I'd bring it over. See you tomorrow." With a wave of her hand, she headed down the walk.

"Thank you," Christa called before glancing at the envelope. Her heart thumped, then slowly iced.

"Who's it from? Gavin?" Susan peered over her sister's shoulder. "Great, but why is the return address a military convalescent center in Texas?"

Unaware of the cold night air rushing into the hall, Christa slit the envelope with her fingernail. A single page fell out. The same sense of foreboding that had troubled her when the doorbell rang returned, only now it was multiplied a hundred times.

"Don't stand there freezing," Susan ordered. She reached past Christa and closed the door. "Come back in the living room by the fire before we turn into icicles."

Christa silently obeyed, the unread letter clutched in white-knuckled hands. She stumbled to a chair, sank into it, and read:

Dear Christa,
　　I was on a reconnaissance mission and our engines caught

fire. We punched out (ejected), but I was blinded. Surgery has restored my sight, but the Air Force has taken me off flight status permanently. This changes everything between us. I am staying in Texas for now. Please don't come. I need time to sort things out.

Gavin.

A postscript read:

Tell Dad and Mom not to worry and not to come to Texas.

The last six words were underlined in heavy black ink.

Chapter 7

Late October shivered into November. Autumn winds stripped deciduous trees of their golden leaves, leaving stark, bare branches to wave against the cobalt sky. Thanksgiving was just weeks away.

Christa's life felt as barren as the trees. How could she give thanks when Gavin's letters and continued insistence that she not come to Texas hovered in her mind? "If he loved me the way I thought he did, Gavin would want me with him," she told Susan after a particularly bad day. The solitude she once cherished while driving gave her too much time to think. Her mind went round and round like a chipmunk in a cage. Now she stared into the fire, watching hope die.

"It's because he loves you so much that he doesn't trust himself to see you," Susan softly said. "Gavin has been through a terrible ordeal. Give him time."

Her sister's wisdom cheered Christa. "All right." Hot

tears stung the insides of her eyelids and tumbled out. "Waiting is so hard."

Susan sighed. "I know. Whoever first said, 'Men go off to fight; women wait' was right on target. Only now, women go off to fight, too." She closed her eyes and her face twisted. "Even those who stay home are engaged in war. You. Gavin's parents. Thousands of others who have loved ones engaged in trying to bring peace and justice to the world." Tears glistened in her long eyelashes. "Think of the army of military wives—and sometimes husbands—who are raising their children alone. They deserve medals, too. Medals for serving on the home front.

"This afternoon a World War II veteran dropped by my office. I'd met him once before. He talked about how his father fought in the First World War and how things haven't changed in over ninety years." She swiped at her eyes. "He said he thought I might like to see something. Then he handed me a piece of yellowed sheet music he said had belonged to his mother. I brought a photocopy home." She took the stairs two at a time and came back clutching a folded page. "We've heard the refrain, but listen to the rest of 'Keep the Home-Fires Burning.'

"They were summoned from the hillside,
They were called in from the glen,
And the Country found them ready
At the stirring call for men.
Let no tears add to their hardship
As the Soldiers pass along
And although your heart is breaking,
Make it sing this cheery song.

"Keep the home-fires burning
While your hearts are yearning,
Though our lads are far away
They dream of Home.
There's a silver lining
Through the dark cloud shining,
Turn the dark cloud inside out,
Till the boys come Home."

Susan's voice turned ragged. It took a long time for her to regain control and go on with the second stanza.

"Overseas there came a pleading,
'Help a Nation in distress!'
And we gave our glorious laddies.
Honor bade us do no less.
For no gallant Son of Freedom
To a tyrant's yoke should bend,
And a noble heart must answer
To the sacred call of 'Friend.' "

Only the crackle of the fire broke the silence that followed. Christa's heart ached. How well the stirring words, penned by Lena Guilbert Ford long ago, fit the turmoil of the twenty-first century! Suddenly Christa felt the burden of a world enmeshed in war. Nation against nation. Truth against the forces of evil, whose goal was to stamp out good—and God. Was this what Jesus had experienced—as recorded in Matthew 23:37—when He stood on the hillside and cried, "O Jerusalem, Jerusalem, thou that killest the prophets, and stonest them which are sent unto thee, how often would I have gathered thy children together, even as a hen gathereth her chickens under her wings, and ye would not!"?

After a long time, Susan brokenly said, "There is a silver lining, Christa, behind every dark cloud. We just have to hang in there and wait until we find it." She hugged the photocopy of the song to her chest, crossed the room, and went up the stairs—leaving Christa strangely comforted.

A week later, Gavin came home.

He hadn't wanted to return. Against his nature, he'd malingered until the Texas powers that be threatened to throw him out. "We need this space for those with problems far more serious than yours," his doctor bluntly told him. "Major Scott, the Air Force needs you. You can't fly for the military, but you can serve in other ways. Forget the past and get on with your future. But first, go home and whip yourself into shape. You're no good to anyone the way you are now." He paused. "You should be thanking God you're alive."

The physician's no-nonsense evaluation stung Gavin, but it also injected a gleam of light into his night-black mood. He hopped a military plane the next day, wishing he were at the controls instead of traveling as a passenger. Yet the constant question, *Where were You when I needed You, God?* never left him. Neither did the obsession that Christa might pity him. All the way to Anchorage, Gavin dreaded what he might see in the blue eyes that had formerly shone with love and trust.

What he actually found shocked him. He hadn't dreamed Christa Jensen Bishop's eyes could flash with such scorn. Or that her first words when he reached his parents' home and she unexpectedly opened the door would be, "It's about time you came

317

home where you belong, Gavin Scott!"

He felt his jaw drop, heard his mother gasp, and his father chuckle.

"Excuse me?" was the best response he could manage.

"You heard me. Why didn't you want me to come to Texas?"

Gavin found himself at a loss for words. "I needed time to—"

"Time to decide if I'm no better than a teenager with a crush on a pilot?"

It was so close to the truth, Gavin felt blood rush to his face. He tried to cover with a poor attempt at a joke. "Well, they say the fancy wrapper sells the goods."

Christa's eyes darkened until they resembled an Arctic night. "I fell in love with *you*, Gavin Scott," she blazed. "Not your uniform. Not your pilot's wings. Got that?"

Never one to cower from even the most direct attack, he was left without a defense—defeated by a woman stronger at that moment than he. The thought did what nothing else could have accomplished. It penetrated the stunned state in which he'd lived since realizing the end of his dream—and caused a reaction so unexpected, he wondered if he might still be feeling the effects of his injuries.

He laughed.

The guffaw began at his toes and gathered force. It came out with the speed of a rocket and just as loud. A quick glance at his parents' startled faces only made him laugh harder, but when he turned back to Christa, his mirth died. Misery had replaced her anger. Her face crumpled and a sob escaped.

Gavin opened his arms, only dimly aware when his mother and father slipped away. "Christa, I am so sorry." He gently pulled her close to him. "It's just that. . ." His voice trailed off.

She sagged against him, her bravado gone. "I know. I really do." All the tears she had tried so hard to keep inside came in a torrent. She wrapped her arms around him and held him as if she would never let him go.

Gavin's homecoming remained bittersweet. Yet Christa's anger had made something clear: Her feelings for him had not changed. Gavin rested his chin on her shining golden brown hair. He forced himself to lay aside his disappointment and concerns for the future. Being encircled by Christa's strong arms—and her love—was enough for the moment. The future would take care of itself.

⚬⚭⚬

Thanksgiving passed in an abundance of turkey and pumpkin pie. December rushed in with thousands of decorative lights. And with trees and Santas and manger scenes. Although fighting continued around the world, carols of joy and the spirit of Christmas present shimmered in the winter air.

Not everyone's heart held peace on earth and goodwill toward men. In spite of Christa's unexpected greeting when Gavin returned home, doubts returned. Doubts about himself. About God, who could have changed things. Even about Christa. Restlessness drove him. Night after night, after he left Christa at the door of the fairy-tale cottage, he tramped the streets until tired enough to fall asleep. "Lord," he prayed, "why can't I just trust You and leave everything in Your hands? I'm sure not doing great on my own."

No answer came. No lifting of the gloom that surrounded him like a cloud-infested Arctic night.

"How can I celebrate the birth of Your Son when I'm feeling torn apart inside?" he demanded. A pang went through him. Christmas had always been special. For the sake of those he loved, he must somehow piece together the raveled edges of his life enough to get through the holiday season.

◦≈◦

Two days later, an unexpected visitor arrived at the Scott home where Gavin was recuperating.

A series of sharp jabs on the doorbell brought him out of a daydream in which he was soaring high in an indigo sky and following the North Star. The rude return to reality irritated him, so he remained parked on the living room couch.

"Gavin, someone wants to see you," his mother called. An odd note in her voice made him wonder, but annoyance at being interrupted overrode his curiosity.

"I'm coming."

"You'd better be. I don't have time to stand here all day," someone retorted. The next instant, a grinning, red-haired Air Force captain strode into the room.

Surprise left Gavin speechless, but only for a few seconds. "Ben! What are you doing here?"

"You invited me, remember?" Ben looked innocent. "Fine thing. I travel thousands of miles and all he can say is, 'Ben, what are you doing here?'"

His parrotlike imitation of Gavin's voice was perfect. It elicited a giggle from Jean Scott and a reluctant smile from Gavin. He leaped from the couch and pounded his friend's back. "Be serious, Burgess Benjamin."

"Knock off the name-calling. Mind if I sit down?" He sat and continued. "I'm here because I'm on leave until those torn ligaments are completely healed." He smirked. "I'm too valuable to the military for them to take chances."

"Yeah, yeah. So how long can you stay? Until after Christmas, I hope."

Ben cocked one eyebrow at Gavin's mother. "Sure, if I won't be an imposition."

Jean beamed at him. "Imposition? You're as welcome as spring. Now if you'll excuse me, I'll leave you two to visit." She started for the door, then turned back to the men. "Gavin, would you like me to call and invite Christa for supper?"

"Great idea. Ask Susan, too." He gave Ben a knowing look. "If she doesn't have a date, that is."

"She'd better not," Ben grumbled after Jean Scott vanished. "You aren't the only reason I came to Anchorage." Never one to beat around the bush, he added, "So, what are you doing hanging around home when you could be using your experience to serve our country?" He sobered. "The way the world is, we're all needed."

"That's for sure." Gavin stood and crossed to the window. Guilt for spending so much time and mental energy worrying about what he could no longer do, instead of focusing on what he might be able to do, swept through him. Before he could tell Ben that his question had slashed through Gavin's regret and self-pity, Mackenzie Scott came into the living room wearing a grin the size of a cruise ship. Gavin's heart-to-heart with Ben would have to wait.

※

One look at Susan Bishop, lovely in pale blue slacks and sweater, robbed Captain Sharp of his bantering. He greeted Christa, appealing in yellow, then eagerly turned back to Susan. At first she seemed rather distant, but by supper's end, she was obviously more comfortable with him.

Under cover of the table conversation, Gavin whispered to Christa, "Ben looks smitten, and Susan seems interested."

Christa slipped her hand into his under the tablecloth. Her

face glowed. "More so than usual. It must be Ben's open face and the admiration in those honest brown eyes. I'm glad he came." She squeezed Gavin's hand.

"So am I." Someday he would tell her just how much, but not now. He still had a lot of things to sort out—and a lot of inner healing that must take place. Yet surrounded by love and friendship, the task before him no longer appeared hopeless.

Chapter 8

avin Scott had never been subject to mood swings. Yet as day followed winter day, he bounced between the heights of happiness and the depths of discouragement like a small plane trying to land on broken asphalt. Time spent with Christa offered solace. Watching Ben Sharp pursue Susan Bishop provided entertainment. Yet when Gavin thought of what he had lost, bitterness returned. In a few weeks Christmas would be over. What would the new year offer?

One afternoon, after he returned from a long and brooding walk, his mother met him at the door. "You have visitors," she said. A puzzled look crept into her face. "A family named Thorsett. The wife says they are here to fulfill a mission."

"A mission?" Sweat trickled down Gavin's neck in spite of the cold day. Had a fellow flier died and left him a bequest? *No, God,* he mentally argued. Then he realized that if that were the case, civilians wouldn't be delivering anything. That was followed by the ominous thought, *They would if personal effects had been given to them.* Dreading what might lie ahead, Gavin stepped into the living room. Relief shot through him. If the contents of the package lying near the hearth contained personal effects of a downed flier, the four strangers seated facing the blazing fire wouldn't be smiling.

"Major Scott? I'm Mark Thorsett. This is my wife, Natalie, and our daughters, Mollie and Amber." He motioned toward the attractive woman and two adorable girls who appeared to be perhaps six and eight.

Gavin held out his hand, noting the firmness of the man's grip. "Have we met?"

"No, but we have something in common." Natalie Thorsett's smile widened. "Mrs. Olivia Forester was my third-grade teacher—and much more. After my mother died, Mr. and Mrs. Forester took me in."

"She was my second-grade teacher," Gavin said. "I kept in touch with her for years. About a year ago, I received a letter from a law firm in Boise saying I had been identified as a 'conditional beneficiary' in Mrs. Forester's will—that I'd be contacted by their office when the conditions had been met." He laughed. "I have to confess I didn't give it much thought, except for feeling sorry she'd passed on. The life of an Air Force pilot doesn't leave much time for speculation."

"The law firm was Graves and Billings, wasn't it?" Natalie asked.

"Yes, but how do you know?"

A smile flitted across her face. "I'm the 'condition.'"

Gavin shook his head. "I don't understand."

She grew solemn. The two little girls edged closer to her, and she dropped an arm around each of them. "Neither did I. This time last year, I was living in Seattle and just this side of down-and-out. I faced eviction and had no idea where Mark was."

Gavin felt a lump form in his throat. The thought of the small girls living on the street touched his tender heart.

"One day I received a letter from a law firm—Graves and Billings. It said Mrs. Forester had left me something in her will." She smiled wryly. "For the first time in weeks, I felt a ray of hope. Anything valuable enough for my old teacher to consider her 'most priceless possession' must have monetary value." She stopped. "I was shocked when I signed the necessary documents and received my 'inheritance.'" She nodded at Mark, who opened the cardboard box the Thorsetts had brought. "This is it."

Gavin felt his jaw drop. This? Who would leave a still-beautiful but worn patchwork quilt to a former student? Had Mrs. Forester grown senile in her final days?

Mark spread the quilt over his wife's lap. The two little girls snuggled under it.

"Major Scott, this quilt is much more than it seems. There were days when I wrapped it around myself and my girls. It felt as if I were literally encircled by my Savior's warm arms. It has brought blessings to my life that I can't even describe. I don't know what blessings it will bring to you, but I'm sure you'll find out."

"To me!" Gavin shook his head. "I don't understand."

"The conditions of the bequest were that I was to keep the quilt for one year, then personally deliver it to someone whose name would be disclosed at the appropriate time. Ample funds to accomplish this would be furnished. I couldn't help wondering who, and why it was important for me to deliver the quilt in person! I still don't know. Anyway, here we are." Her laughter echoed from the walls of the quiet room. "Mr. Graves also sent me a letter I was to bring to you." She opened her purse and took out an envelope.

Gavin wonderingly tore off the corner and removed the contents.

I don't know when or where you will receive this, Gavin, but I somehow feel it will come when you most need it. When I was a young woman living in Texas, a raging fire just before Christmas took my ancestral home and everything I owned except for the family Bible. Insurance replaced "things," but I found it impossible to cope. How could I celebrate the Savior's birth when I had lost so much?

A few weeks later, I was quoted in a national magazine by a reporter doing a series on grief and faith. When asked how faith helped me deal with my loss, I replied, "One day at a time."

Soon afterward, a large package arrived. A Pennsylvania family named Fisher had read the series. They felt God wanted them to send me the patchwork quilt the first Mrs. Fisher had made during her last days on earth. It was a reminder to her husband of her love—and God's. The compassion and concern shown by these strangers filled me every time I touched the beautiful covering. It helped bring comfort and healing.

Now I am nearing the end of my earthly journey. I look forward to meeting the Master Quilter. May my most priceless earthly possession, though worn thin in places from years of hard service, be a reminder: God uses the broken, mismatched bits and pieces of our lives to create something beautiful and lasting, just as Darcy Fisher did long ago.

Affectionately,
Olivia Forester

The words blurred. Coming when he so desperately needed comfort seemed nothing short of a miracle. Gavin managed to thank the Thorsetts and see them out. Then he slumped into a chair and reached for the quilt. He unfolded it and spread it over his knees, idly tracing the tiny stitches and worn pieces of yarn that held it together. Just like the love of God, holding the jagged pieces of his life together until he could again become whole. A feeling of peace stole through him and he wondered, *How can the jagged pieces of fabric—many patched and patched again—make me feel everything is going to be all right?*

Gavin sank back into his chair, still holding his inheritance. He remembered lessons in life he had learned from the teacher who loved her students and challenged them to do their best. He still remembered her insisting life's problems were not as important as the way you handle them. "There's no disgrace in making mistakes and falling down," she said. "Just in giving up and lying there."

Gavin squirmed. What would Mrs. Forester think of him now, falling to pieces because of adversity?

A mental image rose before him: Hubbard Glacier in Yakutat Bay, one of Alaska's largest, most spectacular glaciers. When softened by warm sea air and eroded by seawater, tremendous chunks of ice broke loose—"calved"—from three-hundred-foot-high ice cliffs and crashed into the bay. Gavin had witnessed the spectacle from both ship and plane. Watching the forces of nature at work always brought a feeling of awe at their relentless fulfilling of God's design.

Hands still on the quilt, Gavin felt a great upheaval begin in the depths of his being. It worked upward, churning, building, like an avalanche gathering momentum. Helpless to stem the flow, he could only wait for it to end. It did not. Like a mighty flood that sweeps away whatever is in its path, Gavin's emotions raged in a final protest against the past, against the snatching away of his life's dream.

The feelings subsided. No voice whispered reassurance to his soul, but Major Gavin Scott had won a crucial battle against his worst enemy—himself.

❧

Two years earlier, love had come to Christa and Gavin like a gentle breeze that blew into their hearts and became devotion. Now it attacked Susan and Ben like a March wind determined to sweep obstacles from its path.

Ben had come to Anchorage predisposed toward Susan because of Gavin's glowing description. One look into her aquamarine eyes convinced Ben she was as lovely inside as out. He prepared his strategy to win her as carefully as a general plans a campaign. His opening salvo was to privately tell Christa, "God willing, I plan to marry your sister."

"Good luck," she said. "Just don't think it will be easy." However, she had no answer to his reply that anything worth having was worth fighting for. She also was left speechless when one night shortly before Christmas, Susan ruefully confessed, "I feel as if I've been caught up in a whirlwind." Susan stared into the blazing fire. "I never dreamed my 'Mr. Right' might turn out to have curly red hair."

"Are you serious?" Christa felt compelled to add, "If you marry Ben, it will mean lonely days and nights, raising your children as a single mother when he's away, and having your heart leap to your throat when he's overseas and you don't know where."

"I know. I saw what you went through when Gavin was gone." Susan shifted position in her chair and turned her poignant gaze toward Christa. "It doesn't matter. Don't get me wrong. I'm not going to run off and get married anytime soon." She blushed. "Even if I wanted to, Ben would never agree. He vowed after his parents' messy divorce that he'd never marry anyone unless he knew it was God's plan."

"And you think this may be?" Christa held her breath.

In a twinkling, Susan changed from serious to her usual pert self. "Did I say that?" Little sparkles danced in her eyes. "I don't think so." She sprang to her feet and planted her hands on her hips. "I'll tell you one thing, though. If Ben turns out to be Mr. Right, I'll follow him to the ends of the earth!"

Christa gaped, but Susan wasn't finished.

"Why did I ever think God sent the guy who dumped me?" She cringed, then fiercely added, "I've only known Ben a short time, but he has more integrity in his little finger than the jerk in Seattle has in his whole body."

"Hear, hear!" Christa began singing, "I'm in Love with a Wonderful Guy," but Susan only grinned and waltzed out of the room. Her going left emptiness. The thought of her marrying and leaving brought a pang. They had recently learned the Hagensons wanted to sell the fairy-tale cottage, but with Susan gone. . .

Christa shook her head. Who knew where Ben might be stationed? Or Gavin? She stirred uneasily. Although there had been great improvement in Gavin's attitude since he'd received the quilt, something she couldn't define still lay between them. On impulse, she picked up the phone and called him. "I know it's getting late, but Susan's gone to bed and I need to talk with you." Her heart raced like a jet plane during takeoff.

"What's on your mind?"

"Things don't seem right with us," she blurted out. The stillness that followed confirmed her suspicions. "Gavin, what's going on?"

When he finally spoke, he sounded despondent. "We're facing another hurdle."

Christa felt as if her heart had parked in her throat. "A–a hurdle?"

"Bigger than Mount McKinley. After a lot of prayer, I feel I'm supposed to stick with the Air Force, at least until this crazy world settles down. I don't know how they can use me, but I'm pretty sure I won't be stationed at Elmendorf." He hesitated so long, Christa's nerves screamed. "There's no guarantee there will be a need for a traveling nurse-practitioner where I'm stationed."

Relief sped through Christa like white water through a narrow gorge. "Is that all?"

"All!" His voice sharpened. "How will you feel if you have to give up the freedom of your present job for routine hospital work or private-duty nursing?"

Laughter bubbled out, along with a torrent of happy tears. "Even if it meant I could never practice nursing again—which it doesn't—it wouldn't matter. I can be happy anywhere, as long as we're together."

After a moment, Gavin huskily said, "I love you, Christa. More than life and second only to God Himself. Good night, my darling."

"Good night."

Long after they hung up, Christa curled up on the couch and searched her heart. Everything she had told Gavin was true, but she would miss Alaska. The fairy-tale cottage. Packing her Explorer and heading out to provide medical services to those who needed it, with Aurora in the "co-pilot" seat. Sadness filled her. How much chance was there of Gavin and her taking the malamute with them? Perhaps Gavin's parents would keep Aurora.

"Life is a trade-off," Christa murmured. "Part of my heart will forever remain in Alaska." She bowed her head. "God, Gavin and I know all things work together for good to those who love You, but right now it's hard to see how it applies to his being grounded. Please help us to trust You."

The fire slumbered and died. Her heart at peace without Christa fully understanding why, she deserted her post and went upstairs to a much-needed rest.

Chapter 9

Gavin Scott had always found submission difficult. Even though he'd long ago installed God in his life as his commanding officer, the words "Thy will be done" tended to stick in his throat. "After all," he reasoned, "God gave me a brain, so He must want me to use it."

Yet as Christmas and January rushed at him with the speed of sound, Gavin tired of trying to predict his future. The thought of a desk job appalled him. Pushing pencils was no career for a white hawk, even one that had been grounded. After a sleepless night, he got up, shrugged into warm clothes, and stepped outside, reveling in the frosty morning. He ran for miles. Each ground-covering step brought the growing conviction that he needed to stop trying to fight circumstances beyond his control. He reached a viewpoint overlooking the city just as the sun burst over the mountains, flooding the world with light that penetrated Gavin's self-sufficiency.

"You win, Lord. Whatever You have in mind will be okay with me." He waited, half expecting some kind of sign to show that God had heard and accepted his surrender. None came.

The whitecaps on Cook Inlet continued unabated. The mountains behind Gavin didn't move an iota. He sighed and turned toward home and breakfast.

His mother met him at the door. "A Colonel Foster called."

Gavin's heart lurched. "What does he want?"

"You." She grinned. "His exact words were, 'Mrs. Mackenzie, tell that son of yours to get his b—'" She smiled again, her cheeks showing a modest blush, and then continued, "'Begging your pardon, ma'am—get himself out here to Elmendorf immediately. I need him.'" Her eyes shone. "It sounds as if he has a job for you."

The words, *Hey, God, I really didn't expect an answer so soon*, flitted through Gavin's mind, then, *Too bad I didn't turn the controls over to You sooner.* He showered, shaved in record time, then crammed down a piece of toast to appease his growling stomach. Less than an hour later, he reached Elmendorf Air Force Base, manned by more than six thousand military personnel from all branches of the U.S. and Canadian armed forces.

Colonel Foster's abrupt opening words hit Gavin right between the eyes. "I need someone to command our survival-training program. You've had recent experience in escape and evasion. Not many can say that." His sharp gaze impaled Gavin and made him squirm.

"I was blind, sir. Captain Sharp is the one responsible for getting us to safety."

Colonel Foster snorted. "Doesn't matter. You understand what it feels like to go through such an experience. You've been there. Those you train will respect that. Besides, Captain Sharp's report attributed your survival to your leadership and especially your courage after being blinded. You also know Alaska. So, are you interested?"

Gavin had the insane urge to hug the brusque officer from sheer joy. "Yes, sir!"

"Good." The colonel permitted himself a wintry smile. "Report for duty January 2. Dismissed."

Gavin managed to salute and get back to his car without letting out a *yee-ha*. All the time he'd been wondering how even God could bring good out of his being grounded, this had been pending. Being trained in survival skills made the difference between life and death. He, Major Gavin Scott, would be part of it—because of the accident. His new job also meant he would be based at Elmendorf. Christa could continue her nurse-practitioner work. At times, it might blend with his. And he would fly again—not Ravens hunting for enemies, but small Cessnas on search-and-rescue missions with the Civil Air Patrol.

"Thank You, God!" Gavin's mind raced ahead with rosy plans. He and Christa could begin planning their wedding. He would also look into buying the fairy-tale cottage. He grinned. If the way Susan and Ben looked at each other were an accurate indicator, Susan wouldn't be living there forever!

᠂ᢁᡣ᠂

Winter melted into spring then early summer. With the dwindling snow and ice went the remnants of Gavin Scott's regret. He still felt a pang at seeing military aircraft soaring in the Alaskan skies. Yet the patchwork quilt served as a constant, loving reminder of the way God had picked up the ragged pieces of Gavin's life and had created from them a wholeness. Training men and women how to survive calamitous circumstances could result in saved lives. John 15:13 often came to mind: "Greater love hath no man than this, that a man lay down his life for his friends."

"That's kind of what God has done with me," Gavin mused on his way to meet a new batch of trainees one morning. "I've had to lay aside what I believed was my life, in order for others to live."

While her fiancé settled into his new command, Christa continued her beloved nurse-practitioner duties. Aurora slept away many miles of their travel time. Christa—free from worry about the future—dreamed of the late autumn wedding when she would become "Mrs. Major."

The fairy-tale cottage would be a honeymoon cottage, for Susan had flatly announced, "You're not going to miss out on buying this place because of me." She tossed her blond head. "I have plans of my own." She refused to explain, but the frequency of letters from Captain Ben Sharp and the glow in Susan's face offered undeniable evidence of which way the wind was blowing.

An urgent call late one Sunday night changed everything. Susan hung up the phone, looking dazed. "Ben's been declared fit for duty," she told Christa. "He wants me to marry him next weekend." Excitement replaced shock. "Will you help me?"

Christa's heart thudded. After all their years together, the time for parting had come. She wasn't prepared, but she wouldn't spoil her sister's happy anticipation. "Of course. Will you call Dad and Mom, or do you want me to?"

Six days later, Susan Bishop became Burgess Benjamin Sharp's bride and began life as a military wife. Christa clung to her sister. "Be happy," she whispered.

Nothing could daunt Susan. "I intend to." She sent a loving look toward her new husband. "After all, I married 'Mr. Right.'" They drove away on a wave of laughter.

⊷◈⊶

Summer made way for autumn. Gavin and Christa planned their wedding to coincide with Ben's leave. He and Susan arrived a few days beforehand, and the foursome planned a day of skiing. At the last minute, Christa felt she should check on an isolated patient before leaving on her honeymoon. Susan decided to go with her.

A wicked storm blew up out of nowhere. It caught Gavin and Ben on the slopes. A whiteout followed. Despite having taken precautions, their situation was precarious. Now was the time to use every bit of survival skill they possessed. As they began digging a snow cave, Ben wisecracked, "Talk about déjà vu. Only this time, we're definitely not in the Middle East!"

Gavin grunted. "You can say that again. On the other hand, I can't see any better now than I did then! I just hope Christa and Susan are okay and not out on some back road."

"God can take care of them," Ben reminded. "But it doesn't keep me from wishing we were with them." He continued digging. "All we can do is hunker down and wait."

Miles away, Christa repeated the words. "All we can do is wait. At least we're safe and snug in a winter-proofed home." She smiled at her patient—who was doing fine and was obviously delighted to have the sisters snowed in with her—and looked directly at Susan. "Don't worry about the guys. Both are skilled in the art of survival."

"Yes, but there's a whole lot more snow in the mountains than here. I intend to keep up a barrage of prayers," Susan declared.

"Good idea. In the meantime, we wait."

It wasn't easy. Even knowing no one was better equipped to face a winter storm than Gavin and Ben didn't melt the nagging uncertainty of wondering how their men were faring. It took all of Christa's faith and Susan's "barrage of prayers" to make it through the seemingly endless day, then the next.

On the second morning after the storm, an apologetic sun came out. So did Gavin and Ben, crawling from their shelter like bears after hibernation. They wasted no time in getting off the mountain.

Christa, Susan, and Aurora just as quickly made an exit of their own. They actually made it back to Anchorage a few tense hours before the men returned.

As if to make up for its unexpected assault, the weather stayed beautiful. Two nights later, a curious moon peered down on the church where Gavin and Christa first met—the church where they now took their vows. Gavin looked deep into Christa's blue eyes, humbled by the love shining brighter than the brightest star in the heavens—a God-given love that Gavin knew would never die.

The "white hawk" had never soared higher.

Epilogue

Just before Thanksgiving, Gavin Scott received a letter from the law firm of Graves and Billings, Attorneys-at-Law. The names didn't immediately register. "Do they think I'm going to sue the Air Force?" he grumbled.

Christa laughed. "Hardly. Isn't Graves the name of Mrs. Forester's attorney?"

"Right." Gavin ripped open the envelope and pulled out the single page. "Listen to this:

> *To Amy Fisher Nelson, Natalie Thorsett, and Gavin Scott. Mrs. Olivia Howard Forester left a final request. You and your families are to gather at Sun Valley the weekend before Christmas to share the full story concerning the patchwork quilt. You will also decide who is to keep it. All expenses will be paid.*

Gavin looked at his wide-eyed bride. "Sun Valley? Start packing!"

The weekend before Christmas, the Scotts, Thorsetts, and Amy Nelson and her husband, Tim, eagerly joined Mr. Graves in the large firelit meeting room he had reserved. Amber Thorsett tugged on Natalie's sleeve and pointed to Amy, who sat holding the worn heirloom quilt. "Look, Mom. She's holding our quilt. Do you think she's the one who made it?"

Her mom smiled. "I don't think so, honey, but maybe she knows something about the person who did make it."

"Do you think she'll tell us?" Natalie's other daughter, Mollie, asked.

Before Natalie could reply, Amy nodded her curly, dark head and obligingly began. "Once upon a time, more than sixty years ago, a beautiful lady named Darcy Fisher lived in Easton, Pennsylvania. Just before she went to heaven, she made a quilt for her husband, Dan. Working on it brought great comfort to her. Dan Fisher hung his wife's gift in their used-toy shop, Twice Loved." Amy's eyes grew misty. "My father was killed in World War II, but when I was six, Mama and I met Dan. He and my mother later married. I loved my new daddy, and I loved to cuddle up in the quilt he gave me for Christmas that year."

"So did we," Amber said. "We didn't have anyplace to live, but Mommy and Mollie and I would wrap the quilt around us, and we always felt warm. Our daddy says it protected us when his arms weren't there to protect us. I loved the quilt. Mollie and I wanted to keep it, but Mom told us it was just ours for a year. Dad said now that he was with us and could keep us warm and safe, God knew someone else needed it more."

Amber turned to Gavin. "Did it make you happy?"

Gavin smiled at her earnest face. "Very happy."

Amy went on. "When we read an article about Olivia Howard, who had lost everything except her Bible in a terrible fire, we decided to send her the quilt to make her feel better. Our families became friends. Olivia and her new husband, Nate Forester, came to Pennsylvania and later moved to Boise. I can't help thinking how happy Darcy would be to know all the stories about her quilt."

Natalie looked puzzled. "I still don't understand why Olivia Forester chose Gavin and me to inherit it."

Mr. Graves held up his hand like a schoolboy. "My turn. A few years ago, Olivia insisted I draw up a new will for her. She said God wanted her to do so. You don't argue with that kind of reasoning!" Laughter rippled around the room, and Mr. Graves continued, "Olivia loved Christmas. She loved hearing from her former students, but that year she was saddened by the pain and loneliness that showed beneath the cheery holiday greetings. How could she, with limited resources, help? Besides, she sensed what many of her former students really needed was love, friendship, and to know God.

"Olivia decided she could at least help a few and asked God to help her choose. Gavin, she laughed and laughed at your postscript." He quoted, " 'I've been so busy, I haven't had time to find a woman with whom to share my life. God willing, someday I will.' Feeling all was well with you, she tossed the card aside."

"That was the last Christmas before I met Christa," Gavin interjected.

"One card offered no news," Mr. Graves said. "Just the signature: 'Natalie.' Olivia recognized the writing. She assumed Natalie wasn't married or she'd have signed her full name. In Olivia's own words, 'At that moment a matchmaker was born.'

Gavin and Natalie were fairly close in age. What if she made it possible for them to meet?"

Gavin felt like he'd just been dunked in a glacier-fed lake. "What if she *what*?"

Natalie gasped. "So that's why I had to deliver the quilt to Major Scott in person!"

"Keep in mind, Olivia felt she was doing God's will," Mr. Graves told them.

"What a schemer!" Despite his annoyance at his teacher's outlandish scheme, Gavin couldn't help laughing. "God has some sense of humor! He used Mrs. Forester's matchmaking attempts to get the quilt to Natalie when she needed it—and then to me."

"How could Olivia perceive needs that hadn't yet arisen?" Christa wondered out loud. "All she had to work with were a loving heart, a Christmas card signed 'Natalie,' and a hastily scrawled postscript."

"Olivia only thought she knew," Amy quietly put in. "It was God who really knew."

Mr. Graves looked from face to face. "For six decades, the old quilt has been a comfort and a joy. Now you must decide who will be its keeper. There's one provision: If someone is ever found with a greater need for the quilt, the keeper must pass it on."

Gavin glanced at Amy. Her eyes were soft with memories. Surely she deserved the inheritance. Yet Natalie had suffered. As for him, parting with the patchwork quilt would be like losing a dear friend.

Amy soberly said, "We could split the quilt in three pieces, but that's not what Mrs. Forester requested. I vote for Gavin."

Natalie chuckled. "So do I. It will give our family an excuse to go to Alaska again!" Gavin wordlessly accepted the heirloom.

He draped it over his arm and walked away with Christa, too moved to speak.

One by one, the others said good night and went to their rooms, leaving Mr. Graves to stare into the dwindling flames. He thought of a passage of scripture—Luke 2:10–12—which referred to the long-ago night when Hope had come to earth; a night when angels announced the birth of Jesus to a group of humble shepherds in the fields near Bethlehem: "Fear not: for, behold, I bring you good tidings of great joy, which shall be to all people. For unto you is born this day in the city of David a Saviour, which is Christ the Lord. And this shall be a sign unto you; Ye shall find the babe wrapped in swaddling clothes, lying in a manger."

When the last ember flickered and died, Mr. Graves spoke to his Master. "Lord, I have carried out my task. Olivia's dream has been fulfilled. Peace and friendship surround those who gathered here because of her. Surely these blessings will continue to warm them all, just like the patchwork quilt and the swaddling clothes that once wrapped Your gift to the world."

Then, deep within the faithful servant's heart, a voice whispered in tones so hushed yet clear that Mr. Graves felt as if he were on holy ground. *"Yes, My son, for both the quilt and the swaddling clothes were created in love and bestowed with great joy."*

COLLEEN L. REECE

Colleen Reece learned to read beneath the rays of a kerosene lamp. The kitchen, dining room, and her bedroom in her home near the small logging town of Darrington, Washington, were once a one-room schoolhouse where her mother taught all eight grades!

An abundance of love for God and each other out-weighed the lack of electricty or running water and provided the basis for many of Colleen's 140 books. Her rigid "refuse to compromise" stance has helped sell more than 4.5 million copies that help spread the good news of repentance, forgiveness, and salvation through Christ.

A Letter to Our Readers

Dear Readers:

In order that we might better contribute to your reading enjoyment, we would appreciate your taking a few minutes to respond to the following questions. When completed, please return to the following: Fiction Editor, Barbour Publishing, Inc., P.O. Box 719, Uhrichsville, OH 44683.

1. Did you enjoy reading *Patchwork Holiday*?
   ❑ Very much—I would like to see more books like this.
   ❑ Moderately—I would have enjoyed it more if _____

_____

_____

2. What influenced your decision to purchase this book?
   (Check those that apply.)
   ❑ Cover   ❑ Back cover copy   ❑ Title   ❑ Price
   ❑ Friends   ❑ Publicity   ❑ Other

3. Which story was your favorite?
   ❑ *Twice Loved*   ❑ *Everlasting Hope*
   ❑ *Remnants of Faith*   ❑ *Silver Lining*

4. Please check your age range:
   ❑ Under 18   ❑ 18–24   ❑ 25–34
   ❑ 35–45   ❑ 46–55   ❑ Over 55

5. How many hours per week do you read?_____

Name_____

Occupation_____

Address_____

City _____ State _____ Zip _____

E-mail _____

If you enjoyed

PATCHWORK
HOLIDAY

then read:

CHRISTMAS ON THE *Prairie*

FOUR ROMANCE STORIES
FULL OF CHRISTMAS NOSTALGIA

One Wintry Night by Pamela Griffin
The Christmas Necklace by Maryn Langer
Colder Than Ice by Jill Stengl
Take Me Home by Tracey V. Bateman

If you enjoyed

PATCHWORK
HOLIDAY

then read:

LONE STAR
CHRISTMAS

Someone Is Rustling Up a Little Holiday Matchmaking in Four Delightful Stories

The Marrying Kind by Kathleen Y'Barbo
Here Cooks the Bride by Cathy Marie Hake
Unexpected Blessings by Vickie McDonough
A Christmas Chronicle by Pamela Griffin

Available wherever books are sold.
Or order from:
Barbour Publishing, Inc.
P.O. Box 721
Uhrichsville, Ohio 44683
www.barbourbooks.com

You may order by mail for $6.97 and add $2.00 to your order for shipping.
Prices subject to change without notice.

If you enjoyed

PATCHWORK

HOLIDAY

then read:

angels
for christmas

*Crafty Little Angels Put Their Charm
Into Four Holiday Romances*

Strawberry Angel by Pamela Griffin
Angel Charm by Tamela Hancock Murray
Angel on the Doorstep by Sandra Petit
An Angel for Everyone by Gail Sattler